How often can a heart find love? How many times can it mend from loss? Maureen Russo is an average woman who might be a neighbor or friend. From her darkest days to her brightest joys, "Wounded Angels" tells her story—our stories—of loss and love and moving beyond her "empty existence" to embracing her "new self." Sensitive and moving.

KATHRYN ORZECH, AWARD-WINNING
AUTHOR OF *ASYLUM: A DARK SUSPENSE SAGA*

Chuck Miceli's new novel is an insightful look at the wounds life inflicts on us all – regret, aging, death – and the healing power of friendship. Sensitive and engaging, "Wounded Angels" takes the reader on a journey through the life of Maureen Russo, from the earliest loves and losses of her childhood to her autumn days when, at last, she finds joy once again. It is a powerful journey worth taking.

DEBORAH LEVISON, AUTHOR OF THE MULTI AWARD-WINNING BOOK,
THE CRATE: A STORY OF WAR, A MURDER, AND JUSTICE.

Chuck Miceli is a gifted storyteller with a refreshing and positive writing style. He has a talent for creating compelling situations with familiar characters, many of whom you will quickly care about. In his new novel, *Wounded Angels*, we meet Maureen Russo, a woman who has always been there for friends and loved ones, only to find herself feeling emotionally empty and frantic about what lies ahead. Miceli peppers his tale with an intriguing cast of support players who, along with Maureen, face devastating challenges and discover new meanings for their lives. It is a well told, compelling story.

MARTIN HERMAN, AUTHOR OF
THE JEFFERSON FILES AND SIX OTHER BOOKS

Wounded Angels is a moving account of one Maureen Russo who, at times, appears as fragile as the fraying doily on her faded Davenport, but musters the tenacity to take on life's adversities when confronted head on. *Wounded Angels* will grip your heart and hang onto it to the last page. Powerful. Thought-provoking. Uplifting.

PENNY GOETJEN - AWARD-WINNING AUTHOR OF
THE EMPTY CHAIR – MURDER IN THE CARIBBEAN AND OTHER NOVELS

Wounded Angels, is a novel of resolve, resolution and recovery. Chuck Miceli's "autobiography" of Maureen Bower, traces her life from childhood in 1930s

Brooklyn, New York through near-present day Connecticut. She chronicles her experiences through World War II and the Viet Nam era and the losses that leave her feeling abandoned by those who loved her. One "abrasive" woman simply refuses to let her sink into despondency and in the process, they "save" each other. Based on real-life, *Wounded Angels* provides many points and examples that strike true to the reader's heart and mind. It's an enjoyable, engaging read and well worth the time.

CHARLES I. MOTES, JR., M.S., M.P.H, R.S.
FORMER DIRECTOR OF HEALTH, TOWN OF SOUTHINGTON AND
CITY OF BRISTOL, CT

Writing a memoir that keeps the reader involved and looking for more is an accomplishment. Writing it as a man from the first-person perspective of a woman is a more daunting challenge. In *Wounded Angels*, Chuck Miceli hit upon the perfect formula that kept me engrossed with the story while giving me a sense of family with the characters. Chuck is well on his way to becoming a top-tier author in multiple genres.

BRIAN JUD, AUTHOR OF *HOW TO MAKE REAL MONEY SELLING BOOKS* AND
EXECUTIVE DIRECTOR OF THE ASSOCIATION OF PUBLISHERS FOR SPECIAL SALES

Chuck Miceli has written a dynamic story of Maureen, her young love, Frank, and an unusual influence in her life who shows up just at the right time. You won't want to put this book down!

CAROL KEENEY
AUTHOR OF *BRAND NEW TEACHER* AND *FAIRY DAZE*

There are so few novels that address the lives of older adults as regular people, rather than some sort of flawed and fragile oddity. *Wounded Angels* centers on two terribly mismatched women bonded by what they each believe to be insurmountable personal struggles. What I love about this book is that this is not pitying pabulum. Rather, *Wounded Angels* is a thoughtful and entertaining examination of how the arc of friendship, its endurance and its conflicts, sustains, challenges, and renews us on life's journey, no matter what our age or station.

JEAN MCGAVIN
FOUNDER OF *HISTORYCHIP.COM*

WOUNDED ANGELS

WOUNDED ANGELS

Chuck Miceli

ELM HILL

A Division of
HarperCollins Christian Publishing

www.elmhillbooks.com

Wounded Angels

Published in Nashville, Tennessee, by Elm Hill, an imprint of Thomas Nelson. Elm Hill and Thomas Nelson are registered trademarks of HarperCollins Christian Publishing, Inc.

Elm Hill titles may be purchased in bulk for educational, business, fund-raising, or sales promotional use. For information, please e-mail SpecialMarkets@ ThomasNelson.com.

Publisher's Note: This novel is a work of fiction. Names, characters, places, and incidents are either products of the author's imagination or used fictitiously. All characters are fictional, and any similarity to people living or dead is purely coincidental.

For more information on the book and the author, please visit the *Wounded Angels* website at: authorchuckmiceli.com

Library of Congress Cataloging-in-Publication Data

Library of Congress Control Number: 2019906831

ISBN 978-0-997698640 (Paperback)
ISBN 978-0-997698657 (Hardbound)
ISBN 978-0-997698664 (eBook)

Dedicated to My Mother-in-law, Charlotte
Whose Capacity for Love
Was Greater Than One Lifetime Could Hold

FOREWORD

CHUCK MICELI'S NOVEL, *Wounded Angels*, considers our portrait of God and illustrates the truth that God does not cause human suffering. Rather, as my teacher and mentor, William Sloane Coffin, Jr. stated so eloquently following the death of his son, Alex: "God's heart was the first of all our hearts to break...." In other words, God has compassion when we face the struggles, crises and crucifixions that life thrusts upon us.

One way that God does this is through other people. Hence, it is written: "Do not neglect to show hospitality, for by doing that some have entertained angels without knowing it." (Hebrews 13:2, NRSV) This is the central point of Wounded Angels, Chuck's very engaging story of two broken-hearted women who meet and slowly open themselves to befriending each other, despite significant differences that would normally divide them. While some would say it is sheer coincidence that certain people enter and touch our lives at certain times, the story of these two women testifies to a God who is actively involved in bringing people into our lives to assist us on life's journey. Angels, some would call them, though they are every bit as human as the rest of us. As the relationship between the two women grows and the deeper wounds of each are revealed, their broken hearts begin to heal and new life slowly emerges for each of them.

During my fifteen years as Pastor of First Congregational Church of Southington, Connecticut, Chuck heard me proclaim in various ways that "Jesus is our best portrait of God. We know God best by looking at the life and ministry, death and resurrection of Jesus as they are recorded in the gospels." As an active lay leader in that congregation, Chuck was highly-valued and respected for his insightfulness and creativity. While he professed his beliefs as a Christian, in our private conversations, he also expressed his personal vision of inclusiveness and his desire to focus on the beliefs and values that religions hold in common rather than what distinguishes them.

Wounded Angels is a timeless story, beautifully written, bursting with faith, hope and love. Despite never using a single theological term, Chuck Miceli offers us an authentic, universal example of some of the primary theological pillars that undergird the Christian faith. I have no doubt that the readers of Wounded Angels will love it as much as my wife, Diane, and I did when we read it aloud to one another. We laughed; we cried; we were deeply moved; and we shared lively conversations that led to the insights noted in this Foreword.

Rev. Dr. Gordon E. Ellis
Warwick, Massachusetts
June 23, 2019

PART ONE

ABANDONED

CHAPTER 1

THE WINDOWS WERE open on that sweltering Fourth of July in 1937: the day my father walked out of my life forever.

Mother, my brother, Ralph, and I waited all morning for Father to come home from the shop so we could go to Coney Island. When he finally stumbled through the door in mid-afternoon, he reeked of alcohol and smoke. I was fourteen and while my father was often sad and angry by then, I had never seen him drunk before.

Until the Depression, most of the neighborhood families and stores brought their clothing to Father's tailor shop for mending and tailoring. Each morning he wheeled his clothing rack from the shop filled with beautifully tailored clothes wrapped in cellophane. The sun and wind playing with the plastic made it sparkle like ripples on a pond. To me, Father, tall and trim, looked like a movie star in his finely tailored suit, polished leather shoes, and wide brimmed hat. By noon, he visited each of clothing stores on Atlantic Avenue and Fulton Street and returned with his rack filled with pinned and wax-marked garments. When he didn't have too many stops to make, he would let me walk with him. Even better, he would sometimes say, "My Lady, your carriage awaits," and would invite me sit on the bottom shelf of the clothing rack as he wheeled me through the streets.

On the tree-lined Brooklyn side streets, many of the people sitting on their stoops greeted father with "Good morning, Mr. Bower" and "How do you do, Mr. Bower."

Father returned with "And to you" and "Fine, thank you. Have a nice day."

Occasionally someone asked, "And how is the lovely Miss Maureen this morning?"

I was painfully shy. Father looked down at me, smiled, and replied for me, "Lovely as always." He ended by waving his hand or even better, by tipping his hat just slightly.

"Daddy," I said, "it's like you are the mayor or something," but he quickly corrected me.

"Not at all, my Lady. You are my princess and I am your humble servant."

Stores like the A&P, the bakery, and my favorite, the ice cream parlor, lined both sides of Atlantic Avenue, which we always had to cross quickly. Four lanes of cars sprang forward like racehorses coming out of the gate as soon as the lights turned green. They rushed to pass as many of the streetlights as possible before they turned red again. Meanwhile, women coming out of the A&P wheeled their shopping baskets past the butcher shop and the men smoking out front in their white, bloodstained aprons.

The biggest clothing stores were also on Atlantic Avenue. Father took a few of the plastic wrapped items from his rack into each store and exchanged them for others that were pinned and marked with wax. All of the clothing storeowners looked alike to me. Each of them wore baggy pants, a button down shirt with a collar and a vest. A bar of white marking wax peeked out of the vest pocket and a cloth measuring tape with pins in it hung around their necks. They all spoke with a funny but nice sounding accent.

The smaller clothing stores and my father's tailor shop were on Fulton Street. The elevated train overhead kept the street constantly shadowed. Most of the people living in the third and fourth-floor apartments kept their curtains closed because you could see right inside from the train cars.

The corner candy store was just across the street from the tailor shop and every evening Ralph and I eagerly waited to see what new delights Father bought for us.

"For my princess," Father said as he held up my treat like a prized trophy. It didn't matter what it was. The way he presented it always made me feel special. On weekdays, after school, he and I sometimes walked together to Highland Park. When I was younger, he sat patiently as I played on the swings or monkey bars. As I grew older, I played less and we talked more. We often sat beneath the shade of the tall maple trees at the highest point in the park. From there, we talked for hours and viewed the park and the busy city below. Father said, "It's so much easier to see things clearly from up here." In time, that spot became my favorite place to think, to enjoy the view, and to ponder what the future might hold.

On Saturday nights, Father, tall and trim in his finely tailored suit and Mother, slender and beautiful in her long, flowing dress, walked arm-in-arm to the church dances. Life felt like a fairytale; then everything changed.

After the Depression, many of the regular customers did their own mending or simply made do with what they had. Father worked longer hours at the shop but it didn't help much. He and Mother stopped going to the dances and he stopped bringing home treats for Ralph and me. Then, just when Father's business started to improve again, the news in Europe only made it worse.

Jewish immigrants fleeing the Nazis in Germany settled in the garment district in New York and many of the Jewish-owned clothing stores in our neighborhood moved to the city too. The few stores that remained stopped sending their work to Father's shop. They hired other Jewish immigrants to do their tailoring in-house. Father said they probably distrusted us because we were German. One by one he had to let workers go until it was only him left at the shop. Even then there was never enough money to pay all the bills, and the bank threatened to take the business.

Father looked worried and angry all the time and he started to leave some bills unpaid. Each day more "overdue" notices arrived. On the last day of June, when Mother said that she and I were going to visit my aunt, Father stopped her at the door.

"Good, then you'll be passing the post office," he said. "Make sure you mail this on your way." He handed Mother an open envelope. She looked inside before sealing it. "With all the bills piling up, are you sure you want to do this? This could pay for two week's groceries."

"I'm sure. Just don't forget. It has to be postmarked today."

When Father staggered into the house on that Fourth of July afternoon, Ralph was outside playing with his friends as Mother and I hung the wash out on the line.

"What do you think you're doing?" he shouted at Mother as he entered. Mother looked toward me and then turned back to him.

"It's very hot out. The clothes should be dry in an hour."

"You shouldn't be working on a holiday."

"I didn't know when you would be home. We'll be finished in just a couple minutes."

"You'll be finished now!" Father stumbled backwards against the stove as Mother came in from the fire escape landing and took his arm.

"Maybe you should lie down for a while before we go. You look like you need rest. Let me help you into bed."

He shoved her aside, "I don't need rest. I can't rest. Can't you see that?"

Then he turned, saw me, and stood still for a moment. His lips trembled and a tiny tear trickled down his face. "I'm so sorry, Princess. You shouldn't see me like this."

"It's all right, Daddy. I'm sorry you're sad."

He didn't answer. I reached for his arm but he pushed past me, heading for the door, only pausing a moment to look at Mother, "And you deserve better than this." Then he walked out the door and staggered up the street toward the tailor shop.

I started after him, yelling, "Don't go, Daddy. We're going to the beach together, remember?" but Mother stopped me.

"Your father needs some time to himself," she said gently.

Father didn't return that hot, sticky afternoon, that sweltering night, or the next morning. Several neighborhood women comforted my mother as she paced nervously in the hot afternoon sun. When I couldn't sit still any longer, I walked up to tailor shop but he wasn't there, so I continued on to Highland Park. There was always a breeze on the top of the hill. I hoped that maybe, from under the shade of our maple trees, I might just see him walking along the streets below. I began to sweat as I climbed the hill but the temperature dropped quickly as I entered the tree line. Sitting against the base of a tree, I closed my eyes, tilted my head back, and felt the cooling breeze against my skin. The sun peeking through the canopy played on my eyelids until I opened my eyes and screamed.

Father's eyes, bulging and bloodshot, looked down at me. His mouth and lips twisted horribly like some nightmarish movie monster as he hung from a high branch of a maple tree in Highland Park.

There was something worse than finding Father like that. It was more than my mother's hysteria at the news, or the chaos of the police and newspaper reporters. It was more depressing than the wake and funeral. What haunted me most was that Father had abandoned me. I was his princess. He told me that he loved me more than anything else in the whole world. Then why didn't he love me enough to stay?

After the funeral, Mother found the note Father had left behind. In it he said he was sorry for what he was going to do, but he didn't know of any other way out. He also said that at least now, Mother, Ralph, and I could afford to go on living without him. He left instructions for Mother to contact the life insurance company about his policy, but things didn't turn out the way he planned. Several weeks later, Mother received the letter saying that father's policy did not cover death by suicide. I recognized the address on the envelope as the same one Father insisted we mail on that last day in June. The insurance company didn't even return the last payment Father sent just before he died.

Shortly after, the bank took the tailor shop, forcing Mother to take in sewing at home, as my grandmother had done. Mother looked worried all the time. "I'm sorry, but that's all there is," she said on many nights as she laid the watery soup and stale bread on the table. Then she quickly turned around so we couldn't see her wiping away the tears. Mother relied heavily on her faith, however, and made certain that we prayed the rosary each night and attended Mass every Sunday. That's where she met Benny. He had lost his wife years earlier and treated Mother kindly after Father died. They married the following year and life settled down to a new normal. Benny was a gentle and generous man. Mother appreciated his thoughtfulness, but they never showed the same affection for each other that she and Father had. We continued to attend church services every Sunday. At every Mass for the next three years, I prayed silently that someday I would find someone of my own who would love me always and would never ever leave me.

PART TWO

FRANK

Chapter 2

"MAY I HAVE this dance?"

I recall those words and the way they were said as clearly now as when I first heard them. The Cypress Avenue Roller Rink was popular with neighborhood families and local high school students. For fifteen cents, you could skate all Saturday afternoon. I didn't have to look up to see who asked: I had memorized that voice. Even merged with the rumbling of dozens of roller skaters and Fred Astaire's "They Can't Take That Away from Me" booming through the giant roller rink, it stood out.

"Hey June," I elbowed my best friend sitting next to me, "I think somebody's talking to you." I lowered my head while June looked up.

"Hello June," he said while extending his hand, "My name is Frank—Frank Russo."

June reached out and he shook her hand, "It's very nice to meet you and I hope you don't feel offended, but it was your friend I was asking."

I couldn't breathe. *He must be mistaken*, I thought. After all, June was the pretty one with her silky brown hair and creamy complexion, and she looked even better in her new skating outfit. My reddish waves and matching freckles made me self-conscious, and I'd been wearing the same plaid skirt that my mother made since we started coming to the rink.

June scowled at me, "Thanks a lot, Maureen. Now don't I feel like the fool?"

I looked up to see him staring down at me, smiling. "Are you sure you're talking to the right person," I asked and then immediately regretted saying it.

He looked around and then back to me. "I'm afraid I've already embarrassed your friend and I don't see anyone else here, so yes, you're definitely the right one."

For an instant, I imagined myself making some glib remark like, "Are you kidding? That line might have worked in my mother or grandmother's day, but it's 1940. Don't you think you could come up with something more original?" But that was not going to happen. I felt foolish enough already. I've never been good at playing coy anyway and I would have died if he had walked away. I was too nervous to look into his eyes so instead I concentrated on his face and clothing.

His white Polo shirt looked fresh from the cleaners and his black pants were sharply creased. Now that he was standing next to me, I noticed that his nose tilted just barely to the left and bumped slightly at the bridge. Instead of taking away from his looks, it seemed to me a perfect imperfection. Finally, his dark, curly hair matched his deep brown eyes, almost too gentle for someone so sturdy looking and of course, he wore roller skates.

"So will you dance with me, Maureen?"

"You're not making fun of me, are you? I'm happy I can stand without falling."

"You're being too modest. I've seen you skate before and you're steady enough. With the right technique and a little practice, I'll have you dancing like a pro in no time."

"You sound very sure of yourself."

"I am."

I wondered if Frank might be overconfident but he came across as matter-of-fact instead of bragging. The tiny beads of sweat on his brow also helped to relieve my own nervousness.

"Well, if you're sure you can keep us from falling, I guess…. Wait a second. When did you see me skate before? Have you been spying on me?"

"Why don't we talk about it while we're skating?"

I accepted Frank's hand, stood up, and then looked back at June.

"Don't worry about me," she said. "I can take care of myself, thank you. Besides, see that cute guy in the blue shirt over there? He keeps looking at me. With you hanging around all afternoon, he might never get up the nerve to ask me to skate."

I silently mouthed, "Thank you," as Frank guided me onto the floor.

"Russo?" I asked. "What nationality is that?"

"Italian, through and through."

My heart sank. I wanted him to answer Greek or Swiss or anything but Italian.

Then he said, "I think you're very pretty. I enjoy watching you skate. The way your hair flows across your shoulders reminds me of ocean waves."

The blood rushed to my face and my whole body warmed. Mother warned me about "sex perverts," especially Italians. None of the boys in school talked like Frank and he looked older than they did.

"Maybe this wasn't such a good idea," I said, letting go of Frank and starting to move away.

"Wait. Did I make you nervous?"

"A little."

"I didn't mean to. It's more than the way you look. You're different. I like how, when you skate, you sometimes look like you're not even thinking about what you're doing but just lose yourself in the music. That's why I asked you to dance."

"And when have you seen me skate before?"

"Saturday three weeks ago and every Saturday afternoon since."

Frank's directness challenged me. I had been watching him too. I loved the way he moved with the music. Sometimes he soared across the floor like a hawk in flight. At other times he was as powerful and precise as a machine. He never seemed to notice or care about the other people looking at him. When he skated, it was as though he was alone in the arena.

"Well, I noticed you too," I said, "and to be honest, I was hoping you would ask me to skate, if you don't mind my being *frank*." We both burst out laughing.

"So are you ready for your first lesson?" Frank asked and I breathed a sigh of relief.

He started with the proper stance for dancing and followed with cues for movements and turns. He didn't need to explain much and I didn't have to concentrate hard on what to do. I responded instinctively to his touch and the slightest pressure in any direction caused my body to follow instantly.

"I was right about you being a natural," he said. "You're a fast learner."

Even though I doubted him at first, he was as good an instructor as he said he was.

Then he led me to the far side of the rink where the fellow in the blue shirt was standing.

"Hey, Harv," he said, wrapping his arm around the lanky man's shoulders. "Did you notice that girl in the plaid green outfit over there?" Frank tilted his head in June's direction.

"Are you kidding? Of course, I did. She's a knockout." June was right about his watching her.

"She's Maureen's friend and she thinks you're cute, although God only knows why. Anyway, she'd be happy to pick up a few pointers from you."

Harvey looked toward June as she skated near the edge of the rink, half-stooped over with her legs spread wide and arms flapping like a bird. Her outstretched fingers were always within reach of the support rails. Then Harvey turned to me, "Is he pulling my leg?"

I leaned in and whispered, "She did say it but please, don't tell her I told you."

Harvey slapped Frank hard on the back. "Thanks, Frankie, I owe you one," and shot off in June's direction.

"That was sweet of you," I said.

"Maybe, but then again, you don't know Harvey." The smile on his face told me he was only kidding.

The rest of the afternoon, Frank and I practiced breaks and turns, each a little faster and more complex than the previous.

"I can feel you stiffening," said Frank. "Are you afraid I'm going to lose my grip on you?"

"I'm afraid of something, but I'm not sure what."

"You've made a lot of progress, Maureen, but you can't go further unless you stop trying to control every movement with your mind. Your body knows what to do if you just let it. You have to let go and trust me."

"I'll try. I promise."

As we entered our next turn, I closed my eyes and repeated Frank's request, "Trust me." Then I emptied my mind and focused on relaxing my body.

Frank's strong hands gripped mine and his muscles bulged as he supported me. I abandoned my thoughts about safety or techniques, surrendered control to Frank's lead and imagined myself floating on the rhythm of the music. I had never experienced total trust before and the effect was magical. As our body movements synchronized, Frank Russo and I became one. Practicing our last waltz, I imagined us like a pair of swans gliding across the surface of a still pond. Absorbed in each other and the music, we didn't notice how quiet the arena became. Other skaters had moved off to the sides to watch us and as the song ended, they broke into applause. I turned to Frank who was staring at me, smiling.

"Why are you looking at me like that?" I asked.

His smile widened, "You're blushing."

That made it worse. I felt my face turning bright red and looked away.

"Don't be embarrassed," he said. "I think it makes you look even prettier."

We continued skating and I lost all track of the time until a short, bald-headed man shouted as he skated backwards past us, "Hey, Frankie, you've got about twenty minutes before your 4:30's arrive."

"Sure thing, Mr. Pitrillo, I'll be ready."

"OK, buddy boy; and you, young lady, in case Frank hasn't told you already, the two of you are something else out there. Keep it up and you two could go pro." Then he swung around and sped off ahead of us.

I remembered seeing a movie poster for *Shall We Dance* near the front door of the rink. Under the picture of Fred Astaire and Ginger Rogers on roller skates, the note pasted to the bottom read, FREE LESSONS EVERY SATURDAY AT 4:30.

"Frank," I said more forcefully than I wanted to, "you never said you were a professional instructor."

"That's because I wasn't thinking of you as a student." My heart beat so fast that I wondered if Frank could hear it. I was already falling in love with Frank Russo. Then we skated past the big clock over the desk and I noticed the time.

"I really have to be going soon. I promised my mother I would be home by five."

"Then we've got just enough time to practice one more move." Frank gestured me into a half turn so I ended leading in front of him. As his strong hands pushed down on my hips and his fingers pressed into my flesh, I relished the sensation of my whole body warming and tingling. Then suddenly, my Catholic-school upbringing kicked in and turned my warm tingle into a cold chill.

"Uh, Frank," I stuttered, "I'm sorry, I really have to be going."

I broke away, lifted his hands from my waist, and skated off toward my seat. June and Harvey were sitting together, with Harvey's arm draped over June's shoulder. I shouted that it was time to leave.

"Now?" June pouted.

"Yes, June, now."

While I removed my skates, Frank stood over me with a worried look on his face and asked, "Did I do something wrong? I didn't mean to upset you."

"No, you didn't. Not at all."

As June and I started walking toward the exit, I stopped abruptly. Frank was following so closely that when I turned our faces almost touched and I had to resist the impulse to kiss him. "You were … perfect," I said.

He grabbed my hands and squeezed hard, "Then when will I see you again?"

"Well, we haven't finished my lessons, have we?"

He smiled, "Not even close."

"Then I guess I'll see you again next Saturday, if that's good for you."

"It's … perfect."

Frank told me later that as soon as June and I left the rink, Harvey leaned over and said, "Boy, you sure are sweet on her, Frankie, and I can see why. She's got one killer body."

"Hey, watch how you talk about my wife."

"Your wife?"

"Yes, Harvey. That girl, my friend, is the future Mrs. Russo."

At that moment, Frank couldn't know how the past and the future would conspire to try to keep that from happening.

CHAPTER 3

FRANK AND I continued meeting at the roller rink every Saturday throughout my senior year of school and well into my first year of work. Since I always went to the rink with June, mother never learned about Frank and I made certain never to bring the subject up in conversation.

Each week, June and Harvey practiced cuddling while Frank and I practiced our skate dancing. Then one day Frank suggested we practice lifts.

"But you're already lifting me," I said, referring to how he would twirl me around him until my skates left the ground.

"I'm talking about lifting you over my head."

The sheer thought terrified me. What if his skates slipped? What if he lost his grip? What if he fell while I was above him?

Frank was patient. He dropped the subject and didn't mention it again until several weeks later when I worked up the courage to ask more about it. Then he got excited and explained how we would do it. Some moments in life are so different, so exhilarating, that you can never forget. For me, that afternoon was one of them.

Frank and I normally practiced individual movements until about the last forty-five minutes and then put them all together into our final routine. For the lift, I would skate toward him and just before reaching him, extend my arms above my head, push off, and jump forward as if I were diving into a pool. He would then catch me at the waist and lift me up above his head. My forward momentum would propel us into the turn. I was to keep my body rigid and extend my arms out. Finally, I would lower my right arm so Frank could grasp it and lower me to the ground. Even listening to it terrified me but I felt certain that he would not have suggested it unless he was sure we were ready.

Frank took up his position in the middle of the floor and I skated toward the far end. Our eyes met, he nodded slightly, and I began moving toward him. Then I suddenly froze as Frank's eyes became my father's, staring down at me from the Maple tree in Highland Park. I stood in place, trembling and forcing back the tears. Frank skated back toward me and put his arms around me.

"I'm sorry, Frank. I'm just so scared."

"It's no problem," he said. "I'm not going anywhere. We'll just wait until another day, when and if you feel you're ready."

Frank's words "I'm not going anywhere" shattered the image in my head. He was not going to leave me as my father had done. He was not going anywhere. I took in a deep breath and answered.

"No. I'm better now. Please, let's try again."

Frank returned to his spot and nodded again. This time, I emptied my thoughts of everything but his eyes looking at me. Just before reaching him, I circled my arms above me, bent my knees, pushed off, and lifted into the air. I panicked for a moment when I realized that I was no longer touching the ground. I was leaning too far forward to catch myself from landing face first on the hard wooden floor. Then Frank's hands gripped my waist and started pushing me skyward. When I was only a couple feet off the ground, I felt his arms stiffen. He stopped my forward movement and lowered me back down.

"Are you all right?" he asked.

I nodded because I was too breathless to talk.

"Good," he said. "Then are you ready to try again?" He had explained earlier that we would move toward the final lift in stages and this was the first one.

I nodded again, smiled, and returned to my starting position. As I did, I noticed how quiet it was. Everyone in the rink had skated off the floor. They took positions against the perimeter walls and silently stared at Frank and me.

Frank locked his feet in position, stiffened his body, leaned slightly forward in my direction, and then smiled. I was flush as I began skating toward him. I could feel the sweat dripping down my body. Once again, just before reaching him, I leaped into the air. This time my body went higher until my feet were chest-high on Frank. Then he locked his arms again, halting my ascent and lowered me back down.

My body trembled with excitement. I couldn't stand still. I wanted, I needed to let loose, to break free of any constraints that held me down. "If you want, this can be it," said Frank. I panted as much from exhilaration as exhaustion.

"Yes, Frank! Let's do it."

He smiled, nodded, and motioned for me to return to the start position. Suddenly, the music stopped and everyone stood motionless around the perimeter. The only sound was the wheels of my roller skates and my heart beating so hard I could hear the pounding in my head.

I turned to face Frank. He was in position and ready. Then he gave me a reassuring smile and nodded for me to come. As I skated toward him, I felt outside my own body, conscious only of the sound of my skate wheels and the look in Frank's eyes. Then I realized that I had lost track of my speed. *I'm going too fast*, I thought. He won't be able to stop me. We're both going to come crashing down! There was no time to adjust. I was only inches from Frank so I closed my eyes and jumped skyward.

Then there was nothing. For what seemed like forever, there was no sound at all, not even my heart pounding, nothing but the sensation of floating helplessly in space, praying for support. Then Frank's hands gripped my waist like a vise. His arms arced like the steel beams of a construction crane. My body shot upward. Once again, Frank's arms locked into position but this time, I was directly above his head; I was flying!

I stiffened my body and pushed my arms out to my sides as Frank

20

glided below me in a long, graceful turn. I flew through the air like a hawk soaring on the wind. Suddenly, Tommy Dorsey's orchestra came blaring on the speaker with Frank Sinatra singing *Fools Rush In* and the crowd exploded into applause.

At that moment, Frank Russo and I were the center of the universe. I don't know how long I was suspended, seconds maybe, but it felt like an eternity. Then Frank signaled for me to lower my arm. When I did, he gripped it tight and guided me toward the ground while he completed the turn. The crowd continued to applaud but as Frank looked into my eyes, their sounds faded into nothingness. I hugged Frank's neck, pulled him toward me, and we kissed, long and deep. Nothing else in the world existed.

That was the first of many lifts, many kisses, and a new stage in our relationship. From that afternoon, we wanted to spend all our free time together, which meant Mother would have to know. She was no longer the mother of my youth, however. The elegant dancer in the gown was now my matronly guardian. When we met with her, I focused the conversation on how Frank and I met at the rink, his giving me skate dancing lessons, and how professional we were becoming. Mother had a different focus.

"Russo?" she asked Frank. "And what kind of name is that?"

I hoped that she wouldn't ask him his nationality until she had gotten to know him better and I never mentioned the issue to Frank.

"Italian," he said. "My parents were from Sicily."

That made matters worse. To Mother, gangsters came from Sicily and they all carried knives.

"Thank you for coming and speaking to me about my daughter." With that, she went off and busied herself in the kitchen until after Frank left.

"He acts very nice," she said.

"Oh, he is, Mom. He's thoughtful and considerate, he's very smart and he's Catholic."

"Good. All Italian men act nice at the beginning but after they get comfortable, they change. You cannot keep seeing him."

"What! Mom, you don't even know him."

"I don't have to know him. He's Italian and he can't help it. All Italian men are after the same thing and they are not going to get it from my daughter."

"Frank isn't like that. He's been nothing but a gentleman."

"For now, but you don't hear him when he's talking with his friends and bragging about how far he's getting with you."

"He's not getting anywhere with me and it's not just up to him. Don't you trust me?"

"You think you love him, don't you?"

"Well ... yes."

"Then no, I don't trust you."

When my grandparents first came to America, my grandmother took in sewing and Grandpa helped during the day before going to his night job. Their reputation for reasonable, quality tailoring grew and within a year, Grandpa gave up his maintenance job and started working full-time with Grandma. The business grew and by the time my father graduated from high school, the tailor shop became his full-time job. Eventually he inherited the business, which is where he met and fell in love with Mother. She continued working there during their courtship and early marriage until she became pregnant with Ralph junior. By then she was happy to leave because of the other men at the shop.

At the time, more than a dozen Italian immigrants did tailoring. They were good workers but they were also brazen in their remarks and behavior. They often joked about my mother's looks and her assumed sexual skill. Finally, when one man patted her backside as she walked through the shop, my father quickly fired him and Mother stayed at home. Ralph junior was born eight months later. My mother's experience left her persistently suspicious of Italian men and Frank Russo was Italian.

"That's so wrong!" I shouted. "You haven't even given him a chance. All you have to do is get to know him and you'll see that he's different."

"I'm not going to get to know him because he's not going to be around."

"I'm not going to stop seeing him!"

"So is this how he affects you? Making you disrespect your own mother? No more! Not another word out of you. You can't see him anymore and that's all there is to it."

CHAPTER 4

THAT WASN'T ALL there was to it. I loved Frank and there was no way I was going to stop seeing him. For a while, I covered by saying I was going to the library or out with June and the other girls while Frank and I snuck off together. Then, one day as we watched a movie from the balcony of the Valencia, we saw Mother pacing around in the orchestra seats below us. We chuckled at first as she moved from aisle to aisle, staring at couples and crossing in front of them. Then people started yelling at her to sit down and stop interrupting the movie. Shaking her head, she stormed out of the theater.

Frank halted as we exited the movie, "We can't keep doing this, Maureen."

"Doing what?"

"We can't keep sneaking around like this. We have to tell your mother."

"Can't we just wait a little longer until the time is right?"

"There's never going to be a right time. We need to talk now."

Frank came early the next morning before I left for work. He assured me that he was ready for Mother; she was obviously ready for him.

"So, you finally decided to come out of the shadows," she greeted him at the door.

Frank just smiled. "Good morning, Mrs. Bower."

"What's good about it? That a boy who has been sneaking around with my daughter behind my back comes to my house? Maybe I should call the police."

"Mother," I chided, "you're not even giving Frank a chance to speak."

"Mrs. Bower," Frank said calmly, "you can do that if you feel like you have to. I'll just share what I came here to say while we wait for them to arrive."

"You think you're very funny, don't you?"

"No," Frank answered calmly, "I just love your daughter." Then Frank turned to me, "Maureen, if you don't mind, I think it would be best if I talked to your mother alone."

"I'm not sure that would be such a good idea…," I started but Mother cut me off.

"You heard him. Go off to work. I'll speak to you later."

I waited all morning for Frank to call me at work. By lunchtime, I couldn't stand to wait any longer and I called the skating rink.

"Sorry kid," said Mr. Pitrillo, "Frank called out for the day. If it was anybody else, I'd have sent them packing, but Frank's real solid and he's never called out like that before on such short notice. If you don't mind my asking, is everything all right between you two? He sounded a little stressed on the phone."

My heart sank. I knew Mother didn't want to see me get hurt but she didn't know Frank the way that I did and she had no right to prejudge him. I called Frank's house, but he wasn't there either. What could she have possibly said to him that would make him miss work? I was furious with my mother and I called home to tell her so.

"Mother," I yelled, even before she said hello, "what did you say to upset Frank so much that he couldn't even go to work today? Now I can't even find him."

"What are you talking about?" she answered. "The boy is still here. He refused to leave. Here, you try to talk some sense into him."

"Frank, what are you still doing there? If Mother tells you to leave and you refuse, you're only going to make matters worse. Maybe you should just leave before things go too far."

"Maureen," Frank answered sternly, "do you trust me?"

"Of course I do, but...."

"Then trust me now and let me do this my way. I'll call you as soon as we're done."

Frank didn't call and what I overheard when I got home from work only confirmed my worst fears. As I put my key in the apartment door, I heard the yelling coming from the dining room.

"You can't do that!" Mother shouted.

"I can," Frank yelled back even louder, "and I will!"

I raced into the dining room hoping to intervene before things became impossible, but stopped short at the doorway. Frank and Mother sat opposite each other at the dining room table. Mother had a pad and pencil in front of her and Frank held up a small paper booklet. A half-dozen dice spread across the table separated them.

"Look," Frank said while pointing to the booklet, "the rules say that I have to use at least two for a pair. There's nothing saying I have to use all of them, so I'm taking a pair of twos and rolling the rest of them again."

Mother snatched the paper from Frank's hands, studied it, and nodded. "OK for this time," then she shook her finger at him, "but don't let me catch you cheating." At that point, the two of them broke out laughing and then noticed me standing open-mouthed in the doorway.

"Maureen," said Mother. "Good that you're home. We're almost finished. Come in and sit down. If you want, you can play while I cook. Your Frank is a pretty good Bunco player, but I think maybe he cheats a little." Mother and Frank looked at each other and smiled. "Then you can help me set the table. Your friend is staying for dinner."

As I said, when Frank put his mind to something.... Anyway, that was the end of Mother's objections, which turned out to be the least of our challenges. The real obstacles were not those in our homes or our neighborhoods but the ones that, like some monstrous storm, rumbled toward us from the other side of the ocean.

CHAPTER 5

OUR NEIGHBORHOOD BUZZED with talk about Adolf Hitler. Most of our Jewish neighbors moved away. Even though the remaining neighbors were mainly German or Italian, most of them said Hitler was crazy and should be stopped but they didn't expect that to happen. The European leaders were unable or unwilling to confront him.

Other neighbors whispered that it was about time Germany had a leader who would restore the country to its greatness and finally do something about the Jews. Regardless of which side they were on, most said we should mind our business and let the Europeans solve their own problems.

It all seemed so distant at the time that I didn't give it much thought. The world just stood by and watched when Hindenburg died and Hitler seized power and again when Germany invaded Poland. Then Germany, Italy, and Japan formed the Axis alliance. When Italy attacked Greece and Germany invaded France, everyone started talking about how we needed to support our European allies but they still opposed our getting directly involved. As our country inched closer toward war, we tried to go about our lives as normal.

Frank proposed to me in May of '41 and Harvey and June were engaged in July. We had more than a few laughs over that sequence of events. As summer cooled into autumn, June suggested, "I have an idea. How about we plan a joint wedding for the spring." Frank and I agreed and the four of us began making plans until President Roosevelt came on the radio during an afternoon of board-game playing. Frank turned up the volume.

"Yesterday, December 7, 1941—a date which will live in infamy—the United States of America was suddenly and deliberately attacked by Naval and Air Forces of the Empire of Japan...."

The president described the attack on Pearl Harbor and his request that Congress declare a state of war with Japan. Hitler answered the question of what to do about Germany when he declared war on us four days later.

After Germany's declaration, Harvey suggested that we move up the wedding.

"But what about your munitions plant job?" Frank asked. "You said you were safe from the draft."

"Not any more, Frankie. This changes everything. So, what do you say about moving up the wedding date?"

"I have to think about it."

I didn't say anything at the time but I challenged Frank as soon as we were alone again.

"Until now we've made all of our wedding plans together but when Harvey asked about moving up the date, you said that you, not we, would have to think about it."

"I'm sorry. I didn't mean to slight you but I think we need to cancel the wedding."

Tears welled up in my eyes and I started shaking uncontrollably. "Cancel? I don't understand. I love you and you love me. Why would you even think of cancelling? What did I do wrong?"

"Wrong?" Frank wrapped his arms around me and squeezes tight. "You haven't done anything wrong, Maureen: nothing at all! I love you more than anything else in my life but people die in war and if I don't return, I don't want to hurt you that way."

"What do you mean if you don't return? You haven't been drafted."

"I'm going to enlist."

Something in me snapped. I pushed back and slapped Frank hard across the face. His stunned expression matched my own sense of shock at what I had done. I started crying uncontrollably but then my anger raged back again, "How could you?" I started hitting Frank again and again until he wrapped me tightly in his arms and held me. I buried my head in his chest and sobbed bitterly.

Frank stroked my hair as he spoke, "I'm sorry. I was stupid to be so blunt."

I pushed away, "Why, Frank? Why you? There are plenty of other men who could go."

Suddenly, he looked different. There was a sadness in his expression that I had only seen once before, when we first met.

"Do you remember when you asked me about how I broke my nose?" he asked.

"Of course I do. You shut me off then just like you're doing now." I knew I was being hateful but I didn't care. I wanted to hurt Frank the way he was hurting me. I stepped back farther to look at his nose.

"I've grown so used to it that it's become invisible," then I recalled how angry I was. "What's that got to do with anything anyway?"

"Everything," he said. "I think about it every day of my life. When I was in high school, I used to stop at this little coffee shop on Jamaica Avenue on my way home. One day, while the owner was pouring me coffee, a cop came into the shop and walked up to the counter. The owner turned pale. He stopped pouring halfway through my cup, walked over to the register, took out a wad of money, and handed it to the cop. The cop shuffled through the wad and then complained, 'Is this all?' The owner cowered like a beaten puppy and apologized, saying that it was all he had because business was slow. He spoke low, but everyone at the counter could hear what he was saying. The cop just sneered, 'That's your problem, not mine,' and then he noticed me looking at him.

"'What are you staring at?' he asked.

"I must have been feeling pretty cocky that day and answered, 'I'm not sure.'

"'Come outside,' the cop yelled, 'and bring your donut.' I looked around at the rest of the customers for support but all of them looked away from me and no one moved an inch.

"As soon as I stepped outside, the cop's Billy club crashed into my nose. I fell to my knees and dropped the donut. Blood poured out onto the pavement and for the longest time, I just knelt there crying from the pain.

"'Now what was it you were looking at?' he asked.

"I wanted to challenge him, to say that I was looking at a crooked cop but I was too scared. I whispered, 'Nothing.'

"'I couldn't hear you!' he yelled. 'Speak up!'

"I said it louder, 'Nothing. Nothing at all.'

"'That's right, punk, nothing. Now wouldn't it be a real shame if a young kid like you got locked up for something as small as stealing a donut? Guess you're lucky that you caught me in such a forgiving mood. Now go pay for your stuff and don't let me see you loitering around here again.'

"I never went back to that coffee shop. Months later when I passed, it was boarded shut but I've never forgotten the look in the owner's eyes and the cowering of those other customers. One bully with a badge terrorized us all. Well now, a bigger gang of bullies is terrorizing all of Europe and they're coming after us. Maureen, I'm sorry but I can't sit by and do nothing. It's like Harvey said. This changes everything. I don't want to rush into marriage and then take a chance that I might leave you and not come back. You deserve better than that."

I protested, "And what about me? Don't I have a say in this? I love you and I'm willing to take that chance."

"And what if you got pregnant?" There was anger in his voice that wasn't there before. "How would you support yourself and a baby? With a war on, most able-bodied men will be gone. For the few still around, how many do you think would be willing to take on a wife and a family?" He grabbed my shoulders and squeezed so tight that he hurt me. Then he looked directly into my eyes, "Don't you understand?" His eyes glistened and I could see that he was holding back tears. "It's not that I don't love you enough to marry you. It's that I love you too much."

I desperately wanted to tell him that he was wrong, that we mattered more than some fight on the other side of the ocean, but I couldn't. I realized that if I stopped him from doing this, he might never forgive himself, or me. "Oh, Frank," was all I could get out. I fell into his arms, buried my head against his chest, and cried.

Several weeks after he enlisted, Frank received a rejection letter from the Army because of his broken nose. He was devastated. The very thing that made him so desperate to enlist had also become the reason for his rejection.

In the meantime, Harvey and June moved up the date of their wedding. Harvey asked Frank to be his best man and June asked me to be her maid of honor. It was a beautiful wedding. I pleaded with Frank to stop talking about canceling ours and instead just postpone it until he felt it was safe. We waited until he was satisfied that his deferral would stand and when we finally set the date, we asked the new Mr. and Mrs. Metz to repay the favor. Frank and I married in late September of '42. When we returned from our Atlantic City honeymoon, however, it became painfully clear that we hadn't waited long enough.

CHAPTER 6

BEING SAFE WAS a wish, not a reality. Standing outside of our second-floor apartment in Brooklyn, I set my suitcase down in the hall as Frank searched for the keys. I held a week's worth of mail in one hand and as the door swung open, I reached down for my suitcase with the other.

"Hold on," Frank scooped me up into his arms. "Haven't you heard? The first time a couple enters their new home, it's the husband's prerogative to carry his wife over the threshold."

He continued holding me after stepping into our dining room, kissing me while he did. I hugged him tight around the neck until I felt him stiffen. I loosened my hold to question why when I noticed his strained expression giving way to one of relief.

"Oh, the sunburn, I'm sorry."

"No problem," he answered, "just another souvenir from Atlantic City. A kiss like that is worth a little pain anytime."

He put me down and hugged me tight, which made it my turn to wince. My bra straps chafed against my bright red skin. Frank loosened his hold and laughed, "Boy, aren't we a pair." Then he kissed me softly, "Welcome home, Mrs. Russo."

"Mrs. Russo," I said, "I like the sound of that, Mister Russo."

We each noticed the small beads of sweat forming on our foreheads. Frank said, "I guess I better start opening some windows."

I took in the look and feel of our apartment. The cherry dining room furniture still gleamed from the polishing I did just before we left for our honeymoon. *Our new home*, I told myself. The thought frightened me a little but excited me more.

In our railroad apartment, most of the rooms fell in a row like the cars on a train. At the back end, Frank opened the kitchen window that overlooked the fire escape landing and the small yard we shared with the building's five other families. Clotheslines stretched from each landing to the telephone pole at the far end of the yard. When Frank returned to the dining room and opened the window by me, a wonderful gust of cool air rushed in and I closed my eyes for a moment to relish the breeze. Frank crossed through the tiny living room with its couch on one wall opposite the radio/phonograph console on the other and entered the bedroom. When he opened the final window at the far end of the bedroom, the temperature quickly cooled. Moments later, the rumbling of the elevated train running along Fulton Street briefly filled the apartment.

While Frank busied himself opening windows, I organized the mail into separate piles for bills, advertisements, and letters that looked important. I decided the bills and ads could wait, but I was excited to see what was in the other envelopes. The first one I opened had a typed address to Mr. Frank Russo and Miss Maureen Bower and the return address was from the US Amateur Roller Skating Association. I briefly looked up to our breakfront where a row of our skating competition trophies lined the top. The letter was an invitation for Frank and me to compete in the 1943 National Roller Skating Championship. I excitedly stuffed the letter back in the envelope and placed it on the pile so that Frank could open it again for himself. I stopped and smiled at the next handwritten envelope addressed to Mr. and Mrs. Frank Russo. Meanwhile, Frank retrieved the suitcases from the hall, set them down next to me, and gingerly wrapped his arms around my waist. Then he smiled too as he spied the envelope in my hand. The return address was from Harvey and June Metz.

Frank kissed my neck and began playing with my bra strap. As he moved it to the side, he exposed a thin white line sandwiched between bright pink skin and whispered, "I never realized how sensuous tan lines could be. Why don't we just see how many others we can find?" I trembled with delight as the stack of mail spilled onto the dining room table. I reached up and slid my hand to the back of Frank's neck, tingling with anticipation of what would happen next. But Frank's fingers suddenly stopped moving, he withdrew his mouth from my neck, and I felt his whole body stiffen.

"What's wrong?" I asked, looking into the pained expression on his face. His eyes stared downward, fixed and wide. I followed his gaze to its target and when I reached it, I felt faint. Frank caught me. Then we both stood motionless as the clock ticked away the seconds.

Frank moved first. His hand quivered as he reached for the letter. The return address read *Selective Service, Official Business*. Tears ran down my cheek as he removed the paper from the envelope. The Great Seal appeared at the top and a box to the side contained the stamped name and address of the local draft board. The words beneath the seal read *Order to Report for Induction*.

CHAPTER 7

HARVEY WAS RIGHT: Pearl Harbor changed everything. The government reversed Frank's draft deferral and he joined the ranks of the other *able-bodied* men. Following the instructions in his draft notice, he reported for duty on December 8, 1942, exactly one year after the president's radio address. At the train station just before he boarded, Frank handed me a small box. In it was a pair of earrings in the shape of two gold leaves.

"Do you remember when we first saw these?" he asked.

"Of course, Frank, at the artist's studio, but I remember that they cost a fortune."

"I wanted you to have the necklace too, but I couldn't afford it right now. We'll get it in the future and you can wear them each year on our anniversary. In the meantime, whenever you look at these, think of me."

"Just come back to me, Frank." The train started moving. We kissed and then ran together hand-in-hand as Frank mounted the stairs, until our fingers finally slipped apart.

"I love you, Maureen Russo," he shouted and remained at the base of the stairs looking back at me until he vanished into the mist.

We never did respond to the skating championship invitation. Over the next three years, we saw each other for a total of three weeks, one after Frank completed basic training and two more just before he went overseas. On our last night before Frank shipped out to the Pacific, I asked him to promise that he would come back to me.

"As much as I want to, you know I'd be lying if I said could control that."

"I'm not looking for honesty," I yelled. "I want you to tell me that you will come back no matter what."

He answered, "I promise you this, Maureen: I'll do everything in my power to come back to you and if I do, I will never ever leave you again."

We exchanged letters every day. If he was in transit for a time, I wouldn't receive anything for a week or more and then I would get a stack of mail on a single day. Sometimes I reread the letters again until I fell asleep.

For weeks after he left, I couldn't sleep, eat, or concentrate at work. I couldn't even take comfort in the letters he sent. No matter what he said, all I could think about was his moving into harm's way. Then I wrote to Frank that Harvey received his draft notice too. After training and stateside duty, he shipped out to the European theater. It was heartbreaking to see the impact on June. She had felt safe with Harvey's job and looked forward to their uninterrupted life together. They were already talking about their plans for children. Like me, Harvey's induction shattered June's sense of security.

June and I became war brides. While our husbands were half-a-world away, we kept vigil at home. We served in the USO, helped with war-bond drives, and even joined the Cadet Nurse Corps. I didn't stay there very long. The training was rigorous and we both handled the academics well, but when we started interning at the hospital, the reality of the war overwhelmed me. "Hurry it up, Russo," the head nurse yelled as I stared at the mangled stump of a soldier's missing leg, "that dressing isn't going to change itself." Some men were blind, others were terribly disfigured. In addition to the physical wounds, many suffered from severe mental and emotional disorders. Many of them accepted their conditions with unbelievable courage but I saw Frank in every one of them and within a few weeks, I dropped out. June, however, stayed on. Unlike Frank,

Harvey promised June that he would return safe and sound and she took comfort in that but I couldn't get over the devastation I would feel if anything happened to Frank.

"You've got to stop thinking like that," June scolded. "You need to trust that our men are doing everything they can to come back to us."

June and I met every day after work. I told her about my activities at the USO and the many entertainers I met there. She reviewed the tasks she did for the men at the hospital, like reading them letters or helping them to reconnect with relatives. She never said so, but I knew that she carefully avoided discussing nursing those with serious wounds. We exchanged stories about the many men who made passes at us until we told them we were married. We sometimes laughed as we secretly imagined what it might be like to take some of them up on their offers.

When we weren't busying ourselves with our volunteer duties, June and I still went roller-skating but it was different without Frank and Harvey. It was also a stark reminder about the war.

"It sure ain't like it used to be," said Mr. Pitrillo. "This place used to be loaded with folks of all ages. Now it's just women, young children, and old men like me. All the young men are gone."

June and I passed some of the time by going to the movies. The newsreels before the main feature showed the progress of our soldiers in the war.

"See? What did I tell you?" said June. "At the rate our guys are going, they'll be home for Christmas."

We purposely avoided war movies, but one of the films we did see made a lasting impression on me. During one scene, a group of people became stuck in an elevator. I worked in a high-rise office building in Manhattan at the time and the thought of being trapped like that terrified me. From that point on, I was leery every time I had to use an elevator.

June guessed wrong. Our men didn't come home for Christmas. As time passed, I continued to write Frank detailed letters every day but his came less often and when they did, they were short and often cryptic. It was what he didn't say that worried me most. June and I often read portions of the letters we received to each other. Harvey's were more upbeat. It seemed like he adjusted to the rigors of war better than Frank did.

For almost two years I shuddered each time the doorbell rang, praying it was not a messenger from Western Union. Then in a letter to Frank in August 1944, I wrote:

Dearest Frank,

Today a Western Union courier came to June's house. He delivered a telegram from the Department of the Army. It said, "We deeply regret to inform you that your husband was killed in action as a result of a land and sea operation on the morning of 6 June 1944 stop Letter follows stop. Please accept my profound sympathy."

The letter was so cold and impersonal. They aren't even going to return his body. They just buried him near some beach in France. Oh, Frank, it was horrible. After she finished reading the letter, June said she needed to be alone and asked me to leave. When I returned the next day, she wouldn't even talk to me. I tried to reach out to her but each time I visited her house, she refused to answer the door and wouldn't come out. Then, this past week, her mother called to say that June moved away and asked that I not try to contact her again.

Frank, please, please be careful. Please come back home to me. I feel so alone. I miss you, I love you, and I can't even think about living my life without you.

> *Loving you with all my heart,*
> *Maureen*

In the letter, I didn't tell Frank how enraged I was with June. I know she was hurting, more than I could ever imagine, but we were best friends and she wouldn't even let me try to help console her. I was sickened when June's mother gave me the news that she was gone. It was another one of those hot, sticky days and when I returned home, I stood in my apartment and looked out the open window for a long time. I thought about the sweltering afternoon my father left and how June, like him, had just cut me out of her life.

I waited anxiously for Frank's response and grew frantic as the days and weeks passed with no reply. I wrote him every day only to find my own mailbox empty. Then, almost three months later, I received a single sheet of paper from him with these words:

Dearest Maureen,

I am devastated by the news about Harvey. He was my dearest friend and I loved him like a brother.

In war, however, death is not the worst thing that can happen.

I Love You,

Frank

CHAPTER 8

FOR THE REST of his time in the Army, Frank sent me letters more often but they were brief and mostly asked about me rather than talking about him. He came home in late September 1945. I was at the dock when his ship came in and I had to hide my tears as he disembarked. His once smooth face was etched with deep lines and he steadied himself with a crutch as he made his way down the gangplank. Frank returned with a noticeable limp, a deep scar on his right leg, and a partial hearing loss. Otherwise, he looked fit. His wounds earned him a Purple Heart. It was the injuries I couldn't see, however, that worried me more.

During his furloughs after boot camp and again before shipping off to the Pacific, Frank talked nonstop about his training and travels. I loved listening to him, so when he returned from overseas I was excited to hear about all the exotic places he had seen and the interesting people he had met.

"Is the water in the Pacific as blue as in the paintings?" I asked. Frank nodded his agreement.

"And the sky too?"

"Except during the rainy season," he answered. "Then you could go for days or weeks without seeing the sun."

"I think I'd like to see it someday. Where was your favorite place?"

His face tightened, "There was none."

When I asked Frank about his injuries, he shut down completely.

Other than a brief description of his respite in China and the caring treatment he received while he recuperated from his injuries, he would not discuss the events that took place in the Pacific. Worse, he insisted that I never ask about them again.

"You can't just shove me away like that!" I yelled. "The war took away your best friend, but it also took away mine. I waited three years for you, so you can't just decide to build some wall to hide behind." Frank grabbed my shoulders and squeezed so hard it hurt.

"The wall isn't for my protection. It's for yours. Now drop it."

While Frank had returned physically, it took much longer before he was mentally and emotionally home again. For months after, he jerked at the slightest sound or movement. On many nights, he couldn't sleep at all and on those when he did, he often thrashed about in bed.

"No!" he shouted in his sleep, "Stop before it's too...."

I slept at the other edge of the bed, afraid that if I touched him he might react violently. Instead, when he started thrashing, I whispered softly, "Frank, you're home now, you're safe."

Then, when I thought it was safe enough, I reached across the bed and lightly touched his arm. If he jerked suddenly, I withdrew and waited before trying again. When he calmed, I whispered, "It's me, Frank, Maureen. I love you," and slowly moved in closer, gently rubbing his arm until his breathing deepened to a peaceful rhythm. Then I snuggled next to him and stroked his hair. It was often moist with sweat and at times, his whole body was wet. "It's all right," I murmured, "you're safe with me," and then I cradled him in my arms like a child and rocked him gently. As I did, I sometimes heard him sobbing in his sleep, "I'm sorry. I'm so, so sorry."

CHAPTER 9

AFTER THE NIGHTMARES subsided, Frank made good on his promise never to leave me again. With the exception of the birth of our two daughters and the annual men's retreat, we never spent another night apart again: at least not physically.

They say that war sometimes takes something out of a person. Whatever it is, Frank returned without it. He never spoke of the war and whenever the topic came up in conversation, he fell silent but his pained expression made it clear that he was somewhere else. Nevertheless he tried his best to show affection, or at least to accept mine. As we walked together, I held his hand or wrapped my arm in his. At first, he tightened but then he caught himself and stopped resisting. Over time, he accepted my advances and began returning the gestures in kind. Eventually, holding hands in public became our trademark and when we got active in church and civic functions, we did all of our volunteer work together.

We later learned that it was Frank's boss from the roller rink, Mr. Petrillo, who nominated us for that national skating competition and that many of the rink patrons had signed a petition supporting it. The limp in Frank's walk lessened over time and eventually disappeared completely, but the damage to his knee made performing our lifts impossible. We never competed in skate dancing again but we still loved to dance together so we shifted our attention to ballroom dancing.

Before my father's business problems, when he and my mother went to the church dances every week, Mother spent many weekday afternoons teaching me ballroom dancing moves. In turn, I taught the steps I learned to Frank and then he and I created new ones of our own. We practiced our moves at the weekly dances in our own parish and in time, our reputation for ballroom dancing approached that of our skate dancing. Any ideas about competing, however, stopped abruptly with my first pregnancy. The other change it brought about was even more profound.

"What do you think about this?" Frank asked as he showed me a camera ad in the Sunday paper. "It's a little expensive but for the money, it's got a lot of features."

"I really can't say. They all look the same to me. What would you do with it?"

"I'd like to take some pictures of you and the baby."

Our daughter's birth changed Frank. It was as though Bridget severed links that tethered him to the past and helped him to find new meaning in the present. Frank grew calmer and smiled more. He bought that camera, took night courses in photography, and subscribed to photo magazines. The quality of his photographs consistently improved and the more he learned, the more appreciation he gained for the artistry of his hobby. He even offered some adult education courses of his own at the local high school and eventually, he returned to the Frank that I first knew.

"OK, now hold her in your other arm."

"Frank, don't you think you've taken enough already?"

"Just one more. I love the way the sunlight coming through the stained-glass window is hitting the two of you. The colors are perfect."

His camera became his constant companion as Frank captured the moments of our lives on film. As time passed, his interests broadened and we became only one of the many subjects he photographed.

"What do you think about this?" he'd ask.

"It looks nice, but there's no one in it?" To me, the idea of using good film to take pictures of things instead of people seemed like a waste.

"I like getting pictures of people too, but sometimes I just want to concentrate on the composition. Look at how the shadows from the clouds play on the curvature of the hill."

Frank's eye for detail soon extended to movies.

"When I used to show the films at the base theater, I never appreciated how much went into capturing a scene in just the right way."

That comment sent a shiver through me. It was the first time Frank mentioned anything service-related since he came back from the war. He spoke with a real sense of pride and none of the anguish he normally associated with that period. As we celebrated Frank's thirtieth birthday, for the first time since his return, I dared to believe that my husband was finally home again.

Frank was also a devoted father. He looked forward to spending time with Bridget, teaching and playing with her, and just being a part of her life. The transition from being a couple to a family was easy for me too, that is until I became pregnant with Megan.

Other than morning sickness, the first few months of the pregnancy went by without much notice. As I entered my sixth month, however, a vague uneasiness set in. During my seventh month, that worry became anxiety and as I moved into my eight, the anxiety developed into a full-blown panic. I couldn't eat or sleep and I spent many nights pacing the floor, trying to figure out what was wrong. Was I afraid of the added responsibilities or the increased time another child would require? Was I worried that we wouldn't have enough money to support a larger family? None of that felt strong enough to warrant my dread. Slowly, another question formed and when it finally entered my consciousness, it startled me: was I afraid that I would stop loving Bridget?

Why would I stop loving my own daughter? The whole question made no sense to me. When I shared my concerns with Frank, he said it was probably just the chemical changes caused by my pregnancy: a typical male response and of no help. Then I brought it up in confession and Father asked me to pray for an answer. What did he think I was doing while I was walking the floors all night? Once again, not helpful. Then

I asked my mother what she thought. "That's a funny question to ask. I always loved you, your brother, and your sister the same."

Her response jogged a memory and I shuddered uncontrollably as I recalled it. Of course: the other open window on the scorching day my sister was born!

In the early thirties, maybe people who lived in upstate mansions went to hospitals to have their babies, but in our East New York apartment the doctor came to the house and the midwife assisted. Mother asked a neighbor to watch me during the delivery. We waited in the shade across the street. Even so, the sitter's face was red and dripping wet.

"Now you mind my words and sit still," she barked as I skirted in and out of the cast-iron fences that separated our neighbor's stoops. In between explorations, I glanced up to the second-floor window of my parents' bedroom. The curtains hung limp in the breezeless air.

"Where is your brother today?" she asked.

"At my aunt's house. I didn't want to go. I wanted to stay home with Mommy."

"Well, maybe you should have gone with your brother."

"But then I wouldn't be around if Mommy needed me."

"Well, she certainly doesn't need you running all over the place. From now on, you're going have to act like a big girl."

I glared at her, folded my arms, stamped my foot down, and pronounced loudly, "I am a big girl."

"Well, once the new baby comes, you're going to have to fend for yourself. Your mother isn't going to have time to be chasing after you all day."

My four-year-old-brain struggled to process the sitter's words and what I understood from them was that once the new baby arrived, my mother wouldn't have time to love me anymore. Suddenly, I hated that baby and for good reason.

After my older brother, Ralph, was born, my older sister, Maureen, was stillborn. Then Mother miscarried twice. She thought that she could never have another baby until I came along five years later. Even then, I was several weeks premature and severely underweight. During one of my aunt's visits, she cautioned that I looked sickly and told Mother that she should prepare herself that she might lose me too.

Mother did the opposite. She hovered over me and if she had to leave me even for a few seconds, she asked someone to watch me until she returned. She watched everything I did and guarded me from any danger, real or imagined. For the next four years, I was the center of her world and now, this new baby threatened to steal that from me. I wanted to run into the house and tell Mother to send it back but just then, the baby cried. It was too late! The new baby was here and Mother would never love me the same way again. I sat down on the stoop and cried.

"Isn't that the sweetest thing," another woman said to the sitter. "How precious."

The midwife came to the bedroom window and signaled for me to come up. I stood motionless until the sitter intervened. "Well, go ahead now. You have a new brother or sister to meet."

When I reached the bedroom door, I stood panicked until Mother said, "Climb up here with us, Maureen." She lowered the sheet and patted the mattress next to her. As I entered the sheets, she wrapped her free arm around me. "You have a new baby sister."

She took my hand and gently rubbed it against my sister's face. I wanted to scratch it instead. Then I placed my hand on Mother's belly.

"Is this where she came from?"

"Uh huh."

"Can you put her back?"

"Of course not! Why on earth would I?"

"Now that she's here, you won't have time to love me anymore."

"That's a silly thing to say. Of course, I will. I love you and your brother every bit as much now as I ever have and I always will. What would make you say something like that?"

"Nothing."

It seemed like we lay there for hours: Mother, Sister, and me. Wrapped in my mother's arms I felt safer, but the insecurity lingered.

Looking back on it now, I wish I had told her about the sitter's comment. For years after, I took any sign of attention that she paid my sister as evidence that the sitter was right. It's written on my face in our family photos. Whenever I recalled that day, it's not my mother's reassurance that first comes to mind. It's that feeling of abandonment, looking up to that open window and wishing my sister away.

Reflecting on Mother's comment, I took in a deep breath and, letting it out again, felt my anxiety exit. From that moment on, I turned my attention to welcoming our new baby. I resolved to do everything I could to make certain that Bridget didn't suffer the same jealous feelings that I had. That night and every other night until Megan was born, I slept soundly. At the same time, I thought back to the open windows in my life: on the day my sister was born, on the night my father died, and the day after my best friend walked out of my life. I realized that deep within me, my own fear of abandonment still lingered.

CHAPTER 10

BRIDGET HAD IT harder growing up than Megan did. Being the first, I guess Frank and I learned how to be parents with her. Setting limits was always a challenge because whenever in doubt, Frank took the more conservative route. Bridget, bless her, was for the most part obedient, even when Frank wasn't around. Megan, on the other hand, did not accept rules easily. Whenever there was a limit, she seemed intent on testing it. That carried through grade school, high school, and even into dating.

Bridget developed more like me in looks and behavior. She had my wavy, strawberry-blond hair, slightly curvy frame and even temperament. She also shared similar interests in men. Several of her boyfriends didn't pass Frank's muster. Some were too immature, others too slovenly, and one was much too old, but eventually her selection of Steve was just right. Conservative in looks and behavior, clean-cut and respectful, Steve hit it off with Frank almost from the start. Since Bridget had met Steve through church choir practice, he already had a leg up. That's not to say that there weren't some tense moments. Steve wasn't afraid to speak his mind and confront Frank, especially if he felt that some of Frank's limits on Bridget were unfair. Eventually, that only helped to increase his stature in Frank's eyes. When he asked Frank's permission to marry Bridget before he proposed, that sealed the deal.

Megan inherited more of Frank's attributes with her brown hair, wiry frame and stubborn disposition. Compared to Bridget, her boyfriends were another story altogether. For one thing, there were many more of them. For another, they came in a wide assortment of shapes, sizes, and colors. Some were different religions, others different races, and one had tattoos from head to toe. By the time she started dating Ryan, he was tame by comparison.

Megan and Ryan met at a funeral and they were immediately attracted to each other. When she brought him home to meet her father, however, Frank had a different opinion. To him, Ryan's full beard, bushy mustache, and shoulder-length hair had all the markings of a drug-addicted rocker. His worn leather jacket and ripped, faded jeans didn't help matters either. Still, he had a warm smile and a charming manner about him that I found appealing. The only redeeming quality Frank could see was that Ryan noticed the chessboard in the living room and asked Frank if he played. Nevertheless, Frank had serious doubts that anyone who looked like Ryan could know anything more about the game than the way the pieces looked. Frank told Megan she could not see Ryan and "that was that." Megan being Megan shouted that Frank was a 'sick old man' and stormed out of the house. For Frank, that ended the matter but I knew better. It was easy for me to spot the signs that Megan and Ryan kept secretly seeing each other. When I confronted her about it, she didn't even try to hide it.

"He's wrong about Ryan and you know it too!" she said.

"Don't even try to get me to side with you against your father young lady. It's not going to happen."

Megan stopped yelling and tears welled up in her eyes. "But he really loves me, Mom, and I love him."

I took her in my arms and felt her body quiver as she sobbed. I hugged and kissed her and gently stroked her hair, "It's not hopeless, Megan. I see the good in Ryan and I'm sure that in time, your father will too. But if you want him to change his mind, you and Ryan are going to have to work to convince him."

For more than twenty years, I supported Frank on most decisions but this was different. Megan wasn't a child any longer and I strongly disagreed with Frank. I believed that Ryan was a good person and I could see that he and Megan cared deeply for each other. So I did what any good mother would do: I hid their relationship from my husband.

My strategy worked for a while. Knowing Megan, I also knew that in time Frank would find out. The ruse lasted a few months.

"Maureen," Frank shouted as he came in from work one day, "you're not going to believe who I saw in the ice cream parlor on the corner."

"Megan and Ryan?"

From the look on his face, I knew that Frank knew that I knew. "They've been seeing each other all along."

"You knew about this and you didn't say anything to me?" He was seething.

"Yes, Frank. Megan and Ryan love each other and Ryan has a lot of good qualities if you just let yourself get to know him."

"Oh? And do you consider his sneaking around with my daughter behind my back one of his good qualities?"

"*Our* daughter, Frank, and think about it. If Megan and Ryan wanted to hide their relationship from you, do you think they would have been together at the corner ice cream parlor? Don't you see? Megan wants your approval but she's like you: too proud and too stubborn to ask."

"Well, we'll see about that. You tell *our* daughter that I want to talk to her boyfriend, alone and pronto!"

The next week, I took Megan on a shopping trip to City Line while Frank and Ryan met. Normally, I'd have to drag Megan away from the stores but that day she was anxious to get back home before things got out of hand. She said she wasn't concerned that Frank might scare Ryan off but rather that she might end up having to choose between her boyfriend and her father. I thought she was being overly dramatic until we reached the top of the landing and heard the shouting coming through the apartment door.

"Listen," we heard Frank yell, "there are rules for the way you go about things and if you can't play by them, then you have no business starting at all."

Ryan answered even louder, "Well sometimes the rules aren't so clear so I go by what I know until I learn otherwise. So what do you want me to do?"

Frank shouted, "You already know what you have to do. Back off and leave her alone."

Megan went ballistic. She shoved the door open and burst into the living room, "What do you mean back off and leave me alone!"

Then she addressed Ryan, "And you, I can't believe you'd agree to...."

Suddenly she stopped talking as she looked into the startled faces of the two men and realized they were sitting across from each other at the chessboard. Ryan held up the rook in his hand, "I'm backing off attacking Frank's queen and not putting him in checkmate because he said I had to clear his check on me first."

"So you two were listening in at the door?" Frank asked. He didn't wait for the answer. He looked at each of us and said, "It seems like everyone in this house is getting a little too good at sneaking around." I cringed for a moment but then the smirks on his and Ryan's face said the rest. We invited Ryan to stay for dinner.

As I stirred the spaghetti, I smiled at the thought of the startled expression on Megan's face when she entered. Then I laughed, recalling my own expression when I saw Frank and my mother playing Bunko more than two decades earlier and how that ended. Frighteningly, the similarities in our relationships did not end there. Three weeks later, Ryan proposed to Megan and they set a wedding date for the following year. As they furthered their wedding plans, however, the Vietnam conflict escalated.

CHAPTER 11

I THANK GOD for answering my unspoken prayer. As events in the Far East escalated, I dreaded that Steve or Ryan might experience the horror of war as Frank had. I ached at the thought that Bridget or Megan might receive the kind of letter that June did. I never formed my thoughts into a prayer but thankfully, I didn't have to.

Steve continued working and taking college courses at night and the draft never picked his name. Like Frank, Ryan didn't want to chance getting married and then being picked, so he requested to have his draft moved up. Megan shared Ryan's plan with her manager who was also a captain in the Marine Corps Reserve. He suggested that Ryan enlist in the reserves so that after his six months active duty, he and Megan could go on with their wedding plans. Ryan followed the suggestion and fortunately the Marine Corps never activated his unit and he never went to Vietnam.

Ryan's relatives lived in Connecticut. After visiting them while she and Ryan dated, Megan fell in love with country living. While Ryan was on active duty, she wrote to him suggesting that they move to Connecticut after the wedding. Following his return, Ryan stayed with his sister and brother-in-law in the Bristol area while he explored job opportunities. By the time of their wedding, he found a secure job and a lovely apartment in Forestville. Not bad for someone Frank thought was a drug-addicted rocker.

It would be fair to say that Megan and Ryan's marriage got off to a stormy start. When the newlyweds returned from their honeymoon, Frank, Bridget and I were at Kennedy Airport to meet them. As soon as they deplaned, Bridget and I rushed to them with welcoming hugs and kisses, but even before we asked the first question, Frank was barking orders. "OK, save the niceties for once we're in the car. Right now, we need to get to the baggage claim area."

Ryan didn't even try to hide his sarcasm.

"Well, it's nice to see you too, Dad."

Frank was not amused. "In case you hadn't noticed, Marine, it's snowing out there."

"And so? It's February."

"All right you two," I intervened. "That's enough sparring. Ryan, I'm sure you and Megan have had more on your minds than the weather, so I suspect you haven't heard."

"Heard what, Mom?" Megan asked.

"This is going to be a really bad snowstorm. It's been on the news for the last two days."

Bridget jumped in, "They're expecting over two feet in the city! All of the news stations are calling it the "Blizzard of 69."

I added, "More than six inches has fallen already and the storm is getting worse by the minute. Your plane was the last one to land until the storm is over."

Frank said, "And to make matters worse, our brilliant mayor decided to save money by holding back the plows. Now they can't keep up with the snow and some of the streets are already impassable."

"Oh," said Ryan sheepishly. "Sorry, Dad, I didn't mean to be a wise-ass."

"Forget it. Let's just hope the roads are better in Connecticut."

Ryan stopped abruptly. "Hold on a second. You're not actually going to try to drive all the way to Connecticut in a blizzard, are you?"

"Aren't you supposed to report to your reserve unit in the morning?

My Ford Galaxy is a boat. I have sand bags and shovels in the trunk. We just have to get moving fast."

Ryan insisted on calling the reserve unit to explain the situation and get permission to move back his reporting time. Frank paced incessantly until he returned. The expression on Ryan's face broadcasted the answer. "The duty officer said no excuses, report on time, or else. I say we spend the night at your house, take off after the storm, and deal with the Marine Corps later."

Frank chided, "Is that what they teach you in boot camp nowadays? When the going gets tough, cave in?"

With that, Ryan's expression moved from embarrassed, to pensive, to resolved, "All right, let's go get the luggage."

As Frank warned, snow already blocked many of the streets. It took us more than an hour to reach the Van Wick Expressway. Frank stopped the car on a hill overlooking the on-ramp where we got out and stood in disbelief. The expressway was a snowfield. The roofs of stranded cars were barely visible and two snowplows were helplessly sinking in a sea of white. To our left and right, the side streets were blocked. Only the way we came in remained open and the snow was falling blindingly fast.

"Looks like that's it," Ryan sighed. "Thanks, Dad. You gave it one hell of a try," but Frank didn't answer. Instead, he circled the perimeter of the cul-de-sac, scanning the area. Then he opened the trunk of the Galaxy, removed the two shovels, and handed one to Ryan.

"See those lights over there. That's a main business street and it's open. We can skirt the expressway until we find an open entrance and then make our way to the Whitestone."

A fifteen-foot span of two-foot high snow lay between the open side street and us. Ryan shook his head and laughed, "OK then. Let's do this." A half-hour later, we were moving again.

We continued for another twenty-five minutes until traffic stopped dead. Frank and Ryan stepped out to investigate. When he returned, Ryan said, "It looks like a tractor-trailer jackknifed at the bottom of the hill and we're pinned in by the traffic."

It was past midnight and Frank added, "There's nothing we can do but wait for the plows. It doesn't look like we're going anywhere for a while." Frank kept the car running with the heater on so the window defroster kept the front windshield clear, but the rest of the car's windows fogged with frost. The men kept vigil while the rest of us nodded off until past five.

When Megan woke, she said, "I'm starving and the donut shop across the street is open."

I suggested, "I think it's about time we heard about Megan and Ryan's honeymoon."

Frank and Ryan chose to stay with the car so I took orders for them and then the girls and I crossed to the store. After supplying the men with coffee and breakfast sandwiches, the girls and I settled into a comfortable window booth.

I placed my hand atop Megan's, "So did you have a good time, honey?"

From that point on, I didn't need to prompt: Megan took over the conversation. "It was wonderful, Mom: everything I could have wished for and more. We went snowmobiling, sledding, skeet shooting and ice-skating. I even learned how to ski. The place was beautiful, the food was great, and the staff couldn't do enough for you. We became friends with two other couples that sat at our table for dinner...."

Megan continued for another twenty minutes until Bridget interrupted. "OK, we get that the place had great resort amenities and everybody was wonderful, but get to the good part, Megan. How was the sex?"

I gave her a nudge, "Bridget, what kind of a question is that?"

"I don't mind, Mom," Megan's face beamed. She leaned in Bridget's direction and lowered her voice, "It was great." Then she whispered something into Bridget's ear and both girls burst out laughing. I smiled at the closeness they shared and at the memories of my own honeymoon.

We continued the conversation unabated for another half-hour, frequently interspersed with shrieks of laughter, until Ryan poked his head into the doorway, "The plow is here. It looks like they almost have the road cleared and the snow is tapering off. Time to go, ladies."

Bridget shouted to Ryan, "Five times in one day? Very impressive, Bro!" Ryan paused, looked confusedly at Megan, then back to Bridget and closed the door. Then he quickly reopened it, stuck his head back in, and smiled. As the door closed again, we heard him laughing.

An hour later, we found an open ramp to the Whitestone Bridge and entered behind three plows that took up the entire highway. They continued slowly but uninterrupted until we passed into Connecticut at daybreak and proceeded without further incident. Amazingly, after driving fifteen hours for what should have been a two-hour trip, when we reached the reserve unit in Hartford, no one was there. We continued on to Megan and Ryan's Forestville apartment where we promptly went to sleep.

Prior to nodding off, I thanked God for the loving relationship Frank and I shared with our two grown daughters and their husbands. I also gave thanks for our adventure's safe ending and feeling secure and contented with my Frank. Meanwhile, however, changes taking place in our society and the Vietnam Conflict threatened to pry open long-hidden secrets and wedge themselves deep into our lives.

CHAPTER 12

FOR MANY OF Frank and my generation, the late 1960s was an excruciating period. Vietnam dominated the news and challenged the very notion of patriotism. Meanwhile, race relations reached the breaking point as entire neighborhoods burned. It also seemed as if everything we once held up as good and decent was under attack. Many of us used to look to the courts to uphold moral standards but it seemed as if every new case struck down more barriers until it felt as if any behavior was acceptable. The news reported that while traditional marriages were disintegrating at an alarming rate, the drug culture and sexual revolution had switched into high gear and the roles of men and women seemed to blur daily.

In 1968, things boiled over. Vietnam War protesters burned the American flag in Central Park while women burned their bras at the Miss America pageant. A minister named Troy Perry founded the first openly gay and lesbian church in Huntington Park, California. Then, Reverend Martin Luther King's assassination in Memphis, Tennessee, set off race riots across the country. The social turmoil challenged everyone but especially those who, like Frank, had served their country during World War II. Regardless of his personal experience in the war, Frank still believed in its necessity. He also believed in service to God and country above all else. The events of that year undermined much of what he held sacred and the most challenging of them all took place in a small Vietnamese village called My Lai.

On March 16, 1968 more than twenty members of Charlie Company, under the command of Second Lieutenant William Calley, marched into the tiny hamlet and killed hundreds of elderly men, women, and children. Soldiers raped women before killing them. They forced many villagers into ditches before machine-gunning them or blowing them apart with grenades. Few of the company's soldiers resisted Lt. Calley's orders. My Lai became the most infamous example of US atrocities in the war.

Because of conflicting statements, obstruction, and outright cover-ups, the investigations into the massacre resulted in different accounts of the incident. Many "official" reports grossly underestimated the numbers killed or cited most of those as Viet Cong soldiers rather than civilians. Several of the senior officers involved actually received citations. By September, however, the army charged Calley with several counts of premeditated murder and indicted twenty-five other enlisted men and officers on related charges.

Back home, we might never have learned about My Lai if not for an Army photographer named Ron Haeberle. He had accompanied one of the company's platoons into the village to document the "battle" between the American and North Vietnamese fighters. When the massacre started, he used his personal camera to capture what really happened. In late November of '69, his hometown newspaper, the Cleveland, Ohio, *Plain-Dealer*, published his pictures. A few weeks later, *LIFE* magazine published a series of his photos and a story about what really happened. It brought the gruesome reality of the war home to us in a way none of us could have imagined. How could our own brothers, husbands, and friends take part in something so horrific?

It took a year from the time the military charged Calley until he came to trial and another four months before they handed down a verdict. In the meantime, war protesters greeted our returning soldiers with shouts of "baby killers" and spit at them as they disembarked from the returning ships. World War II veterans like Frank shook their heads in disbelief. I still shudder when I think about what happened in our own home on the evening of March 29, 1971, the night they convicted Lt. Calley.

Megan and Ryan came for dinner and while Megan helped me clear the table, Ryan challenged Frank to another game of chess. Poor Ryan had never won a game against Frank but that night he had a new strategy: he brought his own chess pieces. They had always played with Frank's traditional looking carved-wood set. The pieces in the set Ryan brought were sleek, modern-looking figures made of shiny plastic. "What do you call these?" Frank protested. "How am I supposed to play when I can't even tell which piece is which?" but Ryan insisted and Frank reluctantly gave in. As they played, images flashed across the television from some program no one was watching but we had set the volume just high enough to signal the start of the evening news.

"OK, Dad," said Ryan as he carefully examined each piece on the board before making his next move, "this time I've got you on the ropes."

"You think so," Frank answered. I could hear in his voice his frustration with Ryan's pieces.

"I know so," Ryan smiled and moved his piece in position to attack Frank's king. Ryan folded his arms, sat back in his chair, and smiled, "Check."

"I don't think so," answered Frank.

"You're not going be a sore loser, are you?"

"No, because I'm not going to lose." As Frank reached for his next piece, Ryan saw the trap his father-in-law had laid and shook his head in disbelief as Frank announced, "Check." Ryan countered with another move and another "Check."

The television interrupted their game playing with the start of the evening news and the headline story. In a matter-of-fact tone, the news anchor announced Lt. Calley's guilty verdict for the premeditated murder of at least twenty people in the My Lai massacre. Frank slammed his fist down hard on the dining room table.

Ryan turned to Frank, "Don't tell me you're surprised by the verdict."

"I'm not just surprised; I'm furious about it and you should be too."

"Why should I be mad because some psychopath was convicted for ordering his men to machine-gun unarmed women, children, and old men? We should be proud that the court didn't cave in to the public pressure and let this murderer off the hook for what he did."

Frank turned red, "What he did was follow orders! That's what you do when you're in the military; you follow orders. OK mister big shot Marine, what would you have done if you were in that platoon? Disobeyed a lawful order?"

"I was only in the reserves. I wouldn't even try to compare myself to the regulars who were in actual combat, but that doesn't excuse killing innocent people."

"Don't be so naïve. There was nothing innocent about them. If they weren't Viet Cong, they were harboring those who were."

"Oh? Including the women who were praying around the altar and the children and infants too?"

Frank hesitated, "Sometimes in war, things like that are unavoidable. They were collateral damage."

"Collateral damage?" Ryan stood up and shoved his chair backwards. "They were herded into ditches and machine-gunned!"

"So I'm asking again, what would you have done?"

"I hope I would have had the courage to shoot Calley!"

We all fell silent and just looked at Ryan. I searched his face to see if he really meant what he said. From his stone expression, it was clear he did.

Frank lowered his voice and said soberly, "You would have been committing treason."

Ryan answered, equally subdued, as if he were just now gaining full awareness of what he had said, "It's not treason to prevent a war crime."

Frank took in a deep breath and lowered his voice further. He sounded almost like a priest in the confessional, "I really do understand how you feel, Ryan. At least when I was in, you knew who the enemy was. It's not like that in Vietnam. The enemy and the civilians all look alike. Some woman or kid walks up to a group of our guys and the next moment they're all dead because that civilian had a loaded grenade strapped to their waist. Even if that weren't the case, unless you've been in combat, you can't imagine what it's like. Day after day, you see your friends picked off by sniper fire or blown to pieces on land mines. You get angrier and angrier and there's no one to take it out on, until…."

Frank moved a piece on the board and sat back in his chair.

Ryan studied Frank's move and then quickly moved one of his pieces and shouted, "Gotcha! Take this, Frank Russo, check and mate!"

As Frank stood, Ryan surveyed the board, puzzled. "Wait a second, Dad. Why did you move your piece there? All you had to do was take my queen and you would have won. You had to have seen that. Did you throw the game?"

"No, Ryan. You won, fair and square," Frank stood slump shouldered and head bent. I had never seen him look so feeble. Then he excused himself, "It's late. I have an early day tomorrow and I need to get some rest. Good night, everyone." He retreated to the bedroom and closed the door.

"Mom, I'm so sorry," Ryan apologized, "I didn't mean to upset Dad like that."

"Don't worry, Ryan. As much as Dad might disagree with you, you said what you honestly believed and he would never expect anything less."

After Ryan and Megan left, I found Frank sitting on the edge of the bed, staring out the window. The tears running down his cheeks glistened in the light of the streetlamp. I kissed him on the top of his head and stood behind him rubbing his shoulders. As I did, I felt his body tremble beneath my touch. "Maureen," he said, "there's something I need to tell you."

I stopped breathing. For many years after Frank returned from the war, I resented his not telling me about his experiences and considered it a lack of trust. As the years passed and I saw the toll it took on him, I came to view his wall of silence as an act of mercy. The argument with Ryan had breached that wall and now Frank had lost the will to hold back any longer. I took in a breath and braced myself as he started.

"They were called the Lilly Corps. High school girls who nursed wounded Japanese soldiers. Every island was tough but Okinawa was the worst. The Japanese dug themselves into bunkers throughout the island. Their machine gun fire cut down so many of the guys I knew. When we got close enough, most of the time we had to clear them out with hand grenades or flamethrowers.

"When the Japs realized they'd lost, they told the students they were on their own. They also said that if we captured them, we would rape and kill them. Some of the girls threw themselves off the cliffs into the ocean. Others tried to make it to the other side of the island. We were coming over a ridge when about a dozen of them saw us and ran into a cave. Our orders were to clear everything as we moved across the island. If we didn't, whenever the Japanese got the chance, they would dig in until we went past them and then attack us from behind. We surrounded the cave. My closest friend in the service was another Brooklyn guy named Jimmy Keifer. We nicknamed him Keys. Jimmy spoke some Japanese, so he tried to coax the girls to come out but they wouldn't budge. They kept shouting something back in Japanese. The sergeant asked what they were saying.

"Jimmy answered, 'Please, we didn't do anything wrong. Please go away.' He kept yelling for them to come out but nothing worked. Finally, the sergeant ordered us to lob in the hand grenades. Jimmy yelled one last time, "Please! You have to come out, right now!" Still nothing, so we threw the grenades in and listened to the screams until they went off. A few minutes later, half a dozen Japanese soldiers came out with their hands up, waving a white flag. They'd been dug in further back in the cave. Afterwards we moved in to make sure everyone else was dead."

Frank paused and took in a deep breath. I was sick to my stomach. I desperately wanted him to stop but I knew that he couldn't, so I forced myself to keep silent.

"The cave walls were covered with blood. One of the girls was still barely alive. She reached out and grabbed my ankle. Then she looked up at me and kept repeating something in Japanese. Her voice was so weak I could barely hear her. I asked Jimmy what she was saying.

"'Let it go, Frank,' he said. 'She's beyond saving, anyway.' I knew he was right, but I insisted so Jimmy answered, 'She's saying, "I'm sorry. Please help me." I told you to let it go, Frank.'

"Then the sergeant gave the order to move out. The girl must have known we were leaving because she talked louder and faster until I pulled away. Then I guess she just gave up because she stopped talking and went limp. She was just a kid and every time I see her eyes in my nightmares, I see them in our daughters' faces."

I felt hot and nauseous and I couldn't stop trembling. "You can't blame yourself, Frank," I squeezed his shoulder with one hand and wiped my tears away with the other. "It's like you told Ryan. We weren't there so we couldn't...."

Frank squeezed my hand, hard. "There's more...."

I didn't want to hear more. I just wanted him to stop, but Frank continued.

"When Jimmy and I got outside, the sergeant yelled, 'Russo and Keys, take the prisoners back and don't waste any time getting back here.' We protested. We didn't want to leave the other guys in our platoon. It was dangerous enough with the few of us that were left, let alone being down another two men but the sergeant said it was an order and told us to get moving.

"Four of the six Japanese soldiers were about our age but two of them looked like they couldn't have been more than fifteen. One of them was guiding another who had a bandage covering his eyes. Two others held up another prisoner with grenade shrapnel in his leg. The last guy just looked like he was in a daze."

Frank paused and took in another breath. Then he just sat silently for what felt like an eternity. I prayed that he couldn't hear my sobbing. Then he continued.

"We tried to hurry them along but we couldn't move fast because of the one with the leg injury. All the while, Jimmy kept saying, 'We should be with our own guys, Frank. We're already down by more than half. They need every one of us.'

"'Shut up, Jimmy,' I said. I was trying to think straight but I kept looking back until our platoon was out of sight. As soon as they were, I looked back to Jimmy. I still had your letter about Harvey in my pocket. Then I thought about Harvey, about all the guys I knew who had been gunned down, and about that young girl in the cave. All I said to Jimmy was 'Do it,' and we both opened fire. When the blind guy fell, the kid that was holding him up turned around and looked right at me."

Frank forced the next sentence out through his sobs. "He had that same look in his eye as the girl did. Then I pulled the trigger … again and again and again." Frank took in a deep breath, composed himself again, and continued.

"A few days later we were sweeping through another cave when a Japanese soldier tossed a grenade between us and the entrance. There wasn't enough time to get out. Jimmy threw himself on the grenade and the explosion riddled my leg with shrapnel. I figured it was God's way of evening the score." Frank looked up into my eyes, "This is the man who came back to you from the war, Maureen. Can you still love a man like me?"

I couldn't answer. The words just wouldn't come out. I straightened up, let go of Frank's shoulder, and walked out of the bedroom. I closed the door behind me and walked straight into the bathroom. My stomach retched and I vomited. That night I slept on the couch and the next morning Frank left for work without saying a word. I didn't want to prolong his pain, but the images were still in my mind and I didn't know how to respond. I also needed to reconcile what Frank said with the man I thought I knew. When he returned from work, he crept straight into the bedroom without saying anything and sat down on the edge of the bed. I followed in after him and wiped my tears away before speaking.

"I'm so, so sorry for what happened in the war, Frank, but please don't ask me to judge you. That has to be between you and God. I wasn't there and I couldn't possibly know what you went through. I only know this: you are a good husband, a good father, and a good man. I've loved you from the moment we met and I can never stop loving you."

Frank wrapped his arms around my waist, buried his face into my stomach, and sobbed bitterly. I stroked his hair until all of the energy drained from his body and he slumped down onto the bed. I nestled down next to him and cradled him in my arms until he cried himself to sleep.

That was the last time Frank and Ryan argued about Vietnam. It was also the last time Frank played chess and he and I never talked about the war again. The events of those few days closed that chapter of our lives forever. It was time to open a new one.

CHAPTER 13

IN 1973, FOUR years after Megan and Ryan moved to Connecticut, Bridget and Steve followed, leaving Frank and me alone in New York. I thought I would die from the loneliness. When Frank walked into our bedroom the Saturday morning after Bridget's move, he found me sitting on the edge of the bed crying hysterically.

"What's wrong?" he asked.

"I can't stand this. Everyone is gone. I feel like they are all dead and we'll never see them again." Looking back on it now, it seems melodramatic, but it didn't feel that way at the time.

"They're in Connecticut, Maureen, not California." That was not what I needed to hear.

My sobs turned into a rant, "Until the girls married, they spent their whole lives with us in these four rooms. Even afterwards, they visited so often that it was as if they never left. Now they might as well be on the moon."

"Get dressed," Frank ordered.

"Why?"

"We're going to take a ride to visit our children."

"Without asking? What if they feel like we're imposing?"

"They've imposed on us their whole lives. It's high time we repaid the favor."

Frank called the girls to make sure they'd be home. I was so happy at

66

the thought of seeing them, I didn't even try to protest. In two hours, we were pulling in front of Megan and Ryan's house. They had lunch ready when we got there and afterwards they took us on a tour of the area.

It was easy to see why Megan fell in love with Connecticut. When she and Bridget were growing up, we escaped the city congestion by spending our summer vacations in places that were lush with green, open spaces, like Virginia and the Catskills. Connecticut had much of the same feel. Forestville was a quaint section of Bristol where the coffee shop doubled as the local news store and bus station. The railroad crossing was just a few feet away and the train tracks ran along a brook that meandered through the town and under a restaurant. We stopped at a pond partially covered with water lilies in full bloom and drove past several parks and shopping plazas. Except for the town centers, large expanses of lawn separated each home. With no subways and few buses, I couldn't imagine living there without a car and everywhere we went, we were going either up a hill or down one.

We ended at Bridget and Steve's for dinner. They were excited to show off their new home and I secretly envied their guest bedroom; we never had one in Brooklyn. Thinking about that spurred a memory of Frank's bathing ritual, which I shared with Steve and Ryan.

"Whenever Frank took a hot bath, our tiny bathroom filled with steam so Frank had to step out into the dining room to finish 'air-drying.' If the girls were home, they needed to either head outdoors or retreat to the bedroom until Frank was finished. We were all used to the routine. When Frank got out of the tub, he'd crack the bathroom door open and yell…," the girls and I all shouted in unison, "STAY OUT!" and then we howled with laughter. Frank shook his head and Steve and Ryan stared in amazement.

After dinner, wine and much conversation, I suggested that we leave so as not to get home too late. Steve and Bridget insisted that we stay in their new guest room. We couldn't think of any good reason to object so Frank and I agreed and we continued with more wine and conversation until well past eleven.

I was feeling tipsy as Frank and I got ready for bed. I hugged him around the neck and asked, "Exactly what did you tell the girls when you called?"

"I just told them how much their mother loved them."

"And…?"

"Nothing of any consequence. Aren't you having a good time?"

"Wonderful, Frank…. Simply wonderful."

That night, we made love in Bridget's guest room and my own love affair with Connecticut began.

The next morning, I awoke before everyone else, tiptoed into the kitchen, and made myself a cup of tea. Then I slipped out the back door. Steam rose from my teacup as I took in the landscape beyond the backyard. I could not sit down because the morning dew left all of the chairs coated with wetness. I didn't mind at all. The morning mist still clung to the ground in places and where it dissipated, the lawn glistened in the early morning sunlight. In the distance, streams of mist meandered upward from the lush green hills toward the clouds that lazily traversed the bright blue sky. I felt my breathing slow down to sync with the serenity of my surroundings.

Even after our lovemaking the night before, it took me a while to fall asleep and I was startled at why. It was the quiet. I realized that in the city, the constant noises lulled me to sleep. Cars raced the lights on Atlantic Avenue. Elevated trains screeched in and out of the station on Fulton Street. Even the talking and laughter of young people walking past our house at night added to the rhythm. Then I heard the crickets. What a beautiful, peaceful sound. Like ocean waves, their chirping swelled louder, then softer and before I could process it further, I drifted off to sleep.

At Frank's request, we ate out for breakfast. He loved breakfast places, especially the "mom and pop" kind, so Bridget and Steve described several and we settled on Grace's.

The restaurant sat in the middle of a small strip mall, perpendicular to the road. It would be easy to miss, but its patron's word-of-mouth kept it bustling. Inside, the brightly patterned wallpaper reminded me of my grandmother's kitchen. Shelves opposite the entrance held books that customers could read or take home. Dinner plates imprinted with images of local churches spanned the topmost shelf and cast-iron trivets hanging near the counter offered sayings like "I Fish, Therefore I Am," and "Life Begins after Coffee." For me, however, the restaurant's most endearing feature was the small pencil sketch of a woman that hung on the wall next to the coffee makers.

"That's Grace," said Bridget. "She started the restaurant. She died a few years ago and her husband runs it now. He keeps her portrait there as a kind of memorial."

After breakfast, Steve and Bridget continued the driving tour. They obviously loved the area as much as Megan and Ryan. Coming from Brooklyn with block after block of connected apartment buildings, I marveled at the amount of open space between the houses and the lawns that were lush with flowers, trees, and bushes. When we met Megan and Ryan at Lake Compounce amusement park, my love affair with Connecticut deepened.

Exiting the cars, we heard the rumbling of the *Wildcat* wooden roller coaster mixed with the delighted screams of the riders as their cars plunged down the first steep hill. We walked through the park sampling carnival food and went on the bumper cars and the huge, antique carousel. Then we took a ride on the miniature railroad. As the train circled the lake, Steve narrated.

"The park got its name from John Compound, an Indian chief who sold the property to the early settlers for some trinkets and a large brass kettle. Legend has it that he drowned in the lake while trying to cross it in that kettle. The darker tale is that his tribe drowned him in the lake for giving away their land."

Ryan continued, "This train is called the Gillette Railroad after an actor who portrayed Sherlock Holmes in silent films and was a bit of an inventor. He designed and built it and at one time had it running on his property along the Connecticut River. The park bought it in the early forties and it's been running along the lake ever since."

As the men continued their history lesson, I closed my eyes, rested my head on Frank's arm, and allowed myself to be lulled by the clickity-clack sound of the train wheels. The flicker of the afternoon sun played on my eyelids. With my Frank, the fear of opening them to see my father's eyes had long since faded from memory. I relished that feeling of safety and contentment.

After the train ride, we played a round of miniature golf on the course between the lake and the large meeting hall and restaurant building. Steve pointed to the second story of the building, "Most of the big bands like Dorsey, Calloway, and Basie played in the dance hall."

Ryan added, "In the spring of '41, the park hit the all-time attendance record when Tommy Dorsey's band featured Frank Sinatra."

Later in the afternoon, while our daughters and their husbands continued on the rides, Frank and I sat by the lake and listened to the country western music of *Slim Cox and His Cowboy Caravan*. I relished the cool afternoon breeze and the sounds of the park and the music. Then I thought about returning alone to our tiny railroad apartment in the city. I turned to Frank and said, "It's time we got out of Brooklyn. I want to move to Connecticut."

CHAPTER 14

IT WAS A long time before we made that move. Having lived through the Depression, Frank was weary of mortgages. He wouldn't buy a house until we could pay for it with cash. Even after we bought the one we wanted, we couldn't leave New York until he retired from the transit authority. We rented the house for seven more years before we finally moved ourselves.

The wait was excruciating. We compensated by spending most of our weekends and many of Frank's vacation days in Connecticut. Thanks to our closeness with the girls and their families, we frequently vacationed with them too. Then Larry Kowalski, Frank's co-foreman at the train yard, introduced us to cruises.

In the highly unionized environment of the subway system, Frank and Larry had become supervisory allies and fast friends. Frank and I took our first cruise to the Caribbean with Larry and his wife, Helen. From then on, they became our constant traveling companions and dearest friends.

Frank took early retirement the day he turned sixty and we immediately started preparing for our move to Connecticut. Although I cherished my time in Brooklyn with Frank, I was overjoyed the day we turned our packed moving truck into the driveway of our new home on Stafford Avenue in Bristol. We lived in a four-room, second-story apartment for more than forty years. Now, Frank and I finally had a home of our own.

The small cape with its attached garage felt like a dollhouse to me. I relished decorating it and there was so much room. We even had a basement all to ourselves!

"Oh no!" I yelled as Steve and Ryan started into the house with one of Frank's many storage containers.

"What are you ranting about?" Frank challenged. "I told them to bring that down to the basement."

As a child, Frank stood on the bread lines during the Depression and never forgot what it was like to go without. He became the ultimate pack-rat. Even after the boys browbeat him into leaving many things behind in Brooklyn, we needed every spare inch of space in the truck to fit what we brought with us.

"Oh no you don't, Frank," I insisted. "We have a two-car garage and only one car. You can use the other side for all that stuff. I don't want it cluttering up our new house." Frank scowled, but when the men finished unloading, they barely squeezed everything into the free side of the garage. Within a few weeks of moving, I had our home nicely decorated just the way I'd always dreamed. The chandelier Frank hung in the dining room glistened on the surfaces of our new walnut dining table and hutch. In our television room, we each had our own reclining chairs. The living room sofa could never have fit into our old apartment and every window in the house had beautiful new curtains. We also became established residents of the neighborhood. One aspect of that included joining the Bristol Senior Center, or BSC, as the locals called it. It was only a short distance from our house and we quickly became active members. Several years later, we were the ones who were welcoming new people to the neighborhood.

"Can we borrow a cup of sugar?" Frank joked as we welcomed the newest couple. Larry and Helen stood in the kitchen of their new home laughing at the sight of Frank holding up the empty sugar bowl. After making several visits to see us, Helen also fell in love with Connecticut and convinced Larry to follow us to Bristol. They bought a house several streets away from where we lived. After settling in, they registered at the

BSC and the four of us began taking the trips organized by the center. For almost a decade, we traveled extensively together, from local day trips to overseas vacations, including at least one annual cruise.

Frank's love of midnight buffets, multiple servings of ice cream, and New Your style cheesecake began to show on him. He still maintained his straight, military posture and remained active, but the extra pounds were noticeable in his belly and face. I sometimes ribbed him that his jowls were starting to make him look like a chipmunk. Other than my chiding him about his weight gain, however, our life felt like a dream. We awoke from that dream the day Larry and Helen shared her diagnosis.

CHAPTER 15

"IT'S STAGE FOUR breast cancer," said Helen. "I don't even understand how it could have progressed this far without my knowing. I felt fine up until this cough. I expected the doctor to give me a shot and send me on my way."

"What did he say about treatment?" I asked.

"He wants to start me on chemotherapy immediately, but I said no."

"No?" Frank blurted out. I didn't say anything, but Helen's response startled us both.

"Even with chemotherapy, the doctor said the cancer has progressed too far to save me. He gave me six months at the most. I want to live every minute of the time I have left and not spend my last few months constantly nauseous and fatigued."

"We've talked about it," said Larry, wiping the tears from his face, "and we both agreed. If this is what Helen wants, then this is what we'll do."

Thankfully, Helen did not have to go into the hospital until the end. The four of us had one last trip planned and she insisted on going. She and Larry had never been to the western national parks and since Frank and I had, we acted as their tour guides to Yosemite, Yellowstone, and Bryce Canyon. We rented a car and Frank drove. Several times during the trip, Helen's eyes glistened with tears, but not from the pain.

"Oh my God, Larry, can you believe how beautiful it is?" she said on seeing El Capitan at sunrise.

The park ranger at Yellowstone pointed out that caldera erupted on average every 600,000 years and that we were 30,000 years overdue. "When it finally does erupt," he said, "it could wipe out half the country."

Helen joked, "It looks like you guys might be following me sooner than you think."

As the trip progressed, Helen's stamina declined. I still have the last picture of the four of us standing together in front of one of the hoodoos at Bryce. Helen is smiling widely but the strain is evident in her face. Returning home, Larry and Frank had to support her getting on and off the plane. The next day, she went into the hospital. Larry remained by her bedside constantly, unable to do anything for her except to hold her hand. Frank and I visited often and I frequently sat with Helen while Frank took Larry off for a cup of coffee. For a time, we all prayed for a miracle to save her. In the end, we prayed for an end to her suffering.

Several weeks after the funeral, Larry packed up his camper and headed south.

"I need some time to clear my head and think," he said. "I have some relatives in Florida and Tennessee and right now, I feel like I need to reconnect with family."

Frank and I monitored Larry's house for him and checked his mail while he was gone. It was four more months before he returned. The trip did him good. He was always handsome with the fit, rugged look of an outdoorsman but just before he left, he was ghostly pale and looked emaciated. He returned deeply tanned and fifteen pounds heavier. We wondered if he might tell us he was moving south to be closer to his relatives.

"I thought about it," he said, "but I've decided to stay here in Connecticut. After all, this is where most of friends are and to me, it's still home." Larry returned to the senior center and became a regular again soon after his return. Several months later, he met Ceil there.

"Doesn't Ceil seem like an odd fit for him?" Frank asked me. Helen and Larry were both the outdoor types. Fit and trim, when they weren't traveling with us, they were off hiking, biking, or kayaking somewhere. Ceil was much more sedentary. She preferred a kitchen apron to hiking boots and enjoyed bridge, mahjong, and movies.

"Maybe," I said, "but she has a lot of good qualities of her own. Everyone talks about how great a cook she is and I don't know anyone who can strike up a conversation with a total stranger as easily as she can. Sometimes Larry jokes that he doesn't know what he appreciates more: her companionship or her cooking. I've taken classes with her at the center and I like her."

It was good to see Larry laugh again and Frank and I were grateful for the part Ceil played in that. Several months later, the new couple of Larry and Ceil joined Frank and me as we celebrated the start of the new millennium.

CHAPTER 16

FRANK AND I celebrated the New Year holiday, as we had many times before, at the Southington Aqua Turf Club. The annual pre-New-Year's-Eve dance took place a day before the holiday and climaxed with the countdown at noon instead of midnight. That suited BSC members whose poor night vision, limited stamina, or distain for holiday traffic made the traditional celebrations a problem. With Frank nearing eighty and me in my mid-seventies, I guess that included us too. The main ballroom sat over 700 and in 1999, coupled with the millennium celebration, the event attracted a sell-out crowd. Happily, Frank and I booked our table right after the preceding year's party.

"All right, folks," the bandleader said as Frank and I waited on the dance floor for the next song to start, "we'll take a short break now and be back in just a few minutes."

"I guess that means us too," I said. Frank didn't answer right away. He was panting and tiny beads of sweat trickled down his pale complexion. "Are you all right? You look out of breath. Maybe we should sit out the next set?"

"No need. I just need a few minutes to rest up and after that, I'll be fine."

We didn't know that we were the focal point of conversation at our table until we sat down.

Lorraine Casperetti, my dearest friend at the senior center, started,

"You two are something else out there. When he was alive, it took everything I had to get George up to do a single dance, even at weddings, but you don't stop until the music does." Lorraine was tall, statuesque, and highly opinionated. According to Frank, she also had the demeanor and disposition of a boot camp drill sergeant.

Frank answered, "Maureen taught me ballroom dancing when we were dating. After that, we just kind of improvised." As he continued, I felt relieved to see the color returning to his face and his breathing less labored. "We don't have to work much at getting up. We get restless as soon as the music starts. I guess we're just programmed that way from the skating rink."

"Oh!" cooed Lorraine, "Now that sounds intriguing."

"That was a long time ago," Frank ended, "before I left for the Army."

Ceil changed the subject. "Did any of you see the way that Cantrell woman treated the kitchen staff last week over that roast beef thing? You'd think she was eating at the Waldorf or something."

Lorraine added, "I did. As far as I'm concerned, she was only doing it to get attention. She walks around the center as if she owns the place and the way she pours herself into her dresses with her boobs spilling out, she looks like a streetwalker. Did you see the way all the men gawked at her: like they were dogs in heat? It was disgusting. You know, I don't think she's even supposed to be there. You're never going to convince me that she's old enough to be a member. I think the director should check to see if she lied on her application."

Ceil ended with, "And that Southern Bell accent of hers is about as fake as a three-dollar bill. As far as anyone here knows, she's never lived south of Atlantic City."

"Now aren't you gals being a little rough on her?" said Larry.

"Well of course you'd say that," Ceil scolded him; "You're a man." I felt a little sad for Larry. In all the years that he and Helen were together, I couldn't recall a single time when she rebuked him publically. After only a few months together, Ceil acted more dismissive toward him than Helen ever had.

"Wow," I said, "I feel like I just got back from a trip to the moon. I've never seen this person but from the sound of it, she sounds difficult to miss. Have you seen her, Frank?"

With his hearing aids in, if the music wasn't playing too loud and there weren't too many people talking at once, Frank could just barely make out the conversation. He hated wearing them because he found the background noise annoying but when he left them out, I had to shout for him to hear me, so he put them in for my sake. "No," he said. "But from what I'm hearing, I think I would have remembered if I had."

"Oh you'd remember her all right," said Lorraine, "believe you me. She started coming around about four or five weeks ago, when you two were in Florida and you wouldn't believe the ruckus she's caused in such a short time. She's loud and crass and curses almost every other word. She's awful to the staff and rude to everyone else. You'd better watch out for that one, Maureen. She's bad news. She'd just as soon steal your husband as look at him and then wind up suing you in the process."

"Thanks for the warning, Lorraine. I'll keep my eyes open for her."

"Yea," Frank added devilishly. "I'd like to keep my eyes on her too!" I chuckled and elbowed him in the ribs.

Lorraine returned to Frank, "So you were in the Army? My George was too. When did you go in?"

"Forty-two."

"Oh. So you served during the war. George left in forty-six, after everything was over. Did you go to Germany?"

Frank sat back and fell silent with that same distant expression I had become accustomed to over the years. I ached for him, knowing the private hell he relived each time it happened. I wrapped my arm in his and answered for him, "Frank was in the Pacific. He even received a Purple Heart but he doesn't like to talk about the war."

The orchestra started up again and I tugged at Frank's shirt.

"Listen, Frank, they're playing a waltz." Then I addressed the group, "The waltz is one of our favorites."

"Well, then I guess we'll see you again next year!" Lorraine joked.

79

On the dance floor, Frank smiled and kissed me on the cheek, "Thanks." Then he resumed his strong, steady lead. Being in his arms again, I became oblivious to my surroundings except for him and the music.

The bandleader approached the microphone again. "All right, folks, it's time for the final countdown, so grab your noisemakers and your partners and join us in welcoming in the new millennium! Ready?"

We all counted down in unison: "Ten, Nine, Eight, Seven, Six, Five, Four, Three, Two, One … Happy New Year!"

The clamor of the noisemakers filled the ballroom, intermingled with the orchestra's rendition of "Auld Lang Syne." Frank and I kissed while shouts of "Happy New Year!" rang out around us. It was magical.

I wondered what the New Year and this new millennium might hold in store for us: changes in the family, health, travel, and friends. At that moment, I relished the closeness I shared with Frank and thought that I had to be the luckiest woman alive. I had no idea that before the year ended, that same closeness would become the instrument of my undoing.

CHAPTER 17

"THAT'S IT. THE movie's all set to go," Frank said as he finished cueing up the VCR. I moved the last chair into place as people began to file in.

Wednesday afternoon was movie time at the senior center. The activity included a fair amount of responsibility and more stress than most volunteers were willing to take on.

Most of us at the BSC grew up with "respect" as a central theme in our lives. We respected our parents, the church, the country, the flag, and the community in general. Most members tolerated individual expression so long as it didn't undermine the greater values of God and country. The films of our time reflected those values. Most movies contained only vague references to sex and almost none to drugs. Any movie that contained nudity at all was taboo. Favored topics included musicals and comedies, westerns and World War II films, especially those featuring John Wayne and most of the classics.

Finding modern films that entertained members without offending them was a challenge. The younger center staff tried but members severely criticized many of the selections. At one point, the center administration considered dropping the movies entirely. That's when Frank and I volunteered for the task. We understood the members' tastes but also appreciated modern films. More importantly, we understood that we would almost never please everyone.

After screening potential videos and making the month's choices, I wrote reviews of the selected films for the center's newsletter, the *Bristol Senior Times*. I was always certain to include any cautionary notes regarding questionable content.

Once we finished arranging the room for the normal twenty to thirty moviegoers, ever punctual, Frank started the movie at precisely three o'clock. Then he sat and watched it again, both to make certain that nothing went awry and because he enjoyed viewing a good movie more than once.

"Do you want to stay and watch it?" he asked.

"No, thanks. It's nice and warm outside today. I brought my magazines and I'm going to catch up on my reading."

"Then what do you say we stop at the Oasis after the movie?"

"I'm not really hungry yet. We've already had lunch and it's too early for dinner."

"Then how about we just stop for coffee and a snack? They have New York-style cheesecake on Wednesdays."

"So that's what this is all about. You have to start paying more attention to what you eat, Frank. These cruise vacations are becoming a problem. You've grown way too fond of cheesecake and ice cream lately and you're complaining that your pants are getting too tight."

"Maybe you should stop washing them in hot water."

"Don't joke, Frank. This is serious. You look like you get winded just walking lately."

"All right, all right. I'll be more careful in the future, but if I skip that cheesecake now, I'll just be craving something sweet for the rest of the day. Then afterwards we can go shopping at the mall."

"You want to go shopping?"

"I need a new pair of shoes. I'm going to be doing a lot a walking at the festival and I want them well broken in ahead of time."

"That sounds fine to me," I answered and started for the door. "Just come and get me when you're finished. I'll be out in the courtyard."

Then Frank added, "By the way, lots of folks commented about your write-up in the Senior Times. Some of them said you should be writing the reviews in the Bristol Press. Good job, Maurie."

I stopped short and turned back to him. "Frank, do you remember when we dated, how you hated to be called Frankie?"

"Yes," he answered cautiously.

"Then tell me something. How is it that almost everyone back then called you Frankie and you still ended up as Frank, while no one addressed me as Maurie but that's what you wound up calling me?"

The color drained from his face, "I thought you liked being called Maurie."

"It's a man's name. The only Maurie I've ever known was that comedian we saw perform at Grossinger's."

"It's a nickname: a term of endearment. People use them all the time to show affection."

"Well so is Frankie, but you weren't too thrilled at the thought of being called that, were you?"

"It was a kid's name. I just grew out of it and wanted people to start addressing me as an adult."

"Well, I'm an adult, aren't I?"

"Maureen, after being together for more than fifty years, don't you think you might have mentioned this a little bit sooner?"

Then I noticed the quiver in his mouth and softened. I smiled and pecked him on the cheek. "My poor Frank. You can be so wonderfully gullible at times. It doesn't bother me at all. Coming from you it sounds … perfect."

The seats were filling up. Frank scowled, turned me around, nudged me toward the door, and then patted me on the rear, "Go. Read your magazines."

I looked back to see several of the moviegoers chuckling. "Remember if you need me, I'll be in the courtyard," I said. Then I stopped at the door, faced back into the room and spoke clear and loud so everyone could hear, "See you later … Frankie."

83

CHAPTER 18

BEFORE SCANNING MY magazine articles, I leaned back, closed my eyes, and faced up toward the sun. The courtyard was in the middle of the complex. The high walls blocked the wind and the bright afternoon sun made it feel balmy. The brick walls and institutional windows hid behind lush vegetation on all sides. Brightly colored flowers edged the ornamental bushes and each in their time bloomed, withered, and died only to be replaced by other varieties in a constant succession throughout the growing season. The crocuses had made a brief appearance following the early spring thaw and the azaleas stubbornly waited for a prolonged heat wave before offering up their bloom. Today the daffodils and tulips took center stage.

The center of the courtyard had open lawn cut low to the ground. In the middle of the lawn was a delicate white fountain topped by a slender, lovely angel. A small piece of her upper left wing was missing, broken off during some renovations. I found something about that defect appealing, but I couldn't quite say why. It was not the kind of statuary normally found in municipal buildings. There was no plaque, sign, or inscription but the staff and members knew it was there to honor the memory of John Blake. He was a much loved and admired center director and the founder of the famous *Teddy Bear Jamboree*. Those of us who knew John also knew of his special devotion to angels.

I loved the peacefulness of sitting on the bench in front of John's fountain, listening to the soft bubbling of the water and feeling the warmth of the sunlight on my face.

"Well, if it isn't Ginger! How are you today, darlin?" I looked up to see a woman hovering over me.

"Excuse me," I said, "but I think you have me confused with someone else."

"Nope, you're Ginger all right," her reply came back strong and confident.

"I'm sorry, but I really don't think I'm the person you're looking for. My name isn't Ginger."

"It may not be the one you go by, honey, but from the way you and that man of yours dance, you're Ginger Rodgers herself."

I couldn't help smiling. I was used to receiving all sorts of compliments on Frank and my dancing, but this was a first. As she spoke, I also detected a less than perfect Southern accent.

"So if your name isn't Ginger, darlin, what is it?"

"Maureen Russo," I extended my hand.

"Well, nice to meet you, Maureen. I'm Doris, Doris Cantrell." She took my hand and shook it like a campaigning politician. "You don't mind if I join you, do you?"

The New Year's Eve conversations regarding the infamous Ms. Cantrell flashed through my mind and I hesitated for a moment but then caught myself. I believe in judging a person by their behavior, not by what other people said about them and it disappointed me that I had forgotten that, even if only for a moment. I cleared away my magazines so Doris could sit, "Please."

I normally pride myself on being a good judge of people's age but it was difficult to do in Doris's case. Her looks and mannerisms came off as a person younger than most of the center members. Her slender shape made her look tall, and her clothes were more stylish and revealing than most of the center regulars. She also displayed an unusually large amount of cleavage for the environment. I couldn't help noticing the smoothness of her skin and the uniform color of her dark brown hair, with no signs of salting. I wondered how much of what I was seeing was original and how much credit belonged to the cosmetologist or plastic surgeon. Her most striking feature, however, was her pitch-black eyes. They locked onto me while she spoke and I quickly realized that once she set her gaze on someone, she was not about to turn away first. I didn't take offense, though. I'm not into competing.

"Doris. I don't remember every meeting someone with that name before. It sounds nice."

"It'll do. We all have to be called something, don't we? So where's Fred?" Once again, she had me confounded.

"Fred?"

"Yea, you know, Fred Astaire, your dance partner."

"Oh, you mean Frank. He's in the auditorium showing the movie."

"I see. You two are regular staff members around here, aren't you?"

"Not really. We do volunteer a lot of time, but we enjoy it."

"They must pay you something, don't they?"

"Pay us? Here?" I laughed, "Now that would really be something."

"Well, I'll be. If they ever asked Henry to do something for nothing, he'd bend over and tell them to kiss him where the sun don't shine."

"Excuse me?" I had trouble believing that someone I had just met could act so familiar. At the same time, there was something endearing about this talkative and vulgar stranger.

Doris must have realized that her glib comments were not working, "Listen, I think that maybe I'm getting off on the wrong foot here. I'm working so hard at being clever that I hardly stand myself. Could we just start over?"

"Sure," I said. "I'm going to be here for a while so why don't you tell me a little about yourself."

"All right then," Doris answered, "let me see. I was born in Philadelphia."

"We've vacationed in Philadelphia with the kids. It was a lot of fun."

"I suppose we all have to come from somewhere, but for my money, I've always preferred places like Atlanta or Charlotte. People in the

South are more 'genteel' as they say and the winters sure beat anything up here. What about you?"

"Brooklyn my whole life, until Frank retired from the transit authority. Did you grow up in Philadelphia?"

"Not really. I grew up pretty much everywhere. My father was a salesman and a half-assed one at that. He tried his hand at everything from Amway cleaners to vacuum cleaners but most of the time he sold cars. When it came to separating a woman from her money or her husband, he could be a real schmoozer, at least for a while. Eventually, usually sooner rather than later, the husband of some bimbo he bedded or a bar-bill he'd run up at the local gin mill caught up with him and then we were off again. I don't think I spent more than three or four years in the same house until I was in high school. That's when my mother checked out and I went out on my own. I did okay, though. If I learned anything from Daddy, it was that if you can find out what it is that somebody wants and give it to them, you never have to go hungry. Once I was past puberty, believe me, I had a lot of what some people wanted. I was lucky too. I guess you could say that I was into a kind of high-risk lifestyle. Am I boring you?"

"Hardly."

"'Cause it feels like I'm doing all the talking here."

"That's all right. I'd rather listen than talk anyway."

"Okay then, where was I?"

"Your high-risk lifestyle."

For the next hour, Doris provided a nonstop monologue of her life history. She described her various moves and the final one to Connecticut. She reviewed her lovers until meeting her husband, Henry, at the bank where they both worked. She shared the struggles raising a precocious daughter in the same house as her increasingly greedy and inebriated husband. Then there was the estrangement between her and her daughter, the dissolution of her marriage, and a survey of her new lovers since Henry's departure. She ended with, "So now it's just me and my McMansion and you know what? It is what it is and that's fine with me."

The description of her house made it sound more like a Southern Plantation than a Bristol home. At that point, I wasn't sure of how much of what I was hearing was fact versus fiction.

Actually, I was overwhelmed and somewhat relieved that it was getting time to go. I was also amazed at the amount of ground Doris covered in the span of a single movie.

"Hey, Maurie," Frank's voice interrupted us as he appeared at the courtyard door, "the movie's finished and I'll be ready to go as soon as I put the equipment and chairs away. I'm starving...."

Then he noticed Doris sitting next to me, "Oh! Sorry. I'm Maureen's husband, Frank."

"I know," Doris cooed in a suddenly more pronounced Southern drawl. At the same time, she leaned back on the bench and propped herself up with her outstretched arms. "I'm Doris. It's a pleasure to meet you, Fred."

"Nice to meet you too, but it's Frank."

"I know," Doris drew the words out like a teenager flirting at the high school dance. Her repositioning accentuated her already generous cleavage. From the direction of his gaze, it was clear to me that Frank had noticed too. When I made eye contact with him, I gestured for him to lift his focus.

He pretended to look confused—typical man—shrugged his shoulders, and said, "I've got to finish up inside. I'll be back soon," and then he disappeared again into the building.

"Well it's about time for me to clear out too," said Doris. "Just one other thing. When couples dance really well, half the time they look like they're putting on a show. But you and Fred, it's like you don't even know anyone else is around. You're kind of weird in that respect."

I've kept a diary for most of my life. Every now and then, I enjoy looking back at my reflections on events like the births of our grandchildren or our move to Connecticut. After meeting Doris at the senior center, later that evening I snuggled into my recliner at home and added this entry.

April 5, 2000

What an interesting woman that Doris is! She certainly isn't shy at all. Like Lorraine and the others said, her language is definitely on the rough side and she's more than a bit forward. I can see why she rubs some of them the wrong way, especially given how she dresses. Nevertheless, she seems nice enough to me. She loves to talk about herself, but I don't mind. I'd rather listen than talk about myself anyway.

I don't know if I can believe everything she says but if so, it sounds like she's had a colorful life. Under all the bravado though, she seems sad. Frank says he doesn't know what to make of her, especially after the way she introduced herself. We'll just have to see where this relationship goes, if anywhere.

It was getting late, my eyelids kept drooping, and I couldn't stop myself from yawning or thinking about the curious Doris Cantrell.

CHAPTER 19

WHEN FRANK AND I first started volunteering at the BSC, we got to know John, the center director, who was constantly innovating and had seemingly inexhaustible energy. We worked on craft fairs, tag sales, parade floats, and countless other projects that were interesting, fun, and successful. In the early 1990s, John proposed his most ambitious project: the *Bristol Teddy Bear Jamboree*.

Frank was skeptical at first. He found it hard to imagine that grown adults would get excited about teddy bears. John assured him that people would travel from throughout Connecticut and even other states to attend and exhibit. "It may take a few years," said John, "but it could actually become famous and a real moneymaker for the center."

Even John couldn't imagine just how right he would be. The first festival was a financial, social, and political success and by the mid '90s, the annual *Teddy Bear Jamboree* was a major event. Thousands of visitors from all over the country crammed into Bristol Eastern High School for the weekend-long events and Frank and I became regular fixtures.

I enjoyed working reception table, greeting excited visitors who came year after year. The vendors liked the quick, reliable help they got from Frank, the "security guy." With his bright red baseball cap, he was easy to spot. Even in his late seventies he looked fit, walked straight, and stood military erect. Once the event was underway, he moved constantly from room to room, answering questions, giving directions, and reuniting lost parents with their children.

We continued working the fair even after John's death in 1997, but without his vision and drive the size and scope of the event dwindled and eventually moved from the high school to the BSC. Nevertheless, when the center's doors opened in September 2000 for Bristol's final *Teddy Bear Jamboree*, I was once again at the registration table greeting the visitors. Meanwhile Frank, the security guy, patrolled the event in his bright red baseball cap.

"Hey Maurie," Frank said as he cruised past my station, "it's lunchtime and I'm starving." The smell of the fried food was driving him crazy. "How about taking a break so we can get a hot dog and some fries?"

"I suppose so," I answered. "I'm getting hungry too, but there has to be something better to eat."

"Sure. How about a sausage and pepper grinder and fried dough?" Things were going from bad to worse and Frank could see what I was thinking from my frown.

"We could get the fried dough with tomato sauce and cheese instead of sugar." I held my stare and Frank caved.

"All right, I suppose the cafeteria has soups and salads," he said reluctantly.

"That sounds much better. Do you suppose they have bottled water too? I'm dying of thirst."

Frank shook his head, "I never thought I'd see the day when we'd pay good money for water in a bottle when we can get it right from the faucet. I'll see if I can get a couple cups and get the water from the fountain."

"That's fine and could you get my food to go?"

"Maureen," he protested, "trying to balance waters and food through this crowd is going to be a royal pain. There has to be somebody who could fill in for you for a half hour. I've been running all morning and right now, I need a break."

I could see how important it was to him. "All right. Give me fifteen minutes to finish up and arrange for coverage and I can meet you in the cafeteria."

"Good. I'll make one more round and if you get there before me, order me a chilidog with mustard and sauerkraut, curly fries, and a Coke."

"I thought we just talked about how bad that kind of food is for you."

"OK, then make it a diet Coke." With that, Frank smiled, turned, and walked off into the crowd before I could issue another reprimand.

While I waited for my replacement at the registration desk, another couple approached with a question. I hoped Frank had gotten us a table in the cafeteria. It could get crowded at lunchtime. I also hoped he reconsidered his lunch choices.

"Maureen!" Lorraine came rushing out of the building. "Maureen, you have to come, quick."

"Sure thing, Lorraine. I'll be with you as soon as I've finished with this couple."

"No, Maureen, you need to come with me right now. It's Frank!"

Lorraine was not prone to hysterics so the tone of her voice panicked me. She grabbed my wrist and the two of us raced through the crowd toward the gymnasium.

Frank lay on the ground in the middle of a crowd. Someone had placed a jacket under his head. "Oh, my God! Frank!" I fell down on my knees and grabbed his hand. It was so wet that I had to grip tight to prevent it from slipping. His face was ghostly white and his sweat soaked through my blouse. I gathered him into my arms.

"It'll be all right, Maurie…," Frank struggled to get the words out. His voice was so low that I could barely hear him. Then he couldn't speak any more. His right hand rested loosely around my wrist and I could feel his finger move, pause, and then start to move again.

I looked up and yelled, "Somebody call 911!" Someone said an ambulance was already on its way, so I turned my attention back to Frank. "Don't you even think of leaving me, Frank. You just hold on till they get here, you hear me?" Frank seemed determined to communicate something and his finger started moving again.

"Will the man be all right, Mommy?" I looked up to see a little girl with curly blond hair wrapped in the arms of her frantic-looking mother. The girl was clinging tightly to brown bear with a ripped arm. Once again, I felt the movement of Frank's finger on my wrist but this time, I paid closer attention.

Letters, I thought to myself. He's spelling something! I concentrated on each stroke and tried my best to decipher.

OV (something?) then a pause.

(Something?) OU, another pause.

I, a pause, LO ... then nothing.

Frank's finger stopped moving and his hand went limp. I looked into his face, the face I had woken up next to for more than fifty years and stroked his cheek. It was as wet with my tears and his sweat. Then Frank's head rolled to the side. "Stay with me, Frank!" I yelled.

"Ma'am, please," the strong hand of the young medic pressed firmly on my shoulder. "I'm sorry, ma'am, but you need to move so we can help him." His words were caring but firm. I kissed Frank on the forehead and moved aside.

As I stood up, Lorraine took me into her arms, hugged me tightly, and reassured me. "They'll take good care of him. It'll be all right, Maureen."

"I know," I answered firmly. "He'll be OK," Then I looked directly into Lorraine's eyes, "Frank's strong. He'll be fine." I didn't know if I was trying to convince her or myself.

The medics worked feverishly, checking Frank's vital signs, performing CPR, hooking him up to monitors, and racing him off into the ambulance.

Lorraine drove me to Bristol Hospital where Bridget and Megan met us in the waiting room. I kept pacing back and forth and rubbing my wrist, trying to decipher Frank's message, but before I could, the doctor came out. "Thank heaven," I said rushing to him. "How is he doing?" I asked. "How soon before we can take him home?"

The expression on the doctor's face communicated his answer before he spoke the words, "I'm sorry, Mrs. Russo. Your husband suffered a massive heart attack. We did everything we could." The doctor kept talking but I have no idea what he said. Bridget and Megan rushed up and started asking him questions but I just continued to pace back and forth while rubbing my wrist. Then I concentrated again on Frank's last movements, assembling and rearranging the sequence of the letters until:

I (pause)

LOV (something?) pause,

(something?) OU

I stopped pacing and stood motionless. Frank had said his final farewell and now he was gone. Gone? The realization shook me to my core. Lorraine came up and placed her hands gently on my shoulders. Maybe it was panic or selfishness or I don't know what, but all I could think was that Frank was gone and now I was all alone. I looked into Lorraine's eyes, "What am I going to do without him, Lorraine?" Then I started crying hysterically, "What am I going to do?"

CHAPTER 20

AT THE WAKE, I learned from center staff, members, and friends the details of Frank's last tour of the Teddy Bear Jamboree.

As he continued his rounds, Frank had helped several customers. One was a slight woman with silver-blue hair. Her double stroller contained two teddy bears in western wear and she asked if any vendors were selling bride and groom outfits. "I think it's about time that Roy and Dale got hitched," she said. Frank smiled and supplied several vendors' names and locations. He always prided himself on having correct and timely information. The woman thanked Frank and as she walked away, a large helium-filled balloon made it way up toward the ceiling. Apparently, Frank didn't notice. Instead, he heard the whisper of a tiny voice coming up from below.

"Excuse me, mister," a young girl with curly blond hair asked, "do you know where the Teddy bear hospital is? Mister Brownbear has a tear in his arm."

"As a matter of fact I do," Frank answered. "And what's...."

The balloon reached the ceiling above Frank's head, caught on something sharp, and exploded with a startling bang. Frank jerked violently and a pained expression crossed his face. He clutched his chest with his hand and fell back against a table.

"Excuse me, mister ... mister?" the little girl asked. "Which way is it?"

"Well, uh, let me see." Frank panted as if he were out of breath. Then he looked around, as if he was trying to remember where he was. One of the vendors asked him if he was OK. Frank took in a deep breath and said he was fine. Then he took the little girl's hand, "I'll just take you there," and headed off in the direction of the Teddy bear hospital. Had he been thinking clearly, he would have seen the confusion in the girl's face and asked about her parents. He would have also remembered about meeting me in the cafeteria and realized the hospital was in the opposite direction.

"Susie," a panicked mother ended a conversation with a vendor, turned around, and called out for her daughter. "Susie, where are you? Susie!" The sound didn't reach Frank's ears. His only focus was on the hospital destination.

One of the nearby vendors answered Susie's mother, "Excuse me, are you looking for a girl about this high with blond hair?"

"Please, yes!" her mother gasped. "I only turned around for a second and.... Have you seen her?"

"She was just asking Frank, the security guy, for directions to the Teddy bear hospital. I guess he decided to take her there himself."

"Without talking to me first! That's unbelievable. How could he be so irresponsible?" Susie's mother was livid.

The vendor stammered, "It's not like Frank to act without thinking. Maybe he thought the little girl was lost."

"Well, he's going to have plenty of explaining to do when I catch up with him. Which way is that hospital?"

After getting the directions, Susie's mother headed off.

"Hey, mister," Susie asked, looking up at Frank, "are you hot?"

Frank had opened the top buttons of his shirt, "A little, why?"

"Your face is all wet."

Frank leaned on the displays as he walked, knocking bears and accessories to the floor along the way.

When he and Susie reached their destination, Frank struggled to speak to the hospital staff. "Help ... need ... need a doctor."

"It's for Mister Brownbear," said Susie. "His arm's all torn up."

The shock of the hospital staff gave way to fits of laughter. "Boy, Frank, did you ever have us going," howled "Doctor" David Banks.

"Frank Russo!" chided David's wife, Harriet. "You ought to be ashamed of yourself. You nearly scared us half to death and probably this little girl too."

Another jolt must have hit Frank. His knees buckled and he collapsed onto the ground.

Harriet screamed, "Frank. Frank! Somebody call for an ambulance and quick, somebody get Maureen!"

CHAPTER 21

EVERYTHING ELSE THAT happened in the days following Frank's death is lost to me. The next thing I remember was sitting between Bridget and Megan in the front pew of Saint Matthew's Church. Father Delaney stood behind the altar, his massive frame dwarfing the angel statues to his left and right. He held a silver container suspended by a chain. As he swayed it forward and back while circling the altar, smoke billowed out and the church filled with the sweet aroma of the burning incense.

When he finished, he went to his chair and silently prayed until the altar server moved in front of him, holding a massive red-covered book. The priest rose, raised his arms toward heaven, and began, "Almighty God and Father, it is our certain faith that your Son, who died on the cross, was raised from the dead..." The rest of his words floated past me like the wisps of incense and dissipated just as quickly.

This isn't right, I told myself. *I shouldn't be here. I should be with Frank in our regular place, on the left side, five pews back, next to the center aisle.* I turned around to look at our spot, but the white shrouded casket obstructed my view.

I retreated into my memories of a lifetime ago but each time one finished, I found myself back in the pew until the priest finally took his seat again. He nodded toward Ryan, who crossed the isle to the lectern, smiled at me, and began the eulogy.

"Welcome to the celebration, everyone. For those who might not have known, today is Frank's eightieth birthday and I'd like to share some thoughts on his extraordinary life."

I tried to manage a weak smile but my face muscles felt frozen into place. Ryan shared Frank's family history, including how his father was an orphan and his mother died when he was young. He talked about our marriage, Frank's draft notice after our honeymoon, and our three-year separation. He went on to describe Bridget and Megan, Frank's love of photography, and his habit of hoarding.

"Before most of us were born," said Ryan, "Frank stood on the bread lines during the Great Depression. It made a lasting impression on him and he learned at a young age not to waste anything. Anyone who has seen his garage can certify to what I am saying. Be it strings, paper clips or paper bags, you could accurately say that Frank was an expert at squirreling items away. In fact, when a squirrel made its way under the wheels of his car…," people started chuckling, "You guessed it. He had it mounted and it sits in his garage still holding its last acorn in its paws.

"This need to save wasn't lost on Maureen. More than once she made us promise that if she went before Frank, we were to inspect her casket before it was buried to make sure that she was still there. Otherwise, she was afraid that Frank might have her stuffed and turned into a coat rack."

The church filled with the sound of laughter. When it subsided, Ryan continued.

"One notable trait of Frank's personality was his strength of character. He had a clear, no-nonsense view of what was right and wrong, acceptable and unacceptable. Take it from me: that made dating one of his daughters a real challenge. Once Frank made up his mind, nothing would deter him from completing his mission."

Ryan went on to describe our fifteen-hour car ride to deliver him to his reserve unit during the blizzard of 69. It hurt to listen. The more I did, the more I realized all that I had lost but hard as I tried, I couldn't break away from Ryan's words.

"The one key feature of Frank's life, however, was his unique and fulfilling love for Maureen. They were inseparable. The greatest sign of how perfectly they matched was when they danced. On his own, Frank had all the subtlety of a steamroller. But teamed up with Maureen on the dance floor, they defined poise and elegance.

"No matter the act or effort, Frank was uniquely and wonderfully himself. His life was filled with color and intensity. As Father Delaney so aptly put it during one of our retreats, 'Frank Russo could never be just another face in the crowd.'"

When he finished, Ryan looked at me and smiled. I couldn't bring myself to smile back but I nodded my appreciation for his heartfelt tribute. I thought how odd it was that Ryan, who Frank had such reservations about, had grown so close to him. At the same time, terror gripped me because I knew the service would end soon and then I would have to say good-bye to my Frank.

CHAPTER 22

AS RYAN RETURNED to his seat, I started to tremble and couldn't stop. Father Delaney circled the casket, swaying the incense holder back and forth as he did. The aroma of incense once again filled the church. I wondered if it should raise us a little closer to heaven, where Frank would be, but that didn't help. I was still here, alone. Then Father addressed the congregation, "Let us take our brother to his final resting place."

The organ and soloist began, "Be Not Afraid," but the lyrics didn't comfort me. Only the hymn's somber tone penetrated my consciousness. As the honor guard filed past our pew, Bridget and Megan helped me to my feet and out into the aisle. They locked my arms in theirs as we followed the casket. Ryan and Steve walked behind us.

At the church entrance, Father Delaney blessed the casket one last time and removed the white cover. The honor guard replaced it with the American flag and we exited the church into the bright morning sun.

"It shouldn't be this nice out," I protested.

Steve leaned forward and placed his hand on my shoulder, "Maybe God just wanted Dad to have a great day for his birthday." I sighed but didn't respond.

It was a thirty-five-mile drive from Saint Matthew's church to the State Veterans' Cemetery in Middletown. Frank wanted a military burial. He was as frugal as he was practical. At a veteran's cemetery, the government would pay for the interment, the plot, and even the headstone. Frank never boasted about his military service but he had fulfilled his patriotic duty and felt that he had earned whatever benefits the government saw fit to award to its veterans. The honor guard participated throughout the funeral. A bugler and firing squad would join them at the cemetery. They were fitting symbols for those who left their innocence on battlefields far from home. It was too simplistic to say that Frank left as a boy and returned as a man. War sometimes cuts something out of a person that can never be fully replaced, and Frank was one of those who came home without it.

I hadn't given much thought to the burial location when we first made the arrangements because I had always expected to go before Frank. He was the stronger one and he often joked about his plans to live to be a hundred. After a reasonable mourning period, he would adjust and go on with his life but things didn't go the way we planned. As the procession made its way south along the Connecticut River, my irritation grew. Frank knew that I didn't drive. How often could I impose on my children to make the trip?

I drifted in and out of awareness and lost track of the time. I closed my eyes and felt the sun's warmth coming through the window while the sunlight flickering through the tree leaves danced on my eyelids. The rhythmic beat of the car's tires crossing the joints in the road transported me back into Frank's arms, listening to the clickity-clack sound of the miniature train circling Lake Compounce.

I remembered the miniature golf game we played near the lake and riding the carousel horses. With my horse's galloping legs and fiery mane, I had felt like I was flying through the air on a mythical unicorn. The sound of the Wurlitzer band organ made me think of the skating rink where Frank and I first met and where I actually did fly through the air in his arms.

I recalled the screams coming from the "Wildcat" coaster and how I wondered how the cars managed to stay on the track as they raced through the steep dips and hairpin turns. I also remembered our sitting together on the wooden benches in front of the lakeside stage and listening to the music of *Slim Cox and his Cowboy Caravan*. Finally, I remembered making love in Bridget's guest room and telling Frank that I wanted to move to Connecticut. It all seemed so distant now.

As the funeral cars pulled off the highway and onto the smaller streets, I struggled to stay with my memories. Resting my head against the seat back, I ached to feel Frank's strong forearm rubbing against the back of my neck but then he was gone. The car turned sharply and the humming of the wheels against the pavement gave way to the sound of gravel shifting beneath the tires. Finally there was the soft, muted sound of earth and grass and the smell of freshly mowed lawn. We had arrived.

CHAPTER 23

A GRANITE MARKER greeted us as we exited the car: "Comrades Tread Lightly, You're Near a Hero's Grave." Thinking back to Frank's descriptions of his war experience, I started to understand why he wanted, or perhaps needed, to be here. In this place, there were no ornately carved headstones, no sentimental inscriptions, and no elaborate mausoleums. There were only rows and columns of simple white, identical headstones: thousands upon thousands of them, stretching outward in perfect unison. I imagined it must be like the place where Harvey slept on the other side of the ocean. Here, there was no distinction. Here, Frank was just another soldier, individual but the same: one of many who just did what they had to do. Here, there was no bravado. Everyone and no one was a hero. Here, perhaps, Frank could rest in peace at last.

Someone guided me to the front row of metal folding chairs next to the gravesite. Frank's coffin sat atop the open pit, covered with the crisp new flag and surrounded by sprays of flowers. Father Delaney positioned himself at the head of the casket, opened his prayer book, and began.

"In sure and certain hope of the resurrection to eternal life through Jesus Christ, we commend to Almighty God our brother, Frank, and we commit his body to the ground; earth to earth, ashes to ashes, dust to dust...."

Following the passage, in the distance, someone shouted orders and seven men holding rifles came to attention. In that respect, Frank was

fortunate. At one time, every veteran's funeral would have had a full firing squad. However, the second "Great War" was a distant memory and
like Frank, its veterans were dying out. The more recent "conflicts" did
not share the same importance and many of their soldiers did not feel the
same way about their participation. Now, many veterans were lucky to
get a firing squad of three. The less fortunate ones got audiotaped volleys.

The squad aimed their rifles toward the clear blue afternoon sky and
fired their weapons in unison, three times in rapid succession. As the
echoes of the last volley trailed away, a lone bugler played taps. The
notes were lonely and somber and resonated deep within me.

As the last note faded off into nothingness, the honor guard snapped
sharply to attention and with severity and circumstance, carefully lifted
the flag from Frank's coffin. Then the angular folding began, one crease
on the other until the final tuck formed the flag into a perfect triangle,
prominently displaying the stars and stripes. The head of the honor guard
approached me and gently laid the flag in my hands while expressing the
thanks of a grateful nation. I felt so limp that I could not support the flag's
weight. Fortunately, someone took my arm and lifted me up. He took the
flag from my hands, replaced it with a single red rose, and guided me to
the casket.

I leaned in to place the rose directly over Frank's heart, saying nothing, but as I stood there, I lost sight of the casket and focused instead on
deep, dark pit below. Images flashed through my mind. I imagined Frank
in the cave on Okinawa with that poor young girl and then in another
cave a week later when he saw his friend, Jimmy, blown to pieces. I
began to feel as trapped as when I was caught in that crowded elevator in
New York while Frank was in the service.

The walls of the open grave were only inches larger than the casket
itself. The images of dirt filling the gaps and then piling on top of the
lid filled me with dread. I could feel the earth squeezing in on me, trap-
ping me, choking the life from me. Images from my childhood recalled
watching some relatives restrain others from jumping into the burial pit

with their loved one. But not me! I wanted to be as far from this place as possible but the blood drained from my head and I felt faint.

I started falling forward toward the open tomb when a pair of strong hands gripped me by the shoulders and then escorted me back to the waiting limousine. From my seat, I looked out at the casket sitting by itself against the now gray sky and nodded to myself, *This is as it should be.* I pressed my head against the window and whispered softly, "Goodbye, my love. Once I waited for you, now please, please wait for me."

As the limousine made its way back to the entrance, I nodded once more, knowing that I would never see this place again.

PART THREE

FAMILY, FRIENDS, AND OTHER ACCIDENTS

CHAPTER 24

IN THE WEEKS after Frank died, Bridget and Megan took turns visiting me every day and on some days, they visited together. I don't think they realized, however, that I was no longer the same woman. All I could focus on was how I hated being by myself and how angry I was that Frank had left me alone.

At first, the girls just listened but as the weeks passed, they grew more concerned and tried to steer our conversations into directions that were more positive. That only made me angrier. On some level, I must have appreciated their efforts but I couldn't express that. My need to lash out at the unfairness of it all trumped any positive feelings I might have had. They would tell me that I had to stop dwelling on what I'd lost and start thinking about getting on with my life.

"That's easy enough for you to say," I'd yell. "You still have your husbands so you don't know what it's like. You couldn't; nobody can. Frank is gone and I'm alone and I can't stand it." Too often, the conversations escalated into arguments without any resolution until they just gave up in frustration.

The grandchildren also stopped in to talk and to help me with shopping or household chores, but most of their visits were short. I sometimes managed to ask about school and extracurricular activities but after that, I just couldn't think of anything else to say. Nothing else seemed much worth talking about anyway.

I lost interest in eating and seldom left the house. Conversations with friends and even my pastor didn't help for long. The girls suggested that I talk to a professional counselor but I would have none of it. "What else did you expect?" I'd argue. "After more than fifty years of marriage, it's crazy not to miss someone."

Even with all of the comings and goings, I spent most of each day alone. My most crushing task was passing the empty nights. Bridget's oldest son, Shawn, moved in with me for a while. He was a social work freshman at UCONN and claimed that he could get more studying done at my house than in his noisy dorm but I knew better. I liked making toast or cereal for him. Larger meals were out of the question. Then I realized that I could not uphold any conversation that didn't revolve around my grief at losing Frank. And no matter how many of those conversations we had, nothing changed. After about three weeks, I thanked him for this thoughtfulness but insisted that he return to his dorm room at UCONN and he agreed. I think he also realized the fruitlessness of his efforts.

Once again I was alone, which suited my mood. To me, my empty house mirrored my new existence. Doing anything just didn't matter anymore. *What's the point?* I thought. *Frank's gone, so who's going to notice?*

Frank and I loved going out to eat but eating was never the purpose. We would talk about how the kids and grandkids were doing and who called today. We'd discuss how Steve liked his new job, how Megan was coping with her unexpected pregnancy, or just what was happening this week at the senior center. It was about the millions of small things that added up to a life together. Now eating was just about surviving and doing it alone seemed pointless, so I did it less often.

Then there were the walks. I loved walking with Frank, especially in the rain. Snuggled together beneath an umbrella with his arm wrapped around me, I felt safe and warm no matter what the weather. Now, without Frank, no matter how many layers of clothing I wore, I was always cold. Walking became a necessary drudgery. Shopping and movies were even more pointless. What was the use of shopping for a new dress or blouse when there was no Frank to admire it, and what good was going to a movie alone?

I sat quietly in my kitchen staring out the window and taking in the scene. The bright fall colors had faded into maroons and browns. Brittle leaves lost grip of their branches and floated aimlessly on the autumn breezes until they fell to the ground and covered the roads and lawns. Some trees were already bare. Piles of leaves assembled along the road-sides waited for the city to collect them ahead of the first snowfall. No one had gathered the leaves in my yard, so the grass lay beneath a red-brown carpet. In past autumns, I viewed the flurry of activity in my flower garden. The last few birds would flutter around the feeder that hung from the shepherd's hook. They would peck the suet bare before heading south for the winter. Chipmunks scurried below, gathering the seeds that fell to the ground while rabbits nibbled away at the plant leaves. Occasionally, an enterprising squirrel would hang upside down, trying to penetrate the squirrel-proof feeder.

There was little to see now, however. I hadn't filled the bird feeder in weeks and the flowers lay smothered under the carpet of leaves. Everything was either dead or dying. That to me seemed as it should be.

"Hi, Mom," Bridget cheerfully announced as she entered the kitchen. She and Megan had just returned from an extended weekend in Ogunquit with their husbands. They shared their plans with me beforehand and I insisted that I would be fine while they were gone. All the grandkids had competing activities so other than telephone calls, I was alone for several days. It was my longest period of isolation since Frank died.

"Hello, Bridget," I said without turning toward her.

Out of the corner of my eye, I could see her face tighten, "What's so interesting in the backyard?" she asked.

"Nothing," I turned around, "nothing at all." It was past ten; I was still in my housecoat and I hadn't yet combed my hair.

"Have you had anything to eat?" she asked.

"I don't think so."

Bridget clenched her jaw and began pacing around the kitchen.

111

"All right then, I'll make you something. What would you like: eggs, pancakes, French toast?" As she asked, she scanned the sink filled with dirty dishes and the mail and newspapers that covered the kitchen table. She eyed the cups, silverware, and papers strewn everywhere and as she moved about the kitchen, there was a crunching sound beneath her shoes. I knew that cleaning and organizing were necessary but I just couldn't muster the energy to do them.

Then Bridget noticed the handwritten letter and envelope sitting atop the other papers on the kitchen table. She picked them up and examined them, "What's this, Mom?" I glanced at the letter in her hands as she began to read it and I recalled its contents.

The envelope had caught my attention because of the handwritten address and the return address from Mrs. June Matthews in Akron, Ohio. I couldn't recall anyone by that name or for that matter anyone I knew who lived in Ohio. I had opened the envelope, put on my glasses, and read the letter.

Dear Maureen,

I learned about Frank's passing recently and I can't put into words how deeply I feel for your loss, nor can I begin to express how sorry I am that this letter comes so late. I don't know how you will feel hearing from me after all these years. You and I were so close at one time and hearing about Frank's death, I felt I had to reach out again. Matthews was the name of my second husband, William. You knew me as June Fassig until I married Frank's best friend, Harvey, and became June Metz.

Maureen, I am so sorry for shutting you out of my life. I wish I could find the right words to explain what came over me but I still don't really understand it myself. All I know is that when Harvey was killed, I died too. Somehow, seeing you reminded me of everything I had lost and I just couldn't stand the pain. I know that you tried to reach out to comfort me but I just wasn't able to let you. Believe me, I tried, I really did. When that became impossible, all I could think to do was to run. I know it sounds crazy, but that's the only way I know how to describe it.

For the next couple of years I existed more than lived and firmly believed that I could never love again. Even after the pain subsided, what I felt more than anything else was numbness. I found a job and for the next ten years, buried myself in my work. I was in my mid-thirties when I met Bill. Fortunately, he was kind and understanding and gave me all the time I needed to feel comfortable caring for another man again. I still marvel that he held in long enough for me to grow to love him as much as he loved me. We married and raised three wonderful children. Bill died two years ago. I still miss him terribly, but it's different than it was with Harvey. While I sometimes cry thinking about what I have lost, I also feel grateful for the time we had together and the wonderful gift of my memories and my children and grandchildren.

Over the years, I've learned that you and Frank had two daughters of your own and that you now have several grandchildren. A thousand times I sat down to write or picked up the phone to call you but I felt so guilty and ashamed that I stopped before I started. When I heard about Frank's death, I realized that my embarrassment paled in comparison to your loss and made myself put these feelings into words. I honestly don't know if I am even remotely succeeding but between my tears and my prayers, I hope so.

Maureen, I wouldn't blame you in the least for tearing this up immediately and putting me out of your mind forever. I deserve that, but if you can find it in your heart to forgive me, please allow me to be there for you as you tried to be there for me. My return address is on the envelope and my phone number is at the bottom of this letter. If you decide to use either, I would be overjoyed to hear from you again. If not, I will understand and not bother you again. I will however, always cherish our friendship, keep you in my heart, and pray that God grants you comfort and peace.

Your friend forever,

June

"Mom," Bridget asked, "how come you never mentioned June to me and Megan? She sounds very nice and it seems like you two were really close."

"There was nothing to mention," I answered. "Like she said in her letter, she shut me out of her life and hasn't made contact ever since." Anger welled up inside me. "Now that Frank's gone, all of a sudden she wants to be friends again and pick up where we left off. It sounds to me like she just wants to gloat that I feel as bad now as she did then. Well thanks but no thanks." I walked over to Bridget, took the letter and envelope from her hands, crumpled them up, and tossed them in the trashcan.

"Are you sure you want to do that, Mom? Do you think that maybe...."

"No," I cut her off. "I don't think anything about her. I haven't for fifty years and I don't see any reason to start now."

Bridget looked around the kitchen again, "Tell you what: on second thought, let's go out for breakfast. You get dressed and I straighten out in here."

"I don't know. I'm really not very hungry and I don't have anything to wear."

"Mom!" Bridget's tone left no room for negotiation. "We're going out for breakfast, not to a cotillion. Now go upstairs and get dressed. Wear your beige print dress and bring a sweater with you; it's chilly out. Now hurry up before they stop serving."

"Where are we going?"

"We're going to Rod's." Bridget's answer spurred me into action. Rod's was close by and was one of Frank's favorite breakfast places. As I dressed to go, I couldn't help hoping that by some supernatural quirk or extraordinary mercy on God's part, Frank might just be sitting there, sipping his coffee as we entered.

CHAPTER 25

"MOM," BRIDGET SCOLDED, "if you keep staring at that couple, you're going to make them nervous."

I turned back to her, "I wasn't staring at them."

"Yes, you were. You have been ever since we came in."

"I wasn't looking at them. That's your father's favorite booth."

Bridget scanned the center booth on the opposite wall as I continued. "If they're still here when he comes, he'll refuse to eat until they leave, no matter how long it takes. Then he'll order the same breakfast as always—two eggs over medium with rye toast, crispy home fries, and one pancake. He loves their pancakes."

"Oh," Bridget answered. "Did you forget, Mom?"

"Forget what?"

"Dad isn't coming today."

"No? Why not?"

Bridget placed her hand on top of mine and spoke softly, "Because he's gone, Mom."

I had to stop to concentrate and let my mind catch up. *Where was I? Where was Frank? What was I doing here?* Then slowly, everything settled back into place. I looked into Bridget's eyes and saw the tear running down her cheek.

"Oh … yes … that's right.… I'm sorry, honey.… I just couldn't help feeling that your father was going to walk through the door any moment and say that he's starving."

Bridget wiped away the tear. "You need to start eating more too, Mom. You don't want to get sick and you know that you can't live on coffee alone."

"The coffee is enough for now. Frank loved his coffee. He always drank three cups. The first was regular and the second and third were always decaf. Sometimes I'd be in a hurry to get somewhere but we couldn't leave until he had his last cup. He always had to get his money's worth, just as he did by being buried in that military cemetery in Middletown. I should never have agreed to that. He knows that I don't drive. Now I can't even visit him without someone else driving me. We'll never be together again."

"Someday, Mom."

"When?"

"You know."

I realized that Bridget was only trying to comfort me, but her answer pried open feelings I had been trying hard to suppress. "I only wish I did. I don't know what I believe anymore."

Then the anger welled up inside me and spilled over, "Your father broke his promise to me. He always said he was going to live to be a hundred. He promised that I would go first because he knew that I couldn't go on without him."

"Dad isn't God, Mom. There was no way he could have prevented dying before you unless he killed you first."

"Well, then maybe he should have!" I spoke louder than I planned to. Several patrons looked in our direction briefly and then returned to their meals but I really didn't care.

"For heaven's sake, Mom," Bridget whispered. "Don't say that."

"Why not?" I fought back the tears as I spoke. "Sometimes I feel dead already. I look around me and see people talking and laughing and I think, why don't they just stop. Frank's dead. Don't they know that when a good and decent man like Frank dies, everything should just stop … at least for a while? For most of my life, it was both of us and now it's just me. I don't know how I can go on living without him."

Bridget's eyes reddened. "Mom. You're just lonely. You miss Dad. We all do, but the world doesn't stop because someone dies, even someone like Dad. Good people die every day. The best we can do is remember them and I know this much, Dad wouldn't want to see you like this. He'd want you to go on with your life."

Bridget was trying so hard to be understanding but I needed to fight and unfortunately for her, she was the only one available; "What have I got to live for now?"

"Mom, please, you have to stop thinking like this. You have plenty to live for. What about Megan and me? We need you."

"You both have your own lives and your own families to worry about. The last thing you need is having someone around who can't even take care of herself."

"Now you're just exaggerating; and what about your grandkids? Don't you think they need you?"

I could fend off almost any other argument, but I couldn't dismiss the protective bond I felt toward my grandchildren. "Well, I suppose so, but right now I don't even know how to be there for them, at least not in the way they need me to be."

"The way they need you to be is whatever way you are. Remember, they've lost their grandfather and they're sad and confused too. Have you reconsidered seeing a counselor?"

"I'm not crazy, Bridget."

"I'm not saying you are, but there are professionals who specialize in helping people cope with losing someone they loved. There's nothing wrong with getting help when you need it."

Bridget waited for the response but I refused to reply. Finally, she changed the subject.

"OK then, just one more thing. Mom, you need to take driving lessons."

"What!"

"I know you heard me. It's not that loud in here."

"I haven't driven in over forty years. Your father did all the driving."

"I know and in that respect, I don't think he did you any favors. Now you're a prisoner in your own home."

"Now who's exaggerating? All the stores I need are right on Farmington Avenue and I walk to the senior center all the time."

"Oh, yeah, and when exactly was the last time you did? You haven't been back to the center since Dad died."

"It's more complicated than that. It's not the same without your father. Besides, you said yourself that if I wanted to go anywhere, all I had to do was to call you or Megan and one of you would be happy to drive me, or has that changed too?"

"No, we said it and we meant it and if we're not available, Steve or Ryan will be happy to take you, but that still doesn't give you independence."

Independence: the word had a finality about it that terrified me. Up until that moment, I had never considered myself as an independent person. Deep down somewhere, I guess I knew that she was right and I lost my will to fight. I stopped arguing and just sat back until she broke the silence.

"Neither Megan nor I can teach you. We'd be too nervous but Steve is very patient and he's an excellent instructor. I'm sure he could get you back to driving again without a problem."

"Steve has so many of his own projects. He certainly doesn't need to take me on as another one."

"He doesn't mind at all. We've already discussed it and he said he could make time on Saturday mornings."

"You've already talked about it? Don't I have any say?"

"Frankly, no. You need to get out of the house and driving could help you do that."

"Well, I'll think about it and let you know."

"Good. You can discuss it with Steve; he's picking you up on Saturday morning at eight."

CHAPTER 26

FOR THE FORTH week in a row, Steve pulled into my driveway promptly at eight on Saturday morning. It was a breezy, overcast day and as usual, I challenged him when he walked through the door.

"Steve, you really shouldn't be wasting your time like this."

"Well, good morning to you too, Mom."

He seldom took me too seriously. I liked that in him. His job required long hours and lots travel but he always made the time for Bridget, the kids, and our many family events. He and Bridget were also active in their church and town activities. With his involvement in so many projects, I resisted taking up more of his time but he never seemed to mind. He often joked that he married Bridget partly because of me. He said he figured that when she was my age, she would look as good as I did. Obviously, I was very fond of him.

Steve drove us to the Southington High School parking lot. School was not in session, there were no cars in the lot, and it was large enough to practice braking and turning around the grassy islands. He promised that we wouldn't drive in traffic until I was ready but after three weeks, we were still no closer to leaving the lot.

"All right, Mom," he said as he exited the car. "Slide over here to the driver's side and we'll get started." I slid into position and grabbed the steering wheel. "OK, Mom, what do you say we do a little...? Oh.... So Mom, you might want to try relaxing just a bit."

"I am relaxed."

"Well maybe relax just a little more. Your elbows are locked and knuckles are turning white."

I looked down and let out a sigh.

"That's all right, Mom. Everyone's a little nervous at first. Just take in a few deep breaths…. That's good…. Now loosen your hands a bit…. That's better…. OK, now let your arms relax…. Great. OK, now we're ready so let go of the wheel and fasten your seat belt."

I pulled the seat belt in front of me, but I couldn't get it into that clicker thingy.

"It doesn't work."

I wasn't trying to be difficult. The darn thing wouldn't click.

"No problem. I'll get it." Steve reached across until our faces were almost touching, then he smiled and looked straight into my eyes, "Now don't think I'm trying to take advantage of you." I laughed in spite of myself and calmed down a little. Steve got into the passenger side.

"Good. Now that you're all limbered up, reach down and turn on the ignition."

Once the car started, we sat for a while. Steve said I should just feel the purr of the engine and see that the car was not going to lunge forward on its own. I don't think it helped.

"It's getting awfully hot in here," I said.

"Actually, it feels a bit chilly right now." I gave Steve a stern look and he said, "Tell you what. Let's turn on the air conditioner." The cool breeze felt good to me but I thought I saw him shiver a little.

"OK, Mom, let's practice braking again. Put the car in drive, give it a little gas until it starts moving forward, and then gently brake to a stop. OK? Now push down on the brake pedal. No, not with your left foot. Remember, the right foot does all the work."

"That still seems silly to me."

"It probably is, but everybody does it that way."

I did as he said and put the car into drive.

"Good. Now take your foot off the brake. See, we're not even moving. Now place your foot on the gas and gently depress the pedal.

A little more.... A little more still.... OK, more than that.... A little more, Mom, we're still not moving.

"Ah yes, see? Now we're beginning to roll a bit. Excellent! Now we want to slowly bring the car to a stop, so take your foot off the gas and gently depress the.... Ugh...."

The car jerked to a stop and we both slammed forward against our seat belts.

"All right then.... See, you did it.... Now that wasn't so bad, was it? Now, Mom, there's no need to cry. I'm all right, really."

We continued practicing until the car stopped smoothly each time.

"So what do you think?" Steve asked.

"Well, I guess I'm getting the hang of it."

"Good. Then let's move on to turns." Steve was in a short-sleeved shirt. I was comfortable but he kept rubbing his arms and hands as if he were at a mid-winter football game.

"OK," he said. "Just maneuver the car around these islands going left or right whenever you feel. When you've gone as far as you want, just stop. All right?"

"If you say so."

"OK. Start moving whenever you're ready.... Very nice.... Now you see that island up ahead. Just pick a direction and turn left or right any time you're ready."

"Any time you're ready, Mom.... Any time now.... Now might be a good time.... Either direction is fine.... I'd turn now if I were...."

The car stopped abruptly when its wheels hit the curbing.

"That's all right, Mom.... That's why we practice this kind of thing in a parking lot instead of down on Queen Street."

"Steve, I'm never going to get the hang of this."

"No, no, no. You're doing fine. I'll tell you what. Instead of trying to pick a direction willy-nilly, I'll just tell you which way to turn each time until you're ready to pick your own."

A half hour later, I had successfully circled the lot several times. In the meantime, Steve kept blowing into his hands and rubbing his arms with them.

"He said, "Now let's try a little parking."

"Aren't you tired yet? I'm about ready for a nap."

"Tell you what, Mom. A couple parking maneuvers and we'll stop for breakfast and some really hot coffee. I promise."

"If you insist."

"Good. Now look ahead and pick out a parking spot on the right-hand side. Just pretend that there are other cars parked in the other spots."

"I can't do that."

"Why not?"

"I might hit them."

"They're just pretend, Mom."

"It still makes me nervous."

"All right then, forget about the other cars. The parking lot is empty, OK?"

"OK."

"Good. Then when you reach the parking spot, just turn in so that the car winds up between the white lines when you stop. You'll need to stay a little to the left to give yourself enough room to turn in. That's all there is to it. OK? Do you have a spot picked out?"

"I suppose so."

Poor Steve was turning blue and shivering so bad that he began stuttering.

"All right then, let's g-go for it."

The car inched forward. As it did, I started moving it to the left.

"Mom, you really d-don't need to m-move quite that far to the left," Steve panted as if he was running a marathon. Out of the corner of my eye, I could swear he was turning from blue to red.

"You're getting kind of close to the left-side parking lines. Now you're cutting into them, Mom. You know what: screw the left-side lines. Just turn when you're ready."

I turned the car to the right while looking down at the white line but it started disappearing beneath the car. I was concentrating so much on the line that I didn't realize I was also pressing further down on the gas. Steve did.

"OK, Mom, you might want to slow down a bit here.... A little slower, Mom.... Mom.... For Pete's sake, Mom, HIT THE BRAKES!"

We slammed hard against the seat belts and then bounced from side to side as each wheel rode up the curb and onto the grass before the engine stalled. The line wound up dead center under the car. I looked into Steve's eyes with a stern, "I told you so" look on my face.

Steve just smiled sweetly, "So, Mom, where do you think we should go for breakfast?"

Bridget and Steve had a long talk that afternoon. Steve told her that he wasn't going to be able to help me to drive again and didn't think a private driving school would do any better. He said I needed to master more than the mechanics of driving. After not driving for more than forty years, at seventy-six years old, I was probably not going to be able to learn. I could have told them that.

Their efforts, however, had unintended results. While they were struggling with Steve's seeming failure, I was on the phone asking Megan for a ride Tuesday to the Bristol Senior Center.

CHAPTER 27

MY ANXIETY HEIGHTENED as Megan rounded the circular driveway and stopped in front of the senior center.

"What time should I pick you up, Mom?"

I hesitated, "I'm not sure that this was a good idea. Maybe you should just bring me back home and we can come back another day."

"You're here now. You might as well go in. If it doesn't work out, just call me."

"Where will you be?"

"It doesn't matter. I have my cell phone. You can reach me whenever you want."

I closed the car door and stood still facing the building. I had to lift my collar against the icy chill but I still didn't move. Questions rolled around in my head. How I could face my friends without Frank by my side? What would I say? How would I answer them when they asked how I was doing? What if I started to cry?

A flock of birds passed overhead on their way south and I wished that I could fly away with them. A tear trickled down my cheek.

"It'll be all right, Mom." Megan's voice was soft and sympathetic. I wiped the tear away before looking back toward the car. She leaned across the front seat and talked through the open passenger window, "Really, it will."

I loved my daughters and deeply appreciated their efforts to help me.

For their sake, I at least had to try. I forced a smile, "If you say so," and with that, I turned, prayed for strength, and walked toward the building.

Once inside, I heard the noise of conversation and laughter coming from the dining area. The sound filled me with dread. As I entered the room I gasped, "Oh no!" The brightly colored Christmas decorations assaulted me. The last thing I wanted was to be immersed in an atmosphere of Christmas cheer but before I could react, Lorraine called out to me.

"Maureen!" She rushed up and wrapped me in her arms. "Oh, honey, we've missed you so much."

"Thank you, Lorraine. I've missed you too." It wasn't true; I was too numb to miss anyone.

"Come sit with us." She took my arm and guided me to the table. Larry Kowalski and Ceil were there with two other couples I knew and a woman I had never met before. Lorraine introduced her.

"Maureen, this is Veronica Beecher. We used to work together at Stanley Works and she and her husband, Ted, used to vacation with George and me. Ted passed away in October." Then Lorraine addressed Veronica, "Do you remember the dancing couple I talked about? Well, this is Maureen. Frank passed in September."

I cringed at the casualness of Lorraine's reference to Veronica's husband and Frank. She announced their deaths the way she might report the price of apples at Stop and Shop. How could she be so flip about the loss of a lifelong soul mate?

"Maureen, we're so sorry about Frank," said Larry. Ceil nodded her head in agreement as did the other couples at the table.

"So you lost your husband too?" Veronica asked me so softly it was barely audible.

"Yes, I'm sorry for your loss," I answered. From Veronica's demeanor, I suspected that she was feeling as uncomfortable as I was, "Are you managing all right?" I asked.

"I have my good days and bad. Lately more bad than good."

"I know. My children keep pushing me to get out of the house but they don't understand. It's not that easy."

"No," Veronica answered, "it's not." The two of us sat in silence for a few moments until I asked Lorraine about some of the absent couples.

"Oh, they all went on that Foxwoods trip today."

Then I realized that other than the first few weeks after Frank's death, I hadn't heard from any of our married friends or been invited to any of their regular events. I wouldn't have gone anyway, but it seemed odd to me that no one had even asked. Then it occurred to me that Frank's death had also changed my social status. They were still couples and now I wasn't. Lorraine's voice interrupted my thoughts.

"They had a full bus again today. It seems like they're running those casino trips every week lately and no wonder. How could you go wrong when you get the bus, buffet, and money to gamble with too? Today's trip was even better. It included show tickets for the Jerry Vale concert."

"Jerry Vale?" someone asked, "Is he still singing?"

The question set off a flurry of conversations among the women about him and other entertainers. Which were alive or dead? Which had the best voice? Which were the most beautiful or handsome? The men at the table quickly tired of the banter and launched a separate conversation of their own revolving around household projects, favorite tools, and the best hardware stores.

Veronica and I faded into the background until I felt a tugging at my blouse sleeve and looked up to see Ralph Corbin. Ralph was a regular at most senior center functions. He was a portly man with a constantly rosy complexion and sparse, wiry white hair. No matter what he was doing, he looked constantly out of breath. His rumpled tan suit complemented his equally wrinkled shirt, and the mustard stains on his sleeve evidenced his lunch selection.

"All right, Russo, it's your turn."

Lorraine protested, "Ralph, Maureen might not be ready to start dancing. Today is her first day back since Frank died."

"Nonsense," Ralph answered. "It's like falling off a horse. The best thing you can do is get right back up and start riding again."

I doubted that Ralph had ever ridden a horse in his life.

"Thank you, Ralph," I answered, "but Lorraine is right. I'm really not up to it right now."

"Maureen, I'm not taking no for an answer so you might as well dance with me or I'll just pester you all afternoon."

He yanked me out of my seat and onto the dance floor. I wanted to resist but couldn't muster the energy. Chet Hartman's orchestra was playing a slow foxtrot. Ralph danced in double time while I remained limp but that didn't stop him from maintaining a strong but clumsy lead.

"It's good to see you again, Maureen. You know it's really important to get out again after a tragedy like Frank's death." Ralph's breath carried the scent of stale cigars from his constant smoking.

"That's seems to be what everyone tells me."

"Well, they're right, you know. So how long has it been, I mean, you know, since Frank died?"

"It will be three months this week."

"Three months, huh: so how are you holding up?" I was learning to detest those words.

"As good as could be expected, I guess. I have days when all I can do is cry. Other days, I can't do much of anything at all."

"Well then it's good that you're here among friends. You know, there are plenty of folks here who are willing to jump in and lend a hand. All you have to do is ask."

"Thank you, Ralph. That means a lot."

"Any time. You know, Maureen, I always thought you were a knockout."

The words barely penetrated my consciousness. "I'm sorry, Ralph, what?"

"You know. I just meant that I think you're a really good-looking woman. Some of the gals around here, well, they just let themselves go to pot. They put on weight; they don't fix themselves up; sometimes

127

they show up looking like they're ready to wash windows. But you, you always look like a class act and I appreciate that in a woman."

"Well, thank you, I guess."

"Listen, Maureen, I've been divorced for more than three years now. I know it hasn't been nearly that long for you but neither of us is getting any younger, if you know what I mean."

"I'm sorry, Ralph. I'm not following you."

"Then I'll make myself clear. Maureen, you're an attractive, healthy woman who's been without a man for quite some time now. I'm sure you've got needs and urges that aren't being met and I'm a guy in pretty decent shape who finds himself attracted to you. Are you seeing where I'm going with this?"

I stopped dancing and pulled myself away. "Yes, Ralph. I think you've made yourself very clear and let me make this clear for you. I'm not about to jump into bed with you or any other man for that matter."

"Now don't get me wrong, Maureen. I didn't mean to be disrespectful or anything."

"I think I understand you perfectly, Ralph, but let me give you a piece of advice: don't wait around for the phone to ring."

I stormed off in the direction of the table. I didn't even notice the woman in the black dress until we collided, but the other woman certainly did.

"What the hell! Are you blind? You almost made me…. Oh, Ginger, it's you."

Doris Cantrell's demeanor softened when she recognized me. "I haven't seen you in a dog's age. Was that you up dancing with Ralph? Listen, kid, if you're trying to make Fred jealous, I'd rethink my choices if I were you. I mean Ralph isn't exactly the pick of the litter."

"It's Frank, Doris, and no, I wasn't trying to make him jealous." I fought back the tears and trembled as I continued, "I can't make him jealous anymore. He's dead."

"Dead? When?"

"In September."

"Oh, I didn't know. Tough break, kid."

"Tough break?" I almost choked on the words. How could everyone be so casual about something so tragic? Has the whole world gone mad? And where does this "kid" stuff come from? I'm obviously older than she is, maybe by a long shot. At least Ralph tried to fake concern.

"Excuse me, Doris, but I have to call my daughter for a ride. I've stayed way too long already." I started moving away

"No need, kid. I was just getting ready to go myself. I've about had my fill of Christmas cheer. I'll just get my coat and drop you off on my way home."

"Thanks anyway, Doris, but I don't think that's such a good idea."

As I started to turn, Doris spoke up. There was a note of desperation in her voice.

"Maureen, please, hold on a minute. I'm sorry about that 'tough break' crack. Like I said when we first met, I have this problem about expressing myself and sometimes I come off like a real jerk. It's just that in my own experience, I've never met a man whose dying didn't seem to improve the situation. But you and Fred, I mean Frank, well, you seemed to have had something special. OK, look. If I say anything more, I'm just going to make a bigger fool out of myself. So what do you say? Can I offer you that ride?"

As awkward as her apology was, it seemed genuine and I calmed down. "All right, thank you. I'll say my goodbyes and get my coat."

In the parking lot, Doris directed me to her black and silver Jaguar. It wasn't the typical ride for center members, but then again, nothing about Doris seemed typical. Even in my malaise, the enigma tweaked my interest.

As Doris switched on the ignition, "Have a Holly Jolly Christmas," blared on the radio. She quickly turned it off. "It's got to be really tough losing somebody at this time of year. How are you holding up?"

"I'm not!" I yelled. I could hear the anger in my voice, but I didn't care and somehow I didn't think I needed to with Doris. Thanksgiving had been torture and I was dreading Christmas and New Year's even more.

She apologized, "I guess I just put my foot in my mouth again. Sorry."

"I'm sorry for snapping. I don't think there's anything anyone could say right now that would help. I don't even think the right words exist."

We sat in silence for the rest of the trip. Doris spoke up as I opened the car door in my driveway.

"How about I give you a call some time? Maybe we can, you know, get a cup of coffee or something?"

"Maybe," I held back from saying anything more. "Thank you for the ride."

"Anytime, kid." Doris backed out onto Stafford Avenue and the Jaguar sped off.

As I closed the kitchen door behind me, I stood with my back against it for a time, relieved to be inside the safety of my home again and alone. I took in a deep breath and then retreated to the living room couch where I cried loud and long until I fell to sleep.

CHAPTER 28

LITTLE BY LITTLE, the earth slowed down as it prepared for its long winter sleep. The days grew dark and colder. Birds gathered in threes and fours, then tens and then hundreds until they were everywhere: on branches, along fences, and on power lines. They swarmed like bees, swooped down on berried trees and bushes, and picked them clean. The air filled with the sounds of their chirping. Then, as if responding to some omnipotent command, they blackened the sky in waves of V-shaped formations as they made their way southward. Then they were gone and all fell silent.

Christmas and New Year's came and went. There were dinners, parties and presents but I simply existed through them all and through the icy months that followed.

The gray winter skies suited my mood, as did the periods of solitude imposed by the cold and snow. The trees stood barren. Weeds and flowers withered and died. Everything seemed to be mourning Frank's death, just as it should. Perhaps soon, I thought, I too would be caught up in the cycle of decay and at last rest forever with my Frank, but that didn't happen. The world grew dark and barren but I stayed. The snow came and blanketed everything until all was quiet and still I stayed. I resigned myself to dying, longed for it, and then prayed for it, but still I stayed. Then a painful reality settled in: either I would have to accept my empty existence as it was, or take matters into my own hands to escape it.

The day I first realized that started out as just another cold winter morning. Snow had started falling after dark and continued steady until dawn. The temperature was just below freezing at the start so the early snow came in large, wet flakes that stuck to everything. As the temperature dropped, smaller flakes piled high and fluffy on top of the earlier ones. By morning, white mantled every tree branch and the evergreens along the back line sagged under the snow's weight. Dark patches of green peeked through the white cover so in the early morning sunlight, the trees looked like giant, snowcapped mountains floating in the air.

The city plows kept the streets open but in the process, they constructed waist-high fortifications of snow, sand, and ice along the front of my driveway. It would be hours before someone would come to plow me out. Even if my children wanted to visit, they would not be able to pull into the driveway from the road.

I shivered as the wind groaned outside. The winter's chill had settled deep within me. It was not like previous years when the cold chilled my skin's surface. Even if I sometimes felt goose bumps up and down my arms, as long as I dressed properly, internally I was warm and comfortable. This cold, however, came from within. It was as though a fire deep within my core had extinguished. Now, even the slightest temperature drop chilled me throughout. Drinking hot liquids gave me only temporary relief and the children commented that they usually found my house uncomfortably warm.

I was sipping hot tea at the kitchen table when the front doorbell rang. As I crossed the bay window in the living room, I looked out at the snow-covered scene. A lone set of tracks made their way from the giant pickup truck at the edge of my driveway to my front door.

As I opened the door, Larry Kowalski kicked the snow from his boots.

"Larry, this is certainly a surprise. I never expected to see anyone on a morning like this." As I spoke, I felt a blast of cold air coming in through the open door. "Please come in. Would you like a cup of coffee?"

"That would be great." Larry brushed the snow from his parka before entering.

I added water to the teakettle and placed it on the stove. "I hope instant is all right; that's all I have." I stretched to retrieve the jar from the top shelf of the kitchen cabinet. As I turned around, I caught Larry lowering his eyes and realized that I was still in my housedress. Frank used to tell me how he loved seeing the outline of my body against the thin material.

"Excuse me for just a second," I quickly retreated to the bedroom, took my robe from the closet, and tied it tightly around my waist. As I closed the closet door, I saw in the mirror that I hadn't even combed my hair. Returning, I told Larry, "I'm sorry for the way I look. With the weather and all, I wasn't expecting company this morning."

He smiled, "You look just fine. I should have called first. I just finished clearing my driveway and thought you might need help with yours. I see it isn't done yet."

I was surprised but pleased that Larry would take the time to think about me. I thought to myself that I was also surprised that he and Ceil were still together. Larry was as athletic and energetic as Ceil was sedentary. She confided to me how she pursued Larry after Helen died: how she made him dinners and provided companionship. As he recuperated from his loss, however, he told Frank that he felt confined by the arrangement, especially after Ceil moved in with him. When Frank asked Larry why he didn't just end the relationship, he said that he didn't want to hurt Ceil's feelings. I admired his consideration but questioned his judgment. As I spoke with him now in my kitchen, I couldn't help noticing how ruggedly handsome he looked. At the same time, I couldn't help thinking about my friend, Ceil.

I said, "I'm guessing Ceil preferred to stay indoors this morning."

"She would have but her sister insists they get together at least once a month for breakfast, no matter what the weather and then do something for fun. Today it was the casino. Ceil tried to back out of it but Anita wouldn't take no for an answer. She has a huge SUV and picked Ceil up about an hour ago."

The teakettle started whistling. I made coffee and handed Larry a cup.

Sitting at the kitchen table, Larry blew across the hot coffee, took a sip, and said, "She's been asking about you. Now that you're back at the center, she was wondering if you'll be taking classes with her again."

I hesitated. "I don't know, Larry. Right now, I'm just taking things one day at a time. I wouldn't have gone back so soon if it weren't for my daughters' insistence. They keep pushing me to get on with my life, as if I could somehow erase fifty years of marriage with a wave of my hand. It's just not that easy. Frank is part of me. He's everywhere in this house. He used to drink his coffee out of that cup you're holding." My voice cracked as I pictured Frank drinking his coffee.

"I guess it's been pretty tough on you these last few months. I'm sorry." Larry's voice was soft, gentle and understanding.

I dropped the facade of strength and independence that I was trying to put on and let my emotions surface. "Oh, Larry," my voice quivered as my eyes began to water; "it's been a living hell. I've been so lonely, so lost. Every day is a struggle. I don't know what I'm going to do. I don't know how I'm going to make it through this." I leaned up against the counter and started to cry. Larry rose from kitchen table and crossed over to me. He took me into his arms and rubbed my back gently as he spoke.

"I know, Maureen. I remember what it was like when I first lost Helen. It's harder than anyone could ever imagine. It may seem impossible right now but believe me, someday you'll get past this. Someday, it's going to be all right again."

I laid my head into Larry's shoulder and sobbed freely, "Oh God, I hope so."

Larry stood still, absorbing my sobs. Then he slowly moved back, placed his hand under my chin, and gently lifted my face. As he did, he wiped the tears from my eyes and then bent down and kissed me on the lips. At first, I wasn't fully aware of what was happening; I just felt an odd, yet relaxing sensation of falling. Then I realized that I was kissing

Larry back and pushed away, as much from myself as from him. "What are we doing, Larry?" I asked.

"I'm not sure myself, Maureen. I just wanted to console you: you looked so hurt and fragile and then I guess I just got carried away. I care about you, Maureen."

"Like that, Larry? Is that how you care about me?"

"I care very much for you and to be honest, yes, I guess I'd have to say that I care about you the way a man cares about a woman."

"But you're with Ceil."

"There are all sorts of ways to be with someone, Maureen. Ceil is a good woman. She has a kind heart but she's not what you would call passionate."

"She's what I would call my friend."

"She's still your friend. There's no need for her to know about this."

"There is no this, Larry…. You need to leave."

"Maureen, I'm sorry. Maybe I misread things."

"There was nothing for you to misread."

"All right, but if I could just try to explain…."

"You need to leave, now."

Larry must have seen from the anger in my face that no amount of explaining was going to make any difference. He paused for a moment and then let out a sigh, picked up his coat, and walked back into the living room. He stopped by the front door for a moment, "I'm sorry, Maureen…. I'm truly sorry."

I shut the door after him and just stood there thinking. I thought about how long Frank and I had known him and Helen and about the many trips we took together. I thought about the experiences we had shared and places we had seen. I thought about all of the laughter and, after Helen's death, the tears. I also thought about the many conversations we had shared over the years and maybe, somewhere deep inside me, about the attraction I felt for him.

Then I thought about Ceil. No matter what their relationship, it would be an unforgivable betrayal of our friendship to come between them and what about Frank: what about our memories? Wouldn't it be a betrayal of all of our years together to be having feelings for another man? Larry's callous disregard for my grief and my own selfish weakness had just trampled on all of those memories. Then I pressed my back against the door and whispered to myself, "I'm sorry too, Larry. I'm sorry, too."

PART FOUR

DORIS

CHAPTER 29

AS THE DAYS lengthened, spring ushered in the promise and, for me, the challenge of new life. I sat near the kitchen window taking in the warmth of the early morning sunshine when the phone rang. The stove's clock read 7:15 a.m.

Putting the receiver to my ear, I expected to hear Bridget or Megan's voice but couldn't understand why either of them would call so early on a Saturday morning. I hoped it wasn't bad news.

"Ever gone tag saleing?"

I was dumbfounded, "I'm sorry. Who is this?"

"It's Doris, honey."

"Oh. Hello, Doris, how are you?"

"Just peachy, darlin. So, have you ever been tag saleing?"

"Is that some sort of boat race?"

"Not that kind of sailing: tag sales, you know, like barn or garage sales."

"Is that even correct: tag saleing? If you are going to them to buy things, shouldn't it be tag shopping?

"What are you, a linguist? The term satisfies perfectly well. So have you ever been tag saleing?"

"Maybe once or twice. Frank liked to go sometimes but I never really got into it much, why?"

"Well, the first signs went up yesterday. There should be a ton of great stuff, so I'm inviting you to join me. We can hit a few sales and then go out for breakfast. I can pick you up in five minutes."

"I really can't think of anything I need to buy. To tell you the truth, the things I saw at them always looked like a bunch of junk to me."

"That's just 'cause you didn't know what to look for. Stick with me, kid, and I'll have you shopping like a pro in no time."

I couldn't recall but there was something oddly familiar and even comforting in the phrasing of her comment. "Oh, I don't know, Doris. I'm not even dressed yet.

"Then I'll make it fifteen minutes instead of five. See you then." The phone went dead.

I thought to myself, *That Doris really is an odd one. Well, I guess I'd better go and get dressed.*

CHAPTER 30

I HAD JUST put the teakettle on when the first blast of the car's horn sounded. I looked at the stove's clock again: 7:28. I would have preferred that Doris came to the side door and rang the bell instead. I raced to put on my coat and tried to exit the house before another honk but I was too late. The second blast sounded as I reached for the doorknob.

"Morning, kiddo," she said as I opened the car door.

"You seem very wide awake."

"I should be. I'm on my third cup of coffee already." She pointed to the travel mug sitting in the center console.

"Really? I haven't even had my...." I stopped as I remembered the teakettle. "Just a minute, Doris, I'll be right back."

The kettle was whistling full volume as I reentered the kitchen. *Good*, I thought to myself, *there's still enough for a cup*.

I reached for the travel mug in the corner cabinet and then hesitated. Like the one I had given Larry to drink from, it bore a ship's picture and under the image the name, "Sovereign of the Seas." It was the last cruise Frank and I had taken. I made myself a decaf instant and for a moment, stood at the kitchen counter gently rubbing the cup's rim. I was just closing the refrigerator door when the next blast came from the driveway. "Doris," I whispered as I entered the car, "it's 7:30; you're going to wake the neighbors!"

"So? It's not Sunday," she said while backing out of the driveway.

"Besides, if we wait any longer those white-haired biddies will be all over the first stops like flies on a crap pile." I winced at the gross depiction but Doris continued unabated. "I can hear them now, 'Do you have any Barbie Dolls? I'd love to buy one for my granddaughter,' as if they couldn't get a dozen different kinds at Kmart."

"Wouldn't they be cheaper at the tag sale? I thought that was the whole point."

"Sure, if that was really why they were buying them. But let me tell you, if one out of a hundred of those dolls ever make it into a kid's hands, it'll be a miracle."

"They're not really buying them for their granddaughters?"

"Classic Barbie dolls are hot collectibles. Only most of these women have no idea of what they're buying, so they wind up filling up their garages with a lot of junk."

I thought of my own garage, still filled to overflowing with years of Frank's collections. After he died, I hardly went out there at all. Then, when I finally did to search there for a lightbulb, I came across a box full of Frank's pictures, movies, and slides. He had carefully labeled each box or envelope with the date and the name of the occasion and the people involved. Many revolved around holidays, birthdays, and vacations. I made the mistake of opening an envelope of pictures labeled, *Catskill Vacation, 1967*. The first few pictures were of the girls with their boyfriends, or of me trying to escape the camera. Then, in one picture, someone had managed to get Frank and me having dinner at Koch's Restaurant in Leeds. Seeing us together, smiling and holding hands sent a jolt through me. I started crying uncontrollably and ran out of the garage. The next day I called Bridget and told her I wanted her, Megan, and their husbands to help clear out the garage right away and bring everything to the dump. It was Steve who finally convinced me to wait. He said that there were probably things the girls might want to keep and that he and Ryan might be able to use some of Frank's tools. He also said he was particularly interested in any cheesecake shots Frank might have taken of me. He made me laugh in spite of myself, so the garage remained untouched. Just thinking about it gave me a sinking feeling.

Doris interrupted my thoughts, "We have to get organized. What's the street number of our first stop?"

I looked at the circled and numbered tag sale listings in the *Step Saver*. Before I could respond, Doris added, "Don't bother, there's the sign."

I scanned the ad while checking the clock on the dashboard, "It says the sale begins at 8:00 but it's only 7:40 now. It also says no early birds." Even before I finished, Doris parked the car and headed up the driveway.

"Good Morning, y'al," Doris greeted the couple who were busily setting up for their sale. Her voice had that same chipper ring as her first greeting to me in the morning but with a noticeable Southern drawl.

"I'm sorry," answered the young woman. She was holding a pen in one hand and a handful of tags in the other. "We're really not fully set up...."

Doris interrupted, "Now don't you worry at all about us, dearie. We'll just busy ourselves looking around and leave you to your work."

"Well, if you would like to come back in just a...."

Doris's Southern drawl was suddenly more pronounced, "Oh no, we couldn't possibly do that. We have way too many other stops to make. You just continue with what you're doing and we'll fend for ourselves. Why, you won't even know we're here."

"Well, I guess it'll be all right." The woman went back to her tagging.

I remained seated in the car with the window open, unsure of how the exchange would end. Once I heard the woman's response, I walked up the drive. Doris already had two items in her hands: an odd-looking camera with double lenses marked $10.00 and a boxed Makita drill for the same price. Doris descended upon the young man coming out of the garage with an upholstered chair in his hands.

"Excuse me, but this drill is marked ten dollars. It must be a mistake. I'll give you two for it if you throw in this old camera."

The man put the chair down, straightened his back, and took in a breath, "I'm sorry, I can't do that. That drill is almost new. It cost me over a hundred dollars less than a year ago."

Doris chirped, "I don't know a thing about tools. I just thought my husband might like it. Then how about a dollar for this old camera alone?"

"Uh, yea, I guess so."

"Thank you very much," Doris placed the drill and a dollar bill into the man's hands.

Meanwhile, I was eying a costume jewelry pearl necklace. I hesitated disturbing the couple further but then I directed my question to the young woman, "Excuse me, miss, this necklace is marked $2.50 and I only have bills." I extended three one-dollar bills in the direction of the woman, "Do you have change?"

The words barely left my mouth when Doris pulled me firmly by the arm, "Maureen, we've imposed on these nice people long enough. We really must be going." She yanked the necklace from my hand and tossed it back on the table. Confused, I turned and followed her to the car.

As we started to drive away, I said, "That's an odd-looking camera. Too bad you missed out on the drill."

"I never wanted that old thing. If I want work done around my house, I hire someone to do it."

"But you said you wanted it for your husband."

"Henry? He wouldn't know which way to put the bit in. Anyway, we've been divorced for years."

"Then why did you ask about it?"

"Because I wanted the camera. The double lens is for taking three-dimensional pictures. Collectors will pay plenty for this model even in poor condition but this one looks almost new. By asking about the drill, he didn't even notice that I offered him a dollar for the camera instead of the ten on the price tag. I figured that even if he didn't jump for the dollar, he would certainly settle for two or three and I can get at least sixty for it this afternoon."

I could see that tag saleing was a lot more involved than I had imagined, "If you knew that you could get that much, why didn't you just give the man the ten dollars? Come to think of it, why did you stop me from buying that necklace?"

"For the same reason I didn't give him the $10 for the camera: because, honey, you never offer to pay the asking price."

"Never?"

"If an item is insanely underpriced and they won't budge no matter what, you might have to give in, but I can count on one hand the number of times that's happened."

"So my asking the woman to make change was the wrong thing to do?"

"Instead of asking for change, you just offer less money."

"So I should have offered her two dollars instead of three?"

"Better yet, offer her a dollar and see if she takes the bait. If not, then she certainly would have jumped for two. You just have to perfect your negotiating skills. Don't worry, kid, stick with me and before long, you'll be cashing in like a pro."

"I don't know if I need to cash in. I thought this was supposed to be fun."

"Winning is fun, darlin'. It may just be the most fun there is. Besides, we're doing these people a favor so maybe they should be paying us to take this stuff off their hands."

"I'm not following you."

"Take the camera. Obviously, they're not using it anymore. Why didn't they just throw it in the trash?"

"I guess because they would feel guilty just throwing it away."

"Exactly. Even though it's old, they realize that it still has value for the right person. They just don't know who that is. I did them a favor by connecting it to that person, easing their guilt not even charging them a finder's fee."

We arrived at the next house just as the conversation ended. It was 8:20 and the advertised starting time was 9:00. I was surprised to see the number of women already milling about the front yard.

"See. What did I tell you?" asked Doris.

While I surveyed the sale items, I overheard an exchange between a tiny blue-haired woman and the homeowner.

"Excuse me, sir, but do you have any Barbie dolls? My granddaughter plays with them constantly and I'd love to bring one back for her." At the mention of Barbie doll, four other women lifted their heads and focused in on the conversation.

"Sorry, we only have boys," the man answered.

"Thank you." The woman sprinted away and darted toward her car. The other women quickly turned as well and left without saying a word. I realized that I had a lot to learn about tag saleing. Then I noticed another pearl necklace and picked it up to examine it. It looked even nicer than the first one and the tag read $2.00. Even though I was satisfied with the marked price, I offered the homeowner a dollar and, to my amazement, the woman answered, without hesitation, "Sure." On the way back to the car, Doris congratulated me on my purchase. I didn't tell her that knowing she was within earshot prompted my negotiation. Nevertheless, I was proud of my accomplishment. There was definitely a feeling of satisfaction at getting the best of the bargain.

"See, what'd I tell you, kid. Stick with me and you'll be cashing in big time."

I laughed, "That was actually fun. Even when I was with Frank, I was always intimidated at the thought of bargaining. He would have been so...."

"So proud of you? You bet he would! You kicked butt, girl."

Then it hit me. I was laughing while Frank was in his grave. He was not with me and he would never be again. Suddenly, the guilt flooded in and panic overtook me. I started panting, "Doris, I'm sorry, but I can't do this anymore."

"But we're just getting started. You just closed your first deal and you did great."

"You need to take me home, right now." She caught the desperation in my voice and did as I asked. As soon as we arrived, I darted toward the house.

Doris shouted after me, "Hey, darlin', you forgot something." The pearl necklace dangled from her outstretched hand.

I took the necklace, "Thank you. I'm sorry. I just can't talk anymore," and rushed away.

CHAPTER 31

INSIDE THE HOUSE, I pressed against the kitchen door for a moment as if trying to hold back the outside world and then retreated to the safety of the sitting room. I sat quietly in my chair for a long time and looked over to Frank's recliner. I pictured him sitting there previewing the latest senior center movie, reading the paper, or just talking to me. I could hear his laughter as he told me about the latest goings on at the center.

Newspaper ads and travel brochures covered the small lamp table between our recliners, waiting for our discussions about upcoming vacations. A copy of the *Bristol Senior Times* sat on the floor.

I grabbed the soft knit throw from my chair, moved onto Frank's recliner, pushed it all the way back, and dug myself into its deep crevasses until Frank's presence enveloped me. I took in the indentations of his body and the places turned shiny by his hands and fingers. I inhaled the smell of leather mixed with the lingering aroma of his aftershave. Most of all, I caressed the faded hollow where he laid his head.

For a moment, if only in my mind, my Frank was there again with me. I rubbed my cheek against his, caressed his face, and kissed him softly while tasting the saltiness of my own tears. Finally, I covered myself with the throw, held and caressed my Frank, and cried unrestrained until exhaustion and sleep set in.

When I opened my eyes again, the deep chill that constantly invaded my body had subsided. The late-morning sun pouring in through the sitting room window had heated the chair's leather and the throw that covered me. I sat up in Frank's recliner, retrieved my journal and pen from the lamp table, and began to write.

April 11, 2001

Dearest Frank,

I don't know how much longer I can do this. I miss you terribly and I'm terrified of being alone. I don't know who I am anymore without you. I feel disconnected from everything and everyone. I want the world to stop but it won't. Then I think if only I could stop, but I open my eyes and I am still here.

Are you happy where you are, Frank? Can you see me: hear me? I want to feel your presence, but as much as I try, there is nothing. All my life I've prayed and never received a response but I accepted that, because I never expected one. God was always just there but with you, that's not enough. I need to know that you didn't just vanish somehow when you.... I can't even stand the thought of that. It's crazy I know, but now I even question God Himself. I mean, if you are not there, then have I been wrong about God all this time too? I can't believe that I am even writing this. It's not something that I want to admit, even to myself, but I question everything lately. Without you, Frank, why am I still here? I'm scared to death.

Maybe people are right. Maybe we did spend too much time together. I see other women at the center who lose their husbands and seem to recover so quickly. Some of them even talk about how it's better in some ways now. Then they go on about all the things their husbands did to annoy them. Of course, they used to complain about the same kinds of things before they died and usually their husbands had talked about them the same way. I loved you for not being like that. We had our differences but *they were <u>our</u> differences and they remained between us. I also loved how you never felt self-conscious holding my hand in public and especially overhearing young couples tell each other how cute we looked when they thought we couldn't hear them.*

Everything I'm saying about us is in the past, Frank. What's going to become of me? I hate this life without you. I hate being cold and lonely all the time. I hate feeling scared. Even when I start feeling better, feeling some little bit of happiness, I feel guilty about that too. It's as though my being happy without you is a betrayal of everything we were to each other. Does any of this make any sense? I'm rambling. I don't know where I'm going with any of this. I'm so tired, Frank.

I couldn't write anymore. The tension I was feeling had left and in its wake, only exhaustion remained. By the time I finished, I had barely enough strength to hold the pen. I closed the book and it dropped into my lap. The sunlight had moved off the recliner and spilled onto the floor. Soon it would travel across the roof toward the back of the house. When it did, the room and my world would turn cold again. I pulled the throw up close and tucked it in around my neck. I pushed back on the chair until it fully reclined and once again faded off to sleep, deeper this time. I dreamed and for a little while I was safe and warm and with my Frank once again.

CHAPTER 32

"MOM," MEGAN ASKED, "please hand me that picture of the kids playing on the swing set."

Megan's dining room table was almost invisible under the piles of scrapbook pages, scissors, glue bottles, and stacks of photos. One stack pictured the children: playing, bathing, smiling through a face full of birthday cake, standing tall in a confirmation robe, or under a graduation mortarboard. Another stack recalled vacations including Disney World, sliding in the water flumes along the Kancamagus highway and posing all dressed up while waiting for the Captain's Dinner on a cruise. Then there were the family gatherings at Christmas and the holidays, birthday celebrations, anniversaries, and the big family reunions. I scanned through the images that, for Megan, captured memories of happiness and joy and for me, images of loss and sorrow.

"Mom, the picture please." She sat patiently; glue in hand, scrapbook at the ready, but I was still lost in my thoughts and I didn't respond. Her voice approached a shout, "Mom, are you paying attention to what I'm saying?" She was growing increasingly short at my inability or, to her, unwillingness to focus.

To me, the matter was even more serious than that. "No, Megan. I'm not hearing you; I can't. I can't make out what you are saying. If you want to speak to me, either talk louder or don't bother trying."

"Do you have your hearing aids in?"

"Yes, both of them," I replied in a tone that clearly indicated Megan was not the only one who was losing patience.

"Well, maybe the batteries are dead or they're not working right."

"The hearing aids work fine. Your sister took me to have them checked last week and the technician said they are working perfectly. Everything is working perfectly; the batteries work perfectly, the hearing aids work perfectly, everything works perfectly but me. You and your sister have to face the fact that I'm going deaf."

"You're not going deaf, Mom; you're distracted. You just need to pay closer attention to what people are saying."

"So that's all there is to it? Why, thank you for sharing that with me." I could feel my face flushing red. "You think it's as simple as just paying a little more attention. Well, wouldn't life be just peachy if it was? Did it ever occur to you that maybe it's just a matter of growing old? Everyone's body begins to break down at some point. We can't all stay young forever."

"But really, Mom...."

"Don't but really me. I am getting old, Megan, and so is my body. I don't hear anymore, I can't see right, my feet ache when I walk, and my back hurts all the time. Everything hurts."

The anger I kept bottled up inside me rose to the surface and spilled over, "Living hurts!" With that, the tears streamed down my cheeks and my body quivered.

"I'm sorry, Mom. I'm sorry you feel the way you do. I want to help but to tell you the truth, I don't know how to anymore and neither does Bridget."

"Do you really want to help?"

"More than anything, yes."

"Then I think you and your sister should start looking into a good nursing home for me."

"A what?"

"Someplace where they could take care of me until I go."

"Go where?"

"Now you know perfectly well where."

"I don't even want to hear this."

"That's your problem. You and your sister want to put your heads in the sand and pretend that I'm going to live forever. Well, I'm not. Nobody does."

"Six months ago you and Dad were planning for your next cruise. Now you're talking about dying. You're still young and healthy. You could live for another thirty years."

"Heaven forbid. I dread living like this for another thirty days."

"That's what this is really all about, isn't it? You've given up. You don't want to live anymore."

"Well, what if I don't? Would you if you were me?"

"Yes, Mom, I would."

"That's what you say now. But you'd think differently if you were my age."

"There is another alternative, you know. Now that Denise is up at Northeastern, her room is empty. You could move in with us."

"What? Never!"

"You don't have to make it sound so awful."

"I'm sorry, Megan, but sometimes lately I can't stand my own company, let alone inflict myself on others. You and Ryan need your own space. The last thing you need is me pouting all the time."

From the expression on her face, it looked like Megan realized that I was probably right.

"Well, you wouldn't necessarily have to move right in with us. We have plenty of property. We could put an addition on and you could have your own place." Her voice quivered and her eyes glistened with wetness as tears began trickling down her face.

I softened as I realized how hard she was trying to help. Then I considered the strain my moving in with her and Ryan would be on their life and marriage. I reached out and cupped her cheek in the palm of my hand. "I'm sorry, honey. Sometimes I forget how blessed I am to have daughters that love me so much. I've lived a long and full life with your father but now that he's gone … I just don't know." I let out a sigh and dropped my hand. My shoulders drooped and I slumped forward in the chair. Nevertheless, I managed a half-smile, "Why don't we just drop this for now, OK?"

"All right, Mom."

Megan dabbed her cheeks with a paper napkin. As she did, I tapped her on the arm with the picture of the kids playing on the swing set. She placed the picture in the scrapbook and then sat back in her chair. She looked exhausted. I placed my hand atop hers and we both sat quietly for a long, long time.

Chapter 33

AS MEGAN PULLED out of the driveway, I inserted my key into the kitchen door. This was always the worst part: the emptiness waiting on the other side.

I scanned the room as I crossed to the stove and turned the burner on for the teakettle. A pile of bills waited on the kitchen table. With Frank, the routine had always been the same. He reviewed and organized the bills, we made out the payments together, and I balanced them against our checking account, but that was before. The bills would have to wait. Next to the bills, a pair of scissors held down a stack of clipped coupons atop the *Bristol Press*. Most of them were for our favorite restaurants; I wouldn't need them anymore. Finally, there was the pile of paid bills and receipts waiting to be filed. Now, I couldn't recall how to file them or where.

I poured the water for my tea and then realized that I was out of milk. I was supposed to ask Megan to stop at the convenience store on the way home but I had forgotten. Then panic set in: *Oh God, I can't do this.*

Memories and emotions flooded in too fast and the unattended tasks overwhelmed me. I grabbed the black tea and headed to the safety of the upstairs bedroom. At the top of the stairs, I glanced to my right and saw the foot of our bed through the open doorway. I hadn't slept in it since Frank died. His gray hat waited for him atop the back of the corner chair and his keys and pocket change sat on the dresser. His bedroom slippers and a pair of shiny black shoes peeked out from under the bed and three of his neckties lay across the quilt. The missing fourth was the one the girls chose for him to wear in his casket. Frank was everywhere and, at the same time, he was nowhere at all.

I took a sip of the tea; it was only lukewarm. I hadn't waited long enough for the water to boil, just another example of a life out of control. I turned to the left and headed into the spare bedroom. As I entered, I noticed the bottle of sleeping pills on the table between the twin beds. The doctor had prescribed them for me after the funeral because I spent most nights pacing the floor rather than sleeping but with my aversion to pills, I had refused to take them. I grasped the bottle and studied it. The pills were tiny. Taking several at a time with my tea, I would probably barely even taste them. I imagined myself drifting into a peaceful sleep. Then the fatigue, fears, questions, longings, unanswered prayers and the merciless, unceasing loneliness would all be over.

The children? As quickly as the thought jumped into my head, I countered it. They have their own lives to live. I'm only an added burden now.

The grandchildren? I worked at getting the image of their faces out of my mind. After all, what good is a grandmother who can't do anything but cry all the time anyway?

Sister Ann's voice sounded in my head, "Only God has the right to take a life; suicide is a sin." I wondered: could hell be any worse? What kind of loving God would want to see me living like this?

Then the thought struck me: what would it do to my family when they realized that I had committed suicide? Picturing their faces sent a chill through my body. Then I heard the teakettle whistling. I had put it back on the stove and forgotten to turn off the burner. My first reaction was to rush down stairs and turn it off before it set the house on fire. Then I realized that maybe this was a message from God. Maybe He had answered my unsaid prayer. People would say that in my confusion, I had forgotten the teakettle on the stove and accidentally set fire to the house. No one would suspect anything and after a brief period of mourning, my children and grandchildren could get on with their lives.

I stared at the bottle for a while longer and then picked up my journal to make one last entry. Like me, the fire would consume it, so I wrote:

I'm sorry, Frank. This isn't your way I know but I was never as strong as you were. I've tried but I can't stand it another second. Please understand and forgive me.

God, please give me the strength to do this.

I put the journal down, emptied the pills into one hand, and then raised the cup of tea with the other.

CHAPTER 34

GOD HAD OTHER plans. The phone rang and I stopped breathing.

It rang again…. I remained motionless.

Twice more….

I started to tremble.

Then silence.

If it started ringing again, I might not be able to resist answering. I put the tea down and reached to take the receiver off the phone but it rang again just as I lifted the handset. I froze.

I couldn't just hang up. If they called back and got a busy signal, they might become suspicious or worried and come to the house. I needed a convincing deception. I would just say how tired I was and that I would need to call them back later. Yes, that would work. I lifted the receiver to my mouth to dismiss the caller. "Hello, I'm sorry but I can't…."

"So help me, I'm going to slit his throat!"

"Doris?" I didn't really need to ask. No one else I knew used such language. "Are you talking about Henry?"

"Of course, Henry," she yelled. "Maureen, you won't believe what that pond scum is up to."

"Doris. I'll listen to you, but only if you calm down and stop shouting."

"All right, Miss Manners, but if I could just wring his neck…."

"Doris."

"OK, OK, I'm just furious."

"Why don't you just tell me what happened?"

"Henry just called from Denver. He's landed another of his real estate deals here in Connecticut and he's flying back next week."

"Oh."

"What's more, he wants to stay with me until he closes the deal."

"What did you say to him?"

"I told him no way, but he claims that if this deal falls through, he might have to sell my house. Then he said he just wants to spend some time with me while he's here. Can you imagine?"

"Well, actually…."

"Actually nothing. He's gone for over a year without a word and then calls out of the blue because he wants to spend time with me! At first I just wanted to die and then I thought maybe I should just kill him instead."

"Now, Doris…."

"Seriously, Maureen, I don't know what to do. I thought he was out of my life for good. Now he'll be here in a week and I'm so mad I'm shaking."

I took in a deep breath and released it in a huff before responding.

"Would you like to come over and talk about it?"

"Could I, sweetie? Oh, that would be such a relief. You seem so much more clear-headed about these kinds of things."

I looked down at the pills in my hand. *Not really*, I thought to myself. Then I responded, "All right."

"Thanks. You're a real lifesaver but if you don't mind, I'll pick you up and bring you over to my place instead. Things will make a lot more sense that way."

"That's fine but on your way over, would you pick up a quart of milk for me? I'm out."

"You've got it. Thanks, kid."

I hung up the phone, returned the pills to the bottle, and lifted my teacup. Then I smelled something burning and rushed downstairs to the kitchen. Small wisps of smoke rose from the charred teakettle. I realized that I still had the tea and pill bottle in my hands so I laid them on the counter and turned off the stove burner. The teakettle made cracking sounds as it cooled. I stood silently for a moment watching the smoke rise and recalled the incense floating above the altar at Frank's funeral. Then I realized that Doris was on her way over.

CHAPTER 35

TWENTY MINUTES LATER, I was in the passenger seat of the Jaguar. Doris said, "Thanks again, kid. I was so mad I wanted to hit something."

The statement roused me from thinking about how close I had come to taking the pills and I forced myself to talk. "Doris, you said Henry drinks. Are you afraid that he'll hurt you?"

"What, Henry? Not a chance. The first time he raised a hand to me I squashed him like a bug. Believe me, kid, he's far more afraid of me that I am of him."

"Then what did he do to get you so worked up?"

"Once we get to my place, I think you'll understand." I exhaled deeply as the conversation ended. I didn't have the energy to sustain it any longer.

Doris turned the car into the rear exit of Bristol Eastern High School. As she navigated through the speed bumps toward the front entrance, I recalled images of happier times. I visualized the large banner along the roofline announcing, "Welcome to the Bristol Teddy Bear Jamboree," and the sea of cars sporting license plates from other states. Along the side of the building, I imagined the vendors busily unloading the wares from their vans and children squirming impatiently as their parents bought teddy bear balloons from the toy carts. I recalled smoke billowing out of food stands and the delicious, fattening aroma of deep-fried foods drifting through the air. As the car crossed the entrance doors in the front of the building, I could almost see the bright white tent next to them. I saw myself seated at the registration table looking up at Frank: tall, trim, and handsome in his bright red security cap.

Doris turned left onto King Street past Page Park. At the traffic light, she veered right and shot up a steep hill toward Bristol Hospital. After several more turns, she stopped in front of what looked like the gated entrance of another park and announced, "Home sweet home." She entered between the giant stone posts and drove down a long driveway toward a stately garrison colonial.

I gasped, "This is your house?"

"I live here, honey, but believe me, it's more the bank's house than mine." The car circled a large, multi-tiered fountain. In the center, water spewed from a pitcher held by a bare breasted woman.

As Doris inserted her key into the massive entrance doors, I commented, "I almost expected to be greeted by your butler."

"No such luck. It's only us mice here."

I stood open mouthed as the doors opened to reveal the interior. The white marbled floor stretched from the entrance to the double circular staircases at the far end. Giant paintings in gilded frames lined each set of stairs. The lead crystal pendants of the foyer's chandelier broke the sun's rays into interlacing rainbows that flowed across the room's interior.

I exhaled, "I'm in Tara."

"What?"

"You know, from *Gone with the Wind*."

"It may be much, honey, but it's not that much. Hungry?"

"Actually, I'm famished." I surprised myself with the remark but then realized that I really was very hungry.

"Good. You can hang your coat in the closet and I'll get some things from the frig. I hope you don't have your heart set on gourmet. I've got some cold cuts and maybe some chicken salad."

"That will be fine." As I closed the closet door, I noticed a new-looking fur coat tucked away at the far end.

Doris shouted from somewhere further back in the house, "Give yourself a tour of the place while I get the food out."

"Thanks, I'd love to." I peered into the sitting room with its French provincial furniture arranged around a large Persian rug. A stone-mantled fireplace took up half of the wall at the far end of the room. French doors on each side of the fireplace led to a sun porch with a lion's head wall fountain and bricked floor. I could hear the noise of Doris's lunch preparations and followed sounds of plates and utensils moving. A hallway connected the front and back portions of the house. The first door off the hallway revealed a sparsely appointed bedroom and the next, a bathroom gleaming in marble, glass, and gold. Then came a pantry and finally the kitchen.

With a commercial refrigerator and freezer and an enormous gas range, the kitchen looked well equipped to cater weddings. In the center of the room, huge pots, pans, and utensils hung from a wrought iron rack suspended from the ceiling. Directly below was the large preparation island where Doris was busy arranging lunch on a large silver tray.

As I took in the surroundings, the image of Doris arguing with the senior center staff over the $2.00 roast beef lunch flashed through my mind. "Doris, this house is amazing."

"In a kitschy sort of way."

"The maintenance must be exorbitant."

"Not if you exercise a little creativity." Doris smiled. Seeing the puzzled look on my face, she glanced toward the window. "Take a look at the lawn. This place has over two acres of grass. Stan next door has about half an acre, but he used to spend hours every Saturdays walking behind his push mower. Now if you do enough tag saleing, one thing you're sure to find is a really big lawn tractor in perfect condition that people are practically begging you to take away."

"Really, why?"

"Maureen, do you have a nice big riding mower?"

I smiled and nodded, "No. We got rid of it when Frank turned seventy and paid our neighbor to do it for us."

163

"Exactly. So Stan wound up with a shiny John Deere tractor and I get my lawn cut every time he does his. Jerry across the street got a nice big hydraulic plow to go with his 4x4 pickup and guess who does my driveway every time it snows?"

"Wow, Doris, you've got this down to a science. What did you get for the person who does your landscaping? It looks like a botanical garden around here."

"Oh," Doris smiled, "that's Seb. He owns his own grounds and landscaping business. There was nothing I was gonna find that boy that he didn't already have." Then her smile grew wider. "But what Seb wanted you don't find at a tag sale. Let's just put it this way: I have no complaints about my flower beds and Seb has no complaints about his bed either."

I howled, "Oh, Doris, you really are something!"

"How about some wine with lunch?"

"That sounds nice but can I use your bathroom first?"

"Sure, only you'll have to go upstairs. The one on this floor is on the fritz."

I smiled appreciatively, "Thanks," and went off in search of the bathroom. On the way, I passed through a dining room with a magnificent mahogany breakfront and a matching table with ten chairs. A huge grandfather clock ticked the time away in the far corner.

As I exited the second-floor bathroom, I noticed a door ajar to my right. Peering inside, I noticed the room was empty. I opened a door to the further right to find the same. Returning to the center of the landing, I opened another door on the other side and peered into another empty room.

"Yep," I jumped at the sound of Doris's voice echoing from below. She was standing in the foyer with two glasses of white wine in her hands. "You can check them all if you'd like. They're all empty."

I stiffened, feeling like a child caught doing something forbidden and apologized as I descended the stairs, "I'm sorry, Doris, I didn't mean to pry. I just noticed a door open to one of the rooms..."

"I told you to give yourself a tour. I never said anything about limiting it to the first floor."

"You don't use the upper floor?"

"Floors honey. There are servant's quarters on the third floor. They're empty too. What's the sense of furnishing guest rooms if you don't have guests, or servant's quarters without servants?" Doris handed me my glass of wine. "This isn't a real home, Maureen. A home is where you raise your children and play with your grandchildren, or at least where you entertain family or friends. This place looks pretty, but when you peek behind the curtain, it's just a façade; a theatrical backdrop for Henry's wheeling and dealing. Come on, let's have lunch."

At my request, we sat at the kitchen island rather than the dining room table. As we ate, I noticed more oddities. The dishes were real china and the flatware was solid silver. All of the condiments, however—salt, pepper, ketchup, relish, mayonnaise, and the like—were in individual little serving packets: the kind you get at restaurants. When it came time for coffee, the sugar bowl came filled with small paper packets. I wondered which of Doris's neighbors owned a restaurant and then smiled at the thought of what he might have gotten in return.

As we ate, Doris explained the house's history. "Henry landed this place in a package deal of apartment houses and properties foreclosed for back taxes. He told the city he was going to develop the apartments as senior citizen housing. Then he got the Feds to pay for the renovations and filled them up with section eights. Before the city could balk, he sold them all to pay off the back taxes on this place.

"He sounds like quite a businessman."

"He doesn't have a penny to his name." Doris topped off the wine glasses. "It's all blue smoke and mirrors. He keeps buying and selling places and shuffling the money around. It a big Ponzi scheme that works as long as he keeps the carousel in motion but if it ever stops, game over. That's what did us in."

Doris described living the high life: the cars, the parties, the vacations.

She confessed that she loved it too, even though she realized the more they got, the more they owed.

"When the economy soured, we started getting notices for loan repayments at sky-high interest hikes. Henry kept transferring money from one credit card or bank account to another. Finally, it got to my nerves and I wanted out but for Henry it was never enough. He was addicted to the game and then he started gambling. When Henry goes to Vegas, he gets the royal treatment: front seats at the headliner shows, the penthouse suites, the restaurant comps, everything. He should. He's lost enough money to build one of those places. When it looked like we might lose everything, I insisted that Henry put the house under my name. Later, he tried to have me sign it back to him again. When I refused, he sued me in court but didn't get it back and it'll be a cold day in hell before he does. This is my retirement plan. All I have to do is keep the bill collectors at bay long enough to cash in on it. That is unless Henry drives it into the dirt first."

"But you said it's in your name?"

"Yea, but Henry pays the mortgage. I'd need to work two jobs just to keep up with the taxes. Now he's hooked up with some other Einstein and the two of them are planning on buying some abandoned hospital in Middletown and turning it into a condominium complex. We're talking about millions and that's just for the initial purchase. Then there are the renovations, the sales, the maintenance and heaven only knows what else. While we were married, we had to declare bankruptcy twice but at least then, we didn't have a pot to piss in. At this stage of my life, I don't relish the thought of starting all over again."

"Can you come to some sort of compromise with him?"

"You don't know Henry, darlin'. Besides, the deal is already set. He wasn't calling to ask my opinion. He was calling to tell me about what he was already doing. And the funny thing about us, I could tell him to pound sand over the phone but when we're face to face, I just kind of melt."

"Is that why you didn't want him to stay with you?"

"Yeah, I guess so. He may drive me up a wall at times, but he's still a hunk. And whatever else his faults may be, he can be annoyingly sweet at times."

We talked away most of the afternoon in chitchat. I was amazed at how comfortable it was to talk to someone who was so different than I was and whom I had known for so little time. We moved from one topic to another with the ease of old friends.

When Doris pulled into my driveway, the sun was low in the sky and had deepened to a golden glow. She lowered her car window as I walked toward the house.

"Hay, Maureen, talking to you today really helped. I guess I kind of panicked and blew things out of proportion. Could I call you again sometime, you know, just to talk?"

I smiled and said, "I'd like that."

"Okay then. Thanks for listening, kid. You have no idea how much it meant to me." Then she rolled up her window, backed out of the driveway, and sped away.

Inside the house, I saw the bottle of sleeping pills on the counter, scooped it into my hands, and looked out the kitchen window toward the driveway. I looked down at the pills again and whispered to myself, "And you have no idea how much it meant to me, Doris." Then I tossed the bottle into the trash.

CHAPTER 36

WHEN THE PHONE rang at 6:45 a.m. the following week, I didn't have to ask who it was. "Good morning, Doris."

"You hungry?"

"I don't know. I haven't even had my morning tea yet."

"Well, I'm famished. Henry will be here later today and I've been pacing around the house since three. How about I pick you up in fifteen minutes? Just one thing, I want to enjoy my breakfast so no mention of Henry."

She picked me up right on time and drove us to Lynn's restaurant, across the street from the Bristol Center Mall. When it first opened, the mall bustled with stores and shoppers but with the recession, changing demographics, and newer mega-malls nearby, the downtown mall sat nearly deserted.

By contrast, Lynn's was abuzz with activity. Their $2.50 breakfast special included eggs, toast, home fries, and coffee. Eyeing the plates as we entered, the portions looked huge.

From Doris's behavior, you'd never guess that Lynn's was one of her favorite places, especially given the way she treated the staff. She interrupted the hostess, who was busy cashing out a customer, "We'll take a seat by the window."

"I'm sorry, we don't have any window seats at the moment, but there are a couple of booths available if you'd…."

"We'll wait. Just make sure you don't have us wait too long and here…." Doris shoved two boxes of macaroni and cheese into the hostess's hands. The hostess put the boxes down, frowned, and returned to the waiting customers. Doris must have noticed my questioning expression, "If you bring an item for the local food pantry, they take the dollar for the coffee off the bill."

"That's very nice of you."

"Yea, I'm a regular Mother Theresa. I buy them at Stop and Shop when they have a four-for-a-dollar sale. Where else can you get a two-egg breakfast with coffee for a buck and a half?"

A few minutes later, Doris spotted a couple leaving their table by the front corner window. "Gotta go." With the menus in hand and me in tow, she darted past the *Please Wait To Be Seated* sign and headed straight for the table. On her way there, she shoved past the busboy who was heading to clear off the table. She didn't notice the scowl on his face, not that it would have made any difference.

When the worker reached the table, Doris barked, "We'll have two coffees, regular for me and decaf for my friend, and two glasses of water with lemon but no ice in hers."

"Your waitress is supposed to…," the busboy stopped short when he made eye contact with Doris. He finished clearing the table and immediately headed off to fetch the drinks.

"From what I've seen so far, the food looks pretty good here," I said.

"It's passable," Doris raised her voice, "but the service is as slow as ever."

A perky young waitress approached, "Have you decided what you would like to have this morning?" She asked so sweetly that it didn't appear she heard Doris's comment, which would have been impossible unless she was deaf.

Doris answered, "I'll have the special: eggs over medium with rye toast, but none of those disgusting seeds and make sure the home fries aren't burned to a crisp."

"Of course; and you, ma'am?"

"Oh, I don't know. I used to love having big breakfasts when I ate out with Frank. I really haven't been eating very much lately...."

"For heaven's sake, Maureen! All she wants is your breakfast order, not your life history."

"Oh, all right, then, could you just bring me an English muffin please?"

"Yes, she could," Doris interjected and then addressed the waitress, "And bring her a bunch of butter pats and an assortment of jellies to go with it and rush those orders. I'm starving"

The waitress answered in the same sweet voice, "I'll put those orders right in for you and you'll find the jellies right behind the menu holder."

Doris turned back to me. "Where were we? Oh yea, the drama queen. You can't figure out what to eat because Frank isn't here to order for you."

"You don't have to make it sound so trivial, Doris. I loved Frank. We spent over fifty wonderful years together." My eyes started to well up. "Now that he's gone, it all seems so pointless. I just feel empty inside. Can't you understand that?"

"To tell you the truth, no, I can't. You're all to pieces because Frank died after so many years of marital bliss. It's Henry's still breathing that I have a problem with."

"That's a horrible thing to say."

"Maybe for you, kiddo, but you didn't have to live with him."

"Would you have preferred to be all alone?"

"In a New York minute! It's nice that you and Frank had this wonderful time together, but a guy like Henry could suck the blood right out of you."

"Now who's being dramatic?" I felt a tinge of excitement at having countered one of Doris's comments and pressed on. "Every husband is irritating some of the time. Besides, I thought you didn't want to talk about Henry."

Doris ignored my final comment and continued, "Oh, you are naïve, Sister. When you have to make your daughter pick up the phone or answer the door because you don't want to face the bill collectors, that's irritating. When you have to avoid looking people in the eye because they might try to hound you for the money he owes them, that's more than irritating. When you have to read all the fine print on anything he asks you to sign, that, dear lady, goes way beyond irritating."

"You mentioned your daughter. How is she?"

Doris looked surprised that I noticed her reference. "I have no idea. I get a card from her for Christmas and my birthday but that's it. We haven't spoken in years and she's hardly a child. She's got a kid of her own that I've never even seen, but that's a train wreck that I'd just as soon leave for another time."

"Well, if I could only have my Frank back, I wouldn't care if we were flat broke." I wiped my eyes with my napkin.

"You just don't get it, do you? You think you've got it so bad because Frank died and you wish you had him back again."

"Yes, of course I do. What could be worse than that?"

Doris's facial features turned to stone. She leaned forward and locked eyes with me. I felt my apprehension rising and for the first time since we met and wondered if she was actually capable of violence. Each of her words emerged individually with unnerving intensity. "WISHING AND PRAYING EVERY SINGLE DAY THAT HE WOULD JUST DIE!"

"English muffin?" The waitress returned with the breakfast orders and Doris eased back into her seat.

"Yes, thank you," I said, relieved by the interruption, "the muffin is mine."

"Would you like a refresh on your coffees?" she asked. I nodded yes. Doris just held her cup in the air while still looking at me. The waitress eyed the cup nervously as she filled it and then quickly retreated to the other tables.

In the time it took me to eat half of my English muffin, Doris finished off three of her four toast pieces, half of her home fries, and one of her two eggs. Then she slowed eating and carefully examined the remaining egg as the waitress returned with the coffee pot.

"What do you call this?" Doris asked while pointing to her plate.

"That's your egg order, ma'am, the special with...."

Doris interrupted her, "I said over-medium eggs. The whites on these look like somebody sneezed them onto the plate."

"I'm sorry about that," the waitress returned with an obvious strain in her voice. "Would you like them more well-done?"

"What I would like, dearie, is to get what I ordered the way I ordered it the first time, or did you just figure we were too senile to notice the difference."

I squirmed at being referenced into the conflict.

The waitress answered, "The cook rushed the order for you but I did request them over medium as you asked." Her reply was polite but the perkiness was gone.

"Good, then you eat them."

The waitress's voice faltered. "I'll be happy to replace them if you would like."

"Just refill the coffees, get me a toasted corn muffin in a large to-go container, and take this abomination back. And make sure you don't charge me for something I didn't eat."

The waitress filled the cups and recovered Doris's plate. I looked at the pained expression in her face as she left. When I glanced back to Doris again, I noticed that she was smiling.

"You really don't like her, do you?" I asked.

"What's to like? She's a waitress. If she can't take it, she should go back to school and get a real job."

"Well, I don't see it that way, but I suppose you're entitled to your opinion."

When the bill came, Doris examined it closely. "Would you look at that? She still charged me for the coffee!" Doris placed the exact amount for the coffee and her corn muffin on the table. Then she scooped all of the creamers, butter pats, sugar packets, and jelly containers into her to-go container.

"How much do you normally leave for the tip?" I asked.

"I don't tip for substandard service."

I placed a dollar bill under my plate and when Doris turned to leave, I slipped an extra dollar under hers.

As Doris drove off after dropping me at my house, I stood in the driveway and reflected on the morning. I felt certain that underlying her anger was a deep pool of sadness. What life experiences had ingrained such hostility in my strange new friend?

CHAPTER 37

DESPITE THE ROCKY start when I first returned to the senior center, I didn't give up. I had received a second chance at living and thanks to the prodding and rides from my daughters, I slowly began to reconnect with the people and activities of my former life.

On one particularly nice day with a mild temperature and a slight breeze, I decided to walk to the center for my Thursday morning aerobic class. Following the class, I retreated to the center courtyard and sat on my favorite bench in front of John Blake's angel fountain. There, I soaked in the late-morning sun and the color, fragrances, and sounds of the setting. I pulled out my journal, which was now my constant companion, and jotted down a quick entry.

The center staff placed a tall, double shepherd's hook in one corner of the courtyard. A birdhouse hangs from one hook and a feeder from the other. A pair of starlings built a nest in the birdhouse and the chicks chirp loudly between the constant feedings from their parents. The feeder attracted other birds, including a bright red cardinal, two robins, and a blue jay. The birdseed mix must have contained sunflower seeds. Several large, beautiful sunflowers have sprouted up around the feeder. It's got me thinking about my own bird feeder and that maybe it's time for me to restock it with seeds.

A familiar voice interrupted my thoughts, "Hey, darlin'. How are you doing?" Doris sounded almost as chirpy as the young starlings. I surprised myself at how happy I was to see her and realized that I actually missed her company.

"Hello, Doris. It's nice to see you again. It's been almost a month. Are you taking any classes?"

"Sure am, sugar. I'm taking the painting course. I wasn't sure I could get into it. It's not what you'd call exciting but I'm actually enjoying it."

We chatted about center goings on and my family happenings until I could no longer stand the suspense, "So tell me how it went with Henry?"

"Ohhh, Henry," Doris stretched out the words so they sounded like the candy bar commercial. "Well, he's gone."

"So it didn't work out with you two getting back together?"

"You know, for a couple of days there, I actually thought it might. I told you how good Henry is in bed. Well, he certainly hasn't lost anything in that department and why should he? After all, he's getting plenty of practice."

"Oh?"

"Yea. I should have known better than to think he might want to settle for just one woman when he's used to moving around like a bee pollinating flowers. It turned out that while he was bunking in at my place, he was seeing some bimbo in Middletown, so I sent him packing. Still, I got a few really good rolls in the hay out of it. Let me tell you, darlin, plenty of women would gladly pay for sex like that."

I had to stop laughing before I could continue. "So what are you going to do now? I mean, I read about his complex in the Courant and then I heard about it on the eleven o'clock news. It seems like everyone thinks it's an exciting project."

"Henry has always been good at schmoozing the press. Anyway, he's moving forward with the plans. I've cosigned the loan and put the house up as part of the collateral. It's still in my name, though, so if he and that other genius don't screw up too badly, hopefully, I'll still have it a year from now."

"You do seem to be in a better mood than the last time we talked."

"The way I see it, there isn't much I can do, so why worry. If I were a religious person, I'd say it is in God's hands now. As it is, it's in Henry's, which is far scarier but that's enough about him. Tell me, do you have any plans for tomorrow morning?"

"Not really. Did you have something in mind?"

"Well of course, darlin'," the season is still young and tomorrow is Friday. It's tag-saleing time!"

CHAPTER 38

DORIS ARRIVED BEFORE eight the next day and most Friday and Saturday mornings after that. She came with a marked-up copy of the tag-sale listings from the local *Step Saver* and a carefully planned route for hitting the most profitable-sounding sales in the least amount of time.

On rainy days, she arrived with the "rain or shine" listings. If a "rain date" listing included some juicy items, Doris would simply drag me with her and ring the bell. If the homeowners hesitated, she always had a hardship story and most of the time it worked. We waddled through peoples' garages in our yellow slickers like a pair of ducklings.

On good weather days, we moved with deft precision from one tag sale to the next until about 10:45 when we stopped for breakfast. Doris had a list covering every restaurant with breakfast specials for all of the towns on our route. On Fridays, most of them stopped serving their "weekday only" specials promptly at 11:00. Most charged full price on weekends so if all else failed, we simply played the age card and asked for the senior discount.

Over the course of the spring and early summer, we visited more area restaurants than I knew existed. During our breakfasts, Doris continued coaching me on her "Rules for Tag Saleing." Her rule about *The Three Ds* hit me particularly hard.

"What do you mean the three Ds?" I asked.

"Easy. The best tag sales are those where someone is divorced, demented, or dead!"

"Doris, that's horrible."

"Not at all. The way I see it, I'm doing a community service."

"What!"

"Think about it. Some jerk cheats on his wife and even though she's getting divorced, she's still wasted years of her life on him with no way of getting even. So what does she do? She holds a tag sale and dumps his twenty-five-hundred-dollar autographed guitar and first-edition comic book collection for a song. I take them off her hands, she gets her revenge, and he gets his just desserts."

"You're not kidding, are you?"

"Of course not. Then there are the demented. There are lots of crazies and seniles out there who have no idea what they have or what it's worth and they don't care. All they really want is some tasty fast-food. When I run across one of them, I usually don't even haggle because they're nearly giving the stuff away anyway. So I get a good deal and they get a Super Slam at Denny's or a banana split at Friendly's.

"You're really serious."

"Of course. But the best of them all is death, because then you're really doing them a favor."

"What!"

"Think about it. A couple collects a lifetime of stuff together but to the survivor, a lot of it is just plain junk. How many widows want a garage full of tools or a closet full of model trains? If I didn't buy that stuff, they probably would have to bring it to the dump for nothing or maybe even have to pay someone to cart it away. And lots of the things have memories attached, like the vase they got in Italy, or the mantle clock they got in France. When one of them dies, some of that stuff is just too painful to have around, so I come along and relieve them of all that pain. Sometimes I think I should get a medal for my service."

I sat open-mouthed so long that I think I could have caught flies. Then I thought about our garage and about how desperate I was to remove everything that reminded me of Frank until Steve intervened. If he had not, I might have obliterated every memory of Frank, as though he never existed. I felt suddenly thankful that I didn't get the chance.

When I got home that evening, I took a box of Frank's pictures from the garage. Sitting on the living room couch, I braced myself before opening the first envelope. The snapshots were of the girls and me in Easter dresses. We were walking the grounds or standing in front of the garden clock at Milleridge restaurant on Long Island. I smiled at how young we looked. The next, however, was one of the rare pictures of Frank and me. We sat by the fireplace and toasted with our wine glasses. "Oh, Frank," I said aloud while rubbing his face. The tears flowed, but I didn't try to hold them back. I sobbed freely as I went through one set after another, relishing every memory and feeling thankful for a lifetime of love.

CHAPTER 39

BY MIDSUMMER, I also learned a great deal more about Doris. I learned, for instance, that when she did not have a good morning at tag saleing, it was not likely to be a good experience for the server, and breakfast at the Oasis in Bristol was going to be one of those mornings.

Doris intercepted the approaching waitress, "We'll take that window table."

"Just a moment, please, and I'll see if it's been cleaned."

"That makes no difference. If it hasn't been, then you'll clean it. Just don't leave us standing here all morning."

The waitress's curled-up lip and her tone of voice broadcast her annoyance. "I'll be right back." She went to check on the table and returned a moment later. "The table is clear; right this way." I noticed that she omitted the 'please.' "Coffees?" she asked as we took our seats.

Doris shot her instructions back like a sharpshooter taking aim at her kill. "Black for me and decaf with sugar for my friend. She likes hers light so bring lots of creamers and don't go running off just yet. I'll have water with lemon and she'll have the same, but with no ice."

"Two coffees, one black, one decaf with cream and sugar and two waters with lemon, one with no ice. I'll be right back with those." The waitress's precise repetition probably saved her from more abuse, at least for the moment.

"How do you know how much you should pay for something at a tag sale?" I asked. I marveled at Doris's negotiation skills.

"That's easy: ten cents on the dollar." Doris could see from my expression the short version answer wasn't going to suffice, so she continued. "When you look at an item, you just ask yourself what you would expect to pay for it new. Let's say it was a perfect-looking blender that you could buy new for around fifty dollars. Then you shouldn't have to pay more than five for it at a tag sale. And when you're estimating the new price, think Kmart, not Lord and Taylor; remember there is no such thing as 'service after the sale' at tag sales." I didn't challenge Doris's last statement, but I quickly recalled several occasions on which she returned items because they didn't meet her expectations. Doris continued, "Of course, that kind of estimating doesn't apply for real antiques or art objects. Then you have to know your merchandise and who you're buying it from."

"Who you're buying it from?"

"Of course. Take for instance that painting I bought last week in Plainville."

"The one you bought for the frame?"

The waitress returned with the coffees and a bowl full of creamers. "What can I get for you ladies today?"

"I'll have the egg special," I answered. "Over medium, please, and what kinds of bread do you have?"

"White, wheat, or rye." From the sound of the waitress's response, it must have been the hundredth time she answered that question this morning.

"Does your rye have seeds?" I asked.

"You know, I'm really not sure." Obviously, this was not a question that was asked nearly so often.

"If it doesn't have seeds, I'll take the rye. Otherwise, I'll take the wheat toast please."

The waitress addressed Doris, "And what can I get for you, ma'am?"

"French toast with bacon and low-calorie syrup, and make sure the bacon is very crispy. I hate chewing into raw fat. Also bring refills for the coffees when you come back with the orders." The waitress retreated and Doris continued with her lesson.

"Frame nothing; I was after the painting."

"But you told the woman it looked juvenile and maybe you could at least use the frame."

"That was to get her to drop the price and she did: from seven dollars to four. As soon as I saw that painting, I knew it was a Barrat. I've seen his stuff in galleries all over France and England. The frame thing was misdirection." I was beginning to understand that in Doris's jargon, misdirection was synonymous with lying.

"I see, but I still don't get what you mean about who you're buying it from."

"If that painting was at some large garrison colonial in West Hartford, believe me, it wouldn't have been marked seven dollars: more likely seven hundred. That is if they ever put it out in a tag sale in the first place. Even if they did, I probably couldn't have bargained for much less than four hundred. But take that same painting being sold in that three-family house in Plainville and those people had no clue of what they had."

"And you didn't even pay that!" Since I decided to emphasize my response, Doris ended with some emphasis of her own.

"No, I did not!"

"But if you knew the painting was so valuable, why didn't you just give the woman the seven dollars she was asking for it?"

"Simple, my dear."

I joined Doris in perfect unison, "Never pay the asking price."

We broke out in spontaneous laughter until I caught myself.

"What?" Doris asked.

"I just realized this was the first time I've had a good belly laugh since Frank died."

"You're not going to go all mental on me again, are you?"

I hesitated for a moment, searching for guilty feelings, but I didn't find them.

"I guess not."

The waitress returned with the orders and placed mine down first. "There were no seeds in the rye bread," she said.

"Thank you," I replied as Doris inspected her plate.

"What's this?"

The waitress answered, "That's your order of French toast with bacon, very crispy."

"I know about the bacon, but what do you call this?" Doris speared a piece of the French toast with her fork and held it above the plate as she spoke.

"That's Texas style. That's how they serve it here but they don't charge any extra for it."

"I should think not. If I wanted a loaf of bread dipped in egg batter that's what I would have asked for."

"Would you prefer it on thin bread?" The waitress spoke in slow, measured words, as a mother might with a misbehaving child.

Doris returned with an equally enunciated reply, "I thought that was the point of the whole conversation."

"I'll be right back with another order." The waitress reached for the offending plate.

Doris blocked the plate as she spoke, "You can leave it right here. You'll just have to throw it out anyway. My friend might take a bite or two. Just make sure that you don't charge us for it."

The waitress straightened up to leave, but Doris's intercepted her, "Wait," she ordered, lifting her coffee cup in the air as she did. The waitress filled our cups, turned, and darted off.

"I guess you didn't make out quite as good with your negotiations today," I said.

"Oh, you mean that little snot in the mint-green excuse for a ranch? If she didn't want to part with her precious little figurine, all she had to do was say so."

"She did, several times actually."

"Well, if she didn't want to sell it, she shouldn't have put it in the tag sale in the first place."

"I think she was perfectly willing to sell it for the marked price."

"Well, no one who's running a tag sale should be stupid enough to think that people aren't going to try to Jew them down."

"What did you say? Doris, no one uses that kind of expression any more. I'd be more careful about what I said if I were you. People could take offense and rightly so."

"OK, OK. Boy, everybody's so touchy these days. It doesn't mean any more than if I said someone was a greasy Italian, or a dumb Polack. Speaking of Polacks, did you hear about Ceil?"

"She isn't Polish."

"No, but that guy she was dating was."

"Oh, you mean Larry."

"Yeah. Well anyway, the talk at the center is that he dropped her like a lead balloon and then kicked her out of his house."

"I was wondering why I hadn't seen her in any of the classes lately."

"Well, you probably won't either. From what I heard, she was so embarrassed that she moved right out of Bristol. Typical man: once they get what they want from you, they bolt and leave you high and dry."

I wondered how my conversation with Larry may have affected the way he treated Ceil. While I didn't think they were a good match, I didn't want to see her hurt in that way. Doris interrupted my thought by changing the topic.

"Anyway, there was no need for that woman to get all huffy like that. It wasn't like I was trying to steal the thing. People do, you know."

"At tag sales? You're kidding."

"Just keep your eyes peeled and sooner or later you'll see it."

The waitress returned with the replacement order. "Is this to your satisfaction, ma'am?" She placed the plate in front of Doris who cut through a piece with her knife.

"Just as I thought: dry as a bone. Well, it'll have to do. If I don't eat soon, I'll die of starvation." The waitress retreated in silence, shaking her head as she did.

Over the next half hour and several more rounds of coffee, I learned the rest of Doris's tag saleing rules. She ended with, "And when nothing else works, you come up short in cash, tell them it's all you've got and ask if they'll take it. Now I tried almost every one of those this morning with Miss Susie homemaker and she still wouldn't budge. Then for the topper, she cuts me off right in the middle of our negotiation and sells it to somebody else. How rude can you get?"

"Maybe it was because they offered her the asking price. Do you think you might want to bend your rules once in a while when it's in your own best interest?"

Doris thought for a moment, "Maybe, but I wasn't about to pay her the full three dollars after having invested all that time in the negotiations. You may have a point, though: I probably could have turned around and gotten at least fifty for it this afternoon." I almost lost my last mouthful of coffee.

When the waitress dropped the checks on the table, Doris picked them up and handed me mine. "If you want to give me the cash for your order, I'll pay the total on my charge card: I get mileage." Then she reviewed her check more carefully. "After all that, she still charged me full price for my meal. Huh, well there goes her tip."

"Don't bother including my tip either," I said. I'll just leave the cash."

"Suit yourself."

As the waitress picked up the charge card and checks, Doris stopped her, "When you come back with the slip, bring me a to-go container." Then Doris turned her attention back to me. "How about hitting a couple more sales before we call it a morning?"

"If you'd like."

After Doris signed the charge slip, I noticed that she had crossed out the gratuity space. I inserted the cash for my tip in the holder and placed it back on the table. I didn't mention that I put in enough to cover her tip too.

Doris put the untouched Texas French toast in the to-go container, along with all the unused creamers, jellies, butter pats, syrup containers, and sugar packets. As our eyes met, she smiled wryly, "Dinner."

185

CHAPTER 40

"I'VE GOT AN idea," Doris said as she reached into the last bag of groceries on my kitchen table. "Where does the cereal go?"

I pointed to the bottom corner cabinet, "In the lazy Susan."

"By the way, why did you need to go all the way to Southington for groceries when you've got half-a-dozen stores within shouting distance of here?"

"I have a soft spot when it comes to Top's Market. While Frank and I were doing some volunteer work for the Southington Apple Harvest Festival, trays of food and pastries arrived. Top's had donated the food for the volunteers and I thought that was a lot for a small business to take on. Later, I met the owners and they seemed like really nice people, so I figured the least I could do was to shop there when I can. Did you remember to close the trunk?"

Doris smirked, "Of course not. How else could I get those cute tow truck drivers to show up to recharge my battery?"

I ignored her sarcasm, placed the orange juice in the refrigerator, and continued, "What did you have in mind?"

"It's overcast today and according to the weatherman it's probably going to rain this afternoon…. The peanut butter?"

I pointed to the lazy Susan again. Doris ended, "What about a movie?"

"A movie?" I marveled at Doris's seemingly endless pool of energy. At the same time, I thought about the limits of my own.

"Yea, I've been thinking about that one with Renee what's-her-name: *Bridget Jones Diary.* "

"Rene Zellweger. I heard she gained a lot of weight for the part. No, the jelly doesn't go in the lazy Susan. I like to keep it cool in the frig."

"Whatever," Doris handed me the jelly. "Yea, I heard that too. They say she put on about thirty pounds. It's also got Hugh Grant in it. Now there's a catch."

"I like him too. He's kind of cute."

"Cute? He's drop-dead gorgeous. I wouldn't mind having his shoes under my bed."

I smiled and then asked, "Is it still playing? Seems like it came out a while ago."

"These?" Doris held up the bananas.

I pointed to the yellow glass bowl sitting next to the microwave, "In there, but leave them in the plastic. I hate those fruit flies."

Doris placed the bananas in the bowl, "It's not in the first run theaters but there's an afternoon showing at the Forestville cinemas for a buck ninety-nine. Cheapskates don't give senior discounts for the matinees."

I folded the last paper bag and stored it below the sink, then slumped onto a kitchen chair, removed my shoes, and began massaging my foot. "Doris, I don't know where you get all of your energy from. It sounds like a good movie. Everyone I know who has seen it said they liked it and it's supposed to be really funny."

"So do you want to go?"

"At some point. I'm just not sure about today. Right now, I'm pretty tired and my feet are killing me."

I caught the grimace on Doris's face and suggested, "How about Scrabble? I haven't played in years."

"I don't play games." There was sternness in her voice that I chose to ignore.

"That's all right. It's very easy to learn. I could teach you in just a few minutes."

"No!" She pounced like a blacksmith's hammer coming down on the anvil. "I never said that I didn't know how to play. I said that I don't play—not Scrabble—not any games—period."

"Why is that?"

"Because they're a stupid waste of time that pit people against each other and always end with the same pathetic result: a single gloating winner and a bunch of has-been losers."

"For heaven's sake, Doris, you make it sound like a war."

"Well, isn't it?"

"Not at all. Games can be a great way to spend time together as long as you don't take them too seriously. And they're certainly more interactive than watching television."

"Or a movie?"

"I didn't mean it that way. I wasn't criticizing your suggestion. I love going to movies, but some of my fondest memories involve playing games. I can still remember going to my aunt Clara's house after school. She, Uncle Bill, Cousin Ernie, and I would spend hours playing Monopoly. We would talk and laugh and Aunt Clara would always make red and green Jell-O with whipped cream topping. It didn't matter who won or lost. We just enjoyed each other's company."

"Well, Pollyanna, not all of us shared in your Disneyesque childhood experiences." Her words still carried their anger, but I noticed the sadness that had crept into her tone.

"I don't understand."

"Well then, let me spell it out for you. While you were negotiating for Park Place at your Aunt Clara's, I was marking time while my father beat the crap out of my mother."

"Oh? Your father was a violent man?"

"Not when he was sober. When he wasn't drinking, Daddy was a model citizen, but when he came home from his Friday night binges, well that was a different story all together. At first, it was just verbal. He would rag on my mother for all of the opportunities he had lost: the places he never went, the promotions he was passed over for, the life he should have had." Her eyes moistened.

"It was also pretty clear that I had entered the scene prematurely."

"Our Megan was a surprise. An unplanned pregnancy can be stressful."

"More than unplanned: they were still dating when she got knocked up! In those days, good girls didn't get pregnant unless they were married, so my father did the right thing. He dropped out of school and got some minimum-wage job to support the family. He felt trapped and he let her know it."

I thought about my own father's drinking on the day he walked out of my life forever. It left me weary of men until I met Frank. This was Doris's story, however, so I stayed silent and just listened as she continued.

"At first it was all words. My mother would just send me to my bedroom to wait things out. She tried to coax him to go back to school, or go after promotions, or plan vacations, but none of it worked. He just ragged on how time had passed him by and it was her fault. I think she suspected there were other women too but she was too afraid to ask. Each week he'd come home later and drunker. That's when my mother started farming me out to the old woman next door. She kept me occupied by playing games.

"Then one day he came home in the middle of the afternoon; he'd been fired. For weeks after he'd leave every morning claiming he was out looking for work but he'd come home smelling like a brewery and I spent nearly every afternoon next door playing games. There was something else too. When he got really drunk, he'd look at me funny. I suspected that my mother wanted me out of the house for more than one reason. Then the alcohol let loose the monster and he moved from running his mouth to using his hands and fists. She should have called it quits right then and there but she didn't. She escaped by going out to work. She said she had to keep up with the bills, but that only made him angrier and the beatings got even worse.

This one day, he came home especially mean and Mom ushered me off to the woman next door again. That day the old lady and I played Parcheesi and my pieces were yellow; funny the things you remember sometimes. Even next door, I could hear the yelling until the old woman shut the window and turned up the radio. We were in the middle of the game when my mother came to get me. She had so much makeup on that she looked like a wax museum figure and it still didn't hide all the bruises. When she left for work, my father was passed out cold on the couch. She hugged me so tight I thought she was going to break something and the tears streaming down her cheeks made these little ruts in her makeup. Later that night, the pounding at the door woke me up.

"The cops must have knocked for five minutes before my father finally woke up. He acted all broken up when they told him about the accident. She hit a bridge abutment on her way to work. The car was doing eighty and there weren't even any skid marks. That was a couple weeks before Christmas and we already had the tree up."

"Oh, Doris. I'm so sorry."

"I don't remember much about the next few days. There was a funeral with words about healing and heaven and lots of people around. Then everything was quiet and everyone was gone except for my father and me. He'd been drinking all afternoon and we sat alone in the living room. There were still cookies and finger foods on the coffee table and some genius had lit the Christmas tree as though it might somehow cheer me up. My father reached under the tree, picked up a present, and handed it to me. 'It's from your mom,' he said.

"Now, maybe what followed was just in my imagination, but I don't think so. I developed very early and I was wearing this black dress with a low-cut neckline. I sat still for a while just looking at that box. My father sat real close, rubbing my knee. I thought he was just trying to console me but then his hand started moving up between my legs. When I looked up at him, he wasn't looking at the present at all; he was staring down the front of my dress. I was just barely out of training bras but he was so fixated that he didn't even realize I was looking at him. I should have said something but I must have been in shock or something, so I just ripped the paper off the gift instead. IT WAS A GAME!

"I flung it across the room so hard it blew out the Christmas lights and knocked half the balls off the tree. The game pieces went flying everywhere.

"I walked alone to midnight mass that Christmas Eve. It was snowing and I remember thinking to myself, this must be what it's like when God cries. After everything that happened, I'm surprised I gave him credit for giving a crap or even that he existed at all."

I just nodded my head slightly and didn't say a word. I couldn't. Our family had its problems too, but I could scarcely imagine the kind of world in which Doris grew up. Then something about her description of Christmas Eve resonated with one of my own memories. I recalled how beautiful the weather was the morning of Frank's funeral and how I thought it should be raining. I wanted God to be crying too.

Doris continued, "Within a few weeks my father pawned me off to my aunt here in Connecticut. He gave some excuse about how he was hurting too much to care for me with Mom gone. He sent notes and money for a while but that stopped pretty soon. I never saw or spoke to him again, which is just fine with me and I haven't played another game since. The only thing is…," Doris's eyes glistened, "I never got to say goodbye to her: to know what she was thinking about that night. Was she was hurt, or angry, or did she hate me for being born?"

For the first time since I had met her, Doris broke down and cried. I walked over to her, hugged her, and rocked her gently in my arms. I recalled how I had held Frank in my arms when he died and the kind of loving husband and father he had been. Then I thought about my relationship with my own father: how loving and gentle he was right up until the stress became too much for him. I also thought about my daughters, their husbands, my grandchildren, friends, and the many things for which I could be truly thankful and how, like so many of the things we found at our tag sales, I almost threw them all away. Then I said, "You know what, Doris, I think I do feel like going to that movie after all."

Her demeanor changed almost instantly. She straightened up, wiped her eyes, and looked at her watch. "Well, it's getting pretty late, kid: the movie starts in about forty minutes. We're not going to have much time for lunch."

"That's all right," I said. "We can just stop at a fast food place for some burgers and fries along the way." Burgers and fries? I could hardly believe I had just suggested that. "Just let me change into some more comfortable shoes."

I went upstairs to the bedroom to exchange my flats for the sneakers under the bed. When I finished, I looked over to the empty nightstand and remembered the bottle of sleeping pills that had once been there. I thought about how differently life looked now than it had just a few months ago and realizing how close I had come to losing it all, I prayed a silent "Thank you."

As I held the kitchen door open to exit, I asked, "Doris, I was just wondering. You said your mother worked nights but I don't remember your saying what she did."

Doris answered matter-of-factly, "She was a waitress."

CHAPTER 41

TAG SALEING THE following Saturday was another tough morning for Doris. She had planned to be at the first house by 7:30, at least a half hour before the start. From the ad in the *Step Saver*, it looked to her like a potential gold mine. When she arrived to pick me up, however, I was deep into a phone conversation with Megan. I gestured for her to come into the kitchen as I continued talking. "Yes, Megan, I know it doesn't seem like it now, but sometimes these things work out for the best in the long run. How is Ryan taking it?"

Doris pointed to her watch.

I shrugged my shoulders and then returned to the conversation. "And what did he say to that?"

As I continued with Megan, Doris paced nervously back and forth tapping her watch as if trying to make the time stand still. She also kept looking out the window to her car, still running in the driveway.

"Megan, hold on a second please. Doris is here and I just want to tell her something. No, no, don't hang up. I'll get right back to you, okay? Hold on, now." I cupped the mouthpiece. "Good morning, Doris. I'm sorry but I have to finish this. Tell you what, you go to the first couple of stops and pick me up after that. I'll finish up with Megan and be ready when you get back."

She shot me an annoyed look, "Whatever," and left.

It was 8:55 when Doris's car squealed back into the driveway. She didn't bother to get out. Instead, she honked the horn several times to announce her arrival.

My coat was only half on as I exited the house.

"Doris, it's Saturday morning," I said as I slid into the passenger seat. "Don't you think some people will still be asleep?"

"It's almost nine. Nobody should still be asleep at this hour, no matter what day it is." As she started backing out of the driveway, she said, "My grandmother used to say, 'Any head that sleeps more than four hours should be broken.'"

"Oh?"

"Yep. She was a smart, tough old lady: didn't take guff from anyone."

"Was this your father's mother?"

"Yea, so?"

"Nothing." I decided it was time to change the topic. "So did you find anything good at the tag sales?"

"No, thank you very much." Implicit in her tone was what she didn't say: "But I would have if you had been ready when you were supposed to be."

I decided that under the circumstances, discretion really was the better part of valor and I said nothing.

Doris continued, "At the first one, they were clearing out their parents' estate but they were doing it on their own, so the estate sale sharks weren't there skimming off the cream and tripling the prices on everything."

"But you didn't find anything you wanted?" I knew what was coming but decided it was going to happen anyway, so I might as well let her get on with it.

Doris enunciated each word of the next sentence, "NO, I DID NOT. The place was crawling when I got there. The old biddies had grabbed up all the collectible toys and dolls and the guys with the pickup trucks had picked over all the decent antiques."

"Were you there all this time?"

"Are you kidding? I got out of there in a shot. I went straight to the one on Burlington Avenue. They were supposed to start at 9:00 and it was already 8:30 when I got there. They must have gotten a late start because they were just starting to put the stuff out."

"Oh," I figured that Doris was holding out on her big find until now. "So that was a good one?"

"It would have been," she said with annoyance, "if the guy running it wasn't such a jerk."

I thought to myself, *This isn't going to be good after all*. "What happened?"

"Well, I decided that since they were still arranging things, I might as well take an inventory of the goods. Then this guy gets all pissy about the 'no early birds' thing in his ad."

"That seems odd. I know a lot of them say that, but they usually don't put up too much of a fuss so long as you're not too troublesome." Then a picture started to form in my mind. "You weren't being too disruptive, were you?"

"Well, according to this little Napoleon, I was. I figured that by emptying some of the boxes out on the tables, I was doing him a favor. That way he would have less unpacking to do."

"You went through his boxes before he put them out?" I tried not to sound too judgmental.

"Well, I didn't have all day. Then the little snot tells me that I'm interfering with his setting up and that things aren't marked yet. He says that his wife is getting all upset and then he tells me to leave the driveway and wait in my car until nine. Can you imagine? Whatever happened to respect for your elders? So I paid him for the plate I found and left. Just as well, I guess. When I threw him two bucks for the plate, he put up another fuss. He said it was supposed to go for ten."

"Then what made you think it cost two?" I asked.

"I told him there was no price marked on it, so how was I supposed to know!"

We spent the next hour and a half scurrying from one tag sale to the next. I bought several pieces of costume jewelry and a brown-haired doll.

I was especially proud of the doll buy. When I asked the seller about the price, the woman said $15.00.

"That seems high for a doll," I said with such assertiveness that it pleased as much as surprised me.

"That's a new Cabbage Patch doll in the original box with the birth certificate and everything," the woman said. "It's worth a lot of money to collectors."

I returned, "Maybe to a collector but this is for my granddaughter. Will you take eight?" and the woman took it.

"That was great, kid," Doris complimented as we drove away. "I must have taught you well. With the condition that doll is in, you could get three, maybe four times what you paid for it. And the way you did the granddaughter thing was perfect."

I responded calmly, "Thank you, but I didn't do any granddaughter thing: the doll really is for my granddaughter."

"Oh," Doris frowned. "It must be swell to shop for your grandkids, if they'll let you. Well, this has been the perfect ending to a perfectly lousy morning. I'm hungry. Let's stop for something to eat."

Based on experience, I had a clear image of how Doris might exercise her frustration at the restaurant. Then a thought occurred to me. "Great," I said, "Let's go to Grace's."

CHAPTER 42

THE WAITRESS APPROACHED our table as we settled into the booth. "Good morning, Alice," I said. She didn't return the greeting.

"What do you want to drink?" she asked with all the charisma of a prison guard.

"Decaf coffee for me, please."

"There's only regular brewed. If you want decaf, I'll have to put a pot on."

"That will be fine, I'll wait."

Alice turned to Doris, "What about you?"

"Is your coffee fresh?"

"Yea, I picked the beans myself this morning."

Doris scanned Alice with a wary eye, "I'll take regular."

"Regular what?"

"I thought I made myself perfectly clear."

"Well, you didn't. You want regular with cream, with sugar, or what?"

"Why didn't you ask her all these questions?"

"Because she's been here before and you haven't, or did I just miss your cheery disposition?"

"Regular, no milk, no sugar."

"So you want it black?"

"I thought that's what I said."

"Well, you thought wrong." As soon as Alice placed the menus on the table, I lifted mine to hide my smile.

"What's up her behind?" Doris asked.

"Nothing: that's just her personality. Kind of what you see is what you get."

"Well, we'll see about that. So you've been here before?"

"This was the first restaurant Frank and I ate at when we came to Connecticut. Bridget and Steve took us here. Bridget waitressed here for a while to pay for her tuition at Tunxis Community College." I paused for a moment when I realized that I has just mentioned Frank's name in a casual conversation without cringing.

Alice returned with the coffees and Doris and I both ordered. As Alice turned to go, Doris called out, "I've decided to have milk with my coffee after all."

Alice didn't bother turning around, "Suit yourself. The pitcher is on the table."

Doris found the creamer behind the napkin holder. "What the…," and then returned her attention to me. "So what was the conversation with your daughter about this morning? It sounded like somebody died." With uncharacteristic empathy, Doris twitched noticeably at her reference to someone dying. I appreciated her sensitivity.

"Megan and Ryan have been trying to buy a house near Mount Southington. It's in a beautiful setting but it needs a lot of work."

Doris answered, "Most places near the ski area are pretty pricey. Sounds like it could be a good deal."

"They thought so too, but it's not going to happen. When they added everything up, they realized that they couldn't afford it, so they had to let it go. Megan is very upset."

"And she called you?"

"We talk a few times a week. Nothing special, just normal conversation."

"Maybe for you, kid, but my daughter calling me for advice and comfort would not fall under what I would call normal."

Alice returned with the orders and set them down on the table. Doris looked down at her plate, smiled, and addressed Alice.

"Excuse me, but I ordered rye bread with my breakfast."

"Yea, and that's what you got."

"This isn't rye bread." Doris speared the offending slice and held it up as she spoke.

"It doesn't have seeds."

"And did you ask for seeds?"

"I shouldn't have too. Any good restaurant automatically knows that rye bread always comes with caraway seeds."

"Maybe the next time you're paying fifteen dollars for a two-egg breakfast at the Waldorf, you'll automatically get seeds. Here you don't."

"Well, I do. Take this back and bring me a new plate with seeded rye."

"Can't."

"Why not?"

"Because we don't have any."

"Then bring me an order of French toast instead." I could see in Doris's face the satisfaction of the kill.

"Suit yourself."

As Alice reached for the plate, Doris grabbed it. "You might as well leave this one. It'll just have to go into the garbage anyway."

"You gonna pay for it?"

"I certainly am not. You can't make me pay for something I didn't want."

"You're right, I can't." Alice yanked the plate from Doris's hands, "but then I don't have to serve it to you either."

"Wait." Doris grabbed her plate back from Alice's hands. Her normally aggressive tone gave way to one of resignation. "By the time you get back with another order, I'll probably have starved to death. I'll take these. The eggs are probably cold by now."

"Wouldn't have been if you hadn't wasted so much time jabbering." Alice removed the check from her apron and slapped it down on the table. "Have a sparkling day," and she walked off.

Doris started to eat in silence while I forced back my grin.

"So you've been here before?" she asked again.

"On occasion," I answered.

I wondered if Doris might choose to moderate her restaurant behavior in the future. Either way, for me, this had been a very pleasant breakfast.

CHAPTER 43

IF WE WEREN'T tag saleing, Doris and I were eating out. It was only a matter of time before we got around to Koch's, a favorite restaurant of Frank's and mine for most of our lives. Nestled in the Catskill Mountains foothills, it was a two-hour drive from Brooklyn yet, to us, it felt a world away. Even after our move to Connecticut, the Catskills remained a prime destination for weekend getaways or a lunch or dinner day trip. Thanks to Washington Irving's characters like Rip Van Winkle and Ichabod Crane, the area remained rich in folklore and legend and many of the motels and area attractions reflected the tradition. The land itself was lush with golden pastures, verdant forests, and picturesque waterfalls. Bridget and Megan spent many of their childhood summer vacations there. Frank loved to point out for the girls the carnival of animals and other characters that formed in the billowing white clouds over the mountains.

We spent many of those family vacations in the efficiency cabins at the Lawrence House in Cairo. When Bridget and Megan became serious with their future husbands, the young men joined in the tradition, although they slept in the old farmhouse across the road. The rustic resort was close to entertainment places like The Mystery Spot, Hunter Mountain, Six Gun City and, of course, the Catskill Game Farm. It was also close to many great eating spots and our favorite of them all was Koch's.

Family-owned for generations, Koch's specialized in German-American food. The restaurant sat at the edge of a scenic ravine and there were enough menu choices to satisfy several nights of a weeklong vacation. When we first started eating there, the toilets were outside and around the back. On cold, rainy days, a rest room trip was an adventure in itself.

A mainstay attraction of the restaurant was the painted concrete deer at the edge of the parking lot. The rock outcropping it sat atop jutted up from the pavement like an iceberg in an asphalt ocean. It was there since our first Catskill vacation. Frank insisted on capturing the girls' pictures with it during every trip. He cataloged all of them in a series of family photo albums. When I revisited the albums and rediscovered the photos, I couldn't help smiling at the girls' growth against the statue. In the early pictures, I held the children sitting atop the deer. Later, they rode by themselves and in the awkward teenage years, first Bridget and then Megan, stood beside it with a forced smile.

As the trees started turning their reds and gold, I found myself drawn to the Catskills again and decided to ask Doris about taking a day trip with me to Koch's. I looked forward to the ride as much as the destination. During autumn, few places rivaled the splendor of Route 8 from Waterbury to Winsted.

Crossing from Connecticut to the Hudson Valley on Route 23, I took in the views of the farms, cornfields, weather-beaten barns, and giant hay bales. Traveling the roads through the hilly countryside felt like a roller coaster. What I didn't count on was that to Doris, the Saturday morning Catskills were also a Tag Saler's Mecca.

"Thank heaven we finally broke for lunch," I sighed as we entered Koch's front door. "I'm light-headed from hunger and one more stop and we'd have to start strapping things to the roof."

"Remember, this trip was your idea."

"Yes, Doris. I suggested we visit the Catskills. I never said anything about buying them."

We were both laughing so hard that we didn't even notice the woman behind the counter waiting to seat us, "Will there be two of you for lunch?"

"Yes, please," I answered, "we're famished. Could we get a table by the back windows?" The hostess escorted us to an open table overlooking the ravine.

I asked the hostess if the sauerbraten was on the menu.

"Sorry, ma'am, this weekend we're featuring the goulash." I was only mildly disappointed since I loved both dishes but Doris had that "deer-in-the-headlights" look. It surprised me that she hadn't eaten German food before. After explaining selections like Wiener schnitzel, potato pancakes, and spatzel to her, I ordered the goulash and she opted for the fish and chips.

"With a name like Russo, I wouldn't have pegged you for a German food fanatic," said Doris, but her words failed to enter my consciousness. "Hello," she raised her voice. "Earth to Russo: are you listening at all, or am I just talking to myself?"

"Oh. I'm sorry, Doris. What were you asking?"

"Obviously, nothing important to you. I just hadn't pegged you as such an authority on German food."

"Oh. Well you might not have been as surprised if you knew my original maiden name was Bower, shortened from Browerman. My father was German and my mother was Irish-Scott."

"I see, German, Irish, Scott: you're a regular mutt, aren't you?" I opted to concentrate on her friendly intent rather than her crass choice of words. She continued, "And what's with the window-induced trance?"

I let out a sigh. "Just some old memories. Frank and I have sat at this window so often looking out at these trees: green in the summer, a fall mix like they are now, and covered with snow in winter. I was just thinking about how many important decisions we made right here: children, work, moving to Connecticut; so many conversations over so many years." My voice cracked slightly and my eyes clouded over as I finished. "I still miss him, Doris."

As I picked up the napkin to dab my tears, Doris asked, "You could still love him that much after all those years?"

"I think I love him now more than ever."

203

"It must really be something to feel like that for someone."

"You must have loved Henry like that at some point, didn't you?"

"Not really."

"But the two of you had a child together!" I startled myself with my bluntness. "I mean, doesn't that kind of intimacy imply deep feelings for each other?"

"In case you hadn't heard, kiddo, deep abiding love is not a precondition for getting pregnant. We were both young and reckless and neither one of us was looking to make a baby. Don't get me wrong: I love my daughter, even if the feeling isn't mutual, but planned she wasn't. It's like they say: those who don't learn from history are doomed to repeat it."

"You just lost me."

"Simple: my mother got knocked up and then married the loser and I followed suit. When we started out, Henry got up, went to work, and brought home a steady paycheck like everybody else, but he always dreamed of having his own business. Then he got into those get-rich-quick schemes on late-night television and he fell for every one of them. He did the 'Think-yourself-rich' tapes, took out newspaper ads, sold useless information, and bartered stuff on the Internet. None of it worked for very long and I started ragging on him because it was affecting his full-time job. Then he got on the real estate bandwagon. Henry loved the "No money down" thing. The thought of getting rich on other people's money excited him. I have to admit that, at first, he was really good at it. For a while, we lived pretty high on the hog. Who knows, maybe he could have kept it going forever if the economy hadn't soured. Anyway, when the bills started piling up and Henry started drinking, that really set me off."

"Were you afraid he might act like your father?

"There was no way I was going put up with that! We argued all the time and I told you, at one point, he actually tried to take a swing at me. I grabbed his hand in midair, looked him straight in the eye, and told him that if he ever tried that again, I'd put him in jail, the hospital, or the morgue. I don't think he bought that but when I told him that I would also take him to the cleaners for everything he had or ever would have, believe me that caught his attention.

Then, when I thought about Colleen and my own father and all, I vowed to myself that Henry would never be alone with her again. From that day forward, he never was and you'd better believe there wasn't a game within a mile of the house."

The waitress returned with our meals, after which I returned to the conversation. "Did Henry ever make you think that he might, you know, try to act out sexually with Colleen?"

"Didn't you hear a word I said: the fighting, the drinking, a daughter well past puberty? Should I have waited until he got into bed with her before I did something?"

"No, of course not, but all couples argue, too many men drink and unfortunately, some of them do become abusive. But I have to believe that very few fathers have sexual feelings toward their own daughters, much less act on them."

"Well, I wasn't about to chance it and have her end up the way I did."

I wasn't sure about pressing further. At the same time, Doris seemed relieved at the opportunity to talk about it. I asked, "So what happened?"

She sat back in her chair, "Just what you'd expect, I guess. I lost it all: Colleen, Henry, everything. The more roadblocks I put up, the more distance I put between Colleen and me. When Henry and I finally separated, she wanted to go and live with him and I said, 'Over my dead body.' Henry and I were in court constantly, suing and countersuing and I used Colleen as if she was my personal trump card. As soon as she turned eighteen, she and Henry flew out to Las Vegas for a two-week vacation and when they returned, she moved in with him."

"Did you suspect there was anything between them?"

"After all the hullaballoo I created, I don't think he ever treated her with anything but respect. She stayed with him up until she and Jeff married and moved out to Arizona. I swear they did it to get away from me. I wasn't even invited to the wedding. But you know what really galls me? In all the time since, I've only seen my granddaughter in pictures and I...."

Doris started to tremble, the fork vibrated in her hands, and streams trickled down her cheeks.

"I really loved my daughter ... more than anything. I would have given my life for hers. All I wanted was to keep her safe. I just didn't want her to have to go through the hell that I did. I just wanted her to love me. Is that too much to ask?" She shot up quickly, "You have to excuse me for a sec," and darted off toward the restroom.

I sat quietly, praying for the right words or gestures to use when she returned. I looked at the gold and crimson leaves gently swaying in the afternoon breeze and marveled at the magic these hills contained for fostering such deep conversations. I also thought about how thankful I was for the opportunity to have them, first with Frank, then with my children, and now with my friend. I wondered for a moment what future conversations might occur in these seats: my children's career decisions, issues with my grandchildren, my own future choices. Then I realized that for the first time since Frank's death, I was looking toward the future. How odd that from sharing in Doris's troubled past, I had somehow found hope for my own future. Like so many of the discarded items we picked up tag saleing, I too had a second chance.

"That was silly of me," Doris said as she returned to the table. "Sorry for the dramatics."

"No need to apologize. You really love your daughter."

She shrugged her shoulders. "Not that it does me much good."

"You were only trying to keep her safe, Doris. That has to count for something. Did you ever try to share with her why you acted the way you did?"

"What, about me and my mother and father? Never! Those aren't the kinds of things you tell your kid. How could she understand? How could anyone? I don't even understand it all myself. Outside of me and my father, you're the only person in the world who knows."

The breath shot out of me as if Doris had just punched me hard in the stomach. "You didn't tell anyone! Not Henry, or a minister, or a friend: you've never told anyone?" I tried to fathom the unimaginable burden that she carried throughout her life: her father's abuse, her mother's suicide. I couldn't imagine the terrible guilt feelings trapped inside her with no one, not another living soul with whom to share it.

We both sat quietly for a long, long time. Then Doris let out a soft sigh and leaned forward. She looked into my eyes and said in an uncharacteristically timid voice, "Maureen, you don't really think she'd understand, do you?"

CHAPTER 44

WHEN DORIS INTERRUPTED our shopping excursion at West Farms Mall to suggest I go with her to the senior center's holiday dance, I promptly said no. Like Frank, however, she did not give up easily. I held the black scarf she asked me to hunt down as I returned to the dressing room. "OK, Doris," I called, "I'm back. Are you still in there? I could only find one scarf in black."

Overpowering the piped-in Christmas music, Doris's answer through the dressing room door echoed throughout the women's section. "Yea, I'll be done in a sec. Listen, Maureen: it's been over a year since Frank died. If he were as self-centered as most men, I could see how he might get some satisfaction at watching you waste away at home. But if he's the saint you've painted him out to be, why wouldn't want you to get on with your life, or at least have a little fun every now and then?"

The door popped open and Doris exited and quickly spun around. "By the way, how do you think this looks on me?" The fiery red dress was skintight. With its low neckline and the low-slung back, it was obvious that she wasn't wearing a bra.

"I think you're going to need this scarf," I said. She took it from me and draped it around her neck.

"By the way," she asked, "what is it with you and elevators? How come we had to go clear to the other side of the store for the escalator when the elevator door is right here?"

"I get too nervous to use them. While Frank was in the service, several of us were trapped in one for hours and one of the men had a heart attack and died!"

"Wow! OK then, I get it."

While Doris continued repositioning the scarf, I considered her comment. It bothered me to hear Frank characterized as uncaring and insensitive. "I'm sure Frank would never want to see me suffer," I said. "It's just that somehow it doesn't feel right to think about enjoying myself without him. It feels like I'm cheating on him somehow, as though our years together don't matter anymore. Like I'm...."

"Like you're forgetting him."

That's it! I thought. Doris caught my surprised expression.

"What? Do you think I'm totally incapable of feelings?"

"Not at all. I just...." My mind went numb and I couldn't find the right words to answer.

"Listen, hon, it may seem hard to believe, but I really think I understand what's eating at you. In my own way, I've been there too. After my mom ... well, after she died, I tried to hold on to her every second of every day. I tried to remember every conversation, every expression, every dress she ever wore, even what she smelled like. I was afraid that if I forgot even the slightest detail, somehow she might evaporate completely and then I wouldn't be able to remember anything about her."

"That's exactly what I've been feeling. The more time that goes by, the harder it is for me to remember the sound of his voice, his expressions, even the words of our last conversations. It's as though each day a little more of him is lost and I can't get it back. Sometimes I feel like I'm going crazy."

"You're not going crazy. You're just trying to do the impossible. There's no way that you can keep every detail of Frank's memory alive while you go on living yourself. Believe me, kid, I know. I've tried."

"What happened with your mom? Did you have to let go of her?"

As I spoke, another woman began approaching the dressing room door behind Doris. I hadn't noticed her, but Doris certainly did, "Hey—what, are you, blind? Can't you see it's taken?" The other women jumped and then walked off in a huff as Doris continued.

"No, sweetie, not at all. I guess I realized that if you keep looking too closely, you never really see the whole picture, so I stopped trying so hard. When I did, I got her back. Not every little detail about how she looked or acted, but how it felt to be with her and that's something I can keep. I felt a lot of anger toward her for leaving and that got in the way but I think I'm over that. Don't get me wrong: I still have my demons, but at least now, my mother isn't one of them. You kind of helped me with that, you know?"

My smile must have projected my admiration, which made Doris uncomfortable. She folded her arms and frowned, "What?"

I just stood quietly for a moment as I processed what she had said. At the same time, I couldn't shake Frank's voice in my head: "It'll be all right, Maurie. It'll be all right." Then I looked down to find myself tracing with my finger in the same way Frank had in his last few moments. Once again, I recalled each stroke of his final message: I LOVE YOU.

I stayed quiet for a little while longer, then looked at my friend still modeling her fiery red dress and smiled, "I think that looks great on you and you don't need the scarf. So tell me, Doris, what do you think I should wear for the dance?"

CHAPTER 45

IT WAS DIFFICULT mustering enough volunteers for some senior center events, but there was never a shortage of help for the annual holiday ball. Year-round, the center staff lined the hallways with colorful posters, fliers, pictures of center goings-on and seasonal trimmings, but that paled by comparison to the holiday decorations. Frank and I had attended the dance every year since we joined the BSC and had volunteered to help decorate for most of them. The first Christmas after his death, I avoided every holiday festivity. I hadn't helped with the decorations for the current year either, so as Doris and I entered the front door of the center, the transformation was overwhelming.

The institutional brown and beige walls disappeared beneath a mantle of green garland, red bows, dazzling tinsel, and shimmering ornaments. Decorations draped every door, office window, and bulletin board. Even the water coolers were trimmed and every corner contained another lighted tree hovering over elaborately wrapped boxes. The entrance, however, was only a prelude. The workers had concentrated most of their efforts in the dining hall. Turning into the doorway, I said, "It looks like it's snowing in here!"

Snow-covered tree branches, wrapped in white lights and shimmering crystals, reached up the walls and spilled onto the ceiling. They looked as if they had grown there and just emerged from a midwinter's snowstorm. Round dining tables skirted the perimeter of the room, leaving the center clear for dancing. Snowflakes and glitter covered each tablecloth and bright-colored Mylar balloons floated above them.

Chet Hartman and his orchestra, flanked by more lights and decorations, were playing from the raised stage. As Doris and I made our way to our table, the band was already into its first set of holiday classics.

"Hey, Maurie," said Doris, "would you get a look at this place. Is this the cat's butt or what?"

I halted for a moment and smiled. Doris looked at me and asked, "What now?"

"You called me Maurie."

"So? Did I hit a nerve or something?"

"Not at all. I just haven't been called that in a long time. It sounded nice…. And yes, Doris, I suppose it's every bit of the cat."

"Are you making fun of me?" a familiar voice interrupted us.

"Maureen, honey!" Lorraine rushed up to us and hugged me firmly. "It's so good to see you. We've missed you so much. How have you been? You look wonderful and that dress on you looks stunning."

That was about as many compliments as I could handle in one helping. I was also a little self-conscious in the dress Doris helped me pick out. The low-cut iridescent blue, with its sequence trim, was more form-fitting and revealing than anything else I owned.

"Thank you, Lorraine. You know Doris, don't you?"

Lorraine hesitated a moment before answering coolly, "Of course. Still around, hey Doris?"

Doris returned with an equal lack of enthusiasm, "Sorry to disappoint you, Lorraine. It's a shame you couldn't find a dress in your size. Who's the stud you're sitting with?" When we reached the table, Lorraine introduced us.

"This is my friend Nicholas Germaine." Nickolas smiled as he stood and extended his hand. With his finely tailored, expensive-looking suit, angular facial features, and full head of lightly salted hair, he looked like a mature cover-model for GQ.

Doris returned the greeting while the fingers of her left hand played in her hair and her Southern accent deepened, "Well, hello, Nicholas Germaine. It's a pleasure to make your acquaintance. I'm Doris."

The exchange made Lorraine visibly uncomfortable and she immediately went on the offensive.

"Nick was an officer at Chemical Bank in Manhattan before he retired. We met at the Genealogy Club."

"Oh?" I asked. "I didn't know you were into genealogy."

"George got me started before he died. He gathered lots of information on our ancestry. We planned to share it with our children someday to pass on the family heritage. With all the work he had done, I thought it would be a shame to let it go to waste, so I joined the club. It's really interesting."

"And you, Nick," cooed Doris, "what are you passing along?" she asked the question in the same tone she might use to invite him into her bed.

"Nothing really. After two divorces, my kids don't have much interest in my ancestry. I do it for my own edification."

"And Nick is a famous golfer too," Lorraine added.

"Famous?" I asked. Meanwhile, Doris stood with her hands clasped behind her back while doing deep-breathing exercises. From Nick's stare, it was obviously working.

"Yes," said Lorraine. "He's hit twenty-six holes-in-one at some golf course on Long Island. They even did a story on him in the local paper."

"Twenty-six?" I asked. "That's got to be a record."

"He really loves his golf," Lorraine answered.

"Almost as much as I do Lorraine's cooking," said Nick, smiling. Lorraine beamed with satisfaction at his comment. "Her strawberry rhubarb pie is the best I've ever tasted and her pot roast is to die for." Obviously, the way to this man's heart was through his stomach. Lorraine took the opportunity to regain the advantage. "So, Doris," she asked, "what do you make for dinner?"

Doris didn't miss a beat, "The same thing every night: reservations."

Lorraine smirked and turned away, "Listen, Nick, they're playing 'The Christmas Waltz.' I love this song. Could we dance?"

"Of course," he extended his arm. From the smile on his face, I could tell he knew exactly what was happening between Lorraine and Doris and was enjoying every second of it.

As we took our seats, Doris and I introduced ourselves to the other couples at the table. I surmised that given Doris's taste in men, the other women at our table had nothing to fear from her.

The table next to ours contained women only. Clem Avery, a short, athletic, and loud center regular, swooped down on it like a hawk. "OK, Gracie, it's your turn," he said as he whisked one of the women out onto the dance floor. As he did, he caught sight of me sitting with Doris. "And you're next, Russo!"

"Did you hear that, kid," said Doris. "You haven't been here ten minutes and you're already popular."

"Swell." Besides feeling uncomfortable about dancing, I cringed as I watched Clem with his current victim. At fifty-eight, he was one of the youngest center members, was very physical and, dancing with Gracie, reminded me of Lorraine's description of men mopping the floor with their partners. "Doris, maybe this wasn't such a good idea after all."

"Oh, relax a little. I'm sure Clem isn't going to sweep you off your feet." After we both watched the dancers for a while, she followed with, "Well, maybe he will literally, but at least not romantically. You know, given his height and yours, if you dance close enough you could bury his face between your boobs and that could be interesting."

"Oh, Doris," I laughed through my words. As the music continued, I detected a hint of disappointment in Doris's expression. I guessed that even an offer from Clem was better than none at all. I leaned in toward her. "Did you catch the way Nick looked at your, um, dress?"

She grinned widely, "Why, Maureen Russo! The way you think sometimes." Then she leaned in closer, winked, and answered, "Of course, I did. With women here outnumbering men three to one, this is a buyer's market. The way I see it, if you want to stir up interest in your property, it needs to have some *curb appeal*." I realized that Doris didn't need much in the way of morale building. Then she said, "Well, while you wait for your prince charming to return, I'm going to do a little prospecting. Who knows, if there are any live ones out there, one of them might just get lucky tonight."

As Doris moved off into the crowd, I scanned the program. Then I searched through my purse as I considered my options. It wasn't that I dreaded dancing with Clem. He wasn't bad looking and I could be a strong lead when I needed to be, but I resented being told instead of asked. It also distressed me that this might be a preview of what was to come: a sort of, "Is that all there is?" feeling. Then I thought about Frank: his gentlemanly manners, the way he never made me feel taken for granted, and his marvelous dancing.

NO! I told myself. I won't settle. I will choose what I do and with whom I do it. The tap on my shoulder punctuated my resolution. I took in a deep breath and shot back my answer.

"Thanks all the same, Clem," I volleyed loudly as I turned, "but if you can't offer me the courtesy of…. Oh. Hello, Larry. I'm sorry; I didn't realize it was you."

"I hope not. You sounded like my grammar school teacher dishing out a scolding…. It's good to see you again, Maureen."

The current song ended and Chet Hartman approached the microphone, "OK, folks, we're going to play some of our regular tunes before returning to the holiday music. Here's one of our favorites, 'Young at Heart.'"

Before I could answer Larry, Clem abandoned Gracie on the dance floor, turned toward me, and shouted, "OK, Russo, it's your turn!" He started heading in our direction until Larry put up his hand.

"Sorry, Clem. Not this time."

Clem stopped short, shrugged his shoulders, and turned back to his partner. Gracie, however, was not pleased. She turned in a huff and headed off the dance floor, with Clem trailing behind her, "Awe, come on, Gracie. Don't be like that…."

I laughed and was maybe even a little disappointed that I didn't get the chance to give him my own comeuppance. Larry also grinned widely, then turned back to me and extended his hand,

"Maureen, may I have this dance?"

PART FIVE

LARRY

CHAPTER 46

I THOUGHT BACK to Doris's comments about Larry and Ceil and hesitated for a moment. Then I recalled the first time I heard those same words from Frank and how my initial reaction was to ask if he couldn't come up with a better pickup line. Like Frank, the sincerity in Larry's expression made it clear that he wasn't trying to be coy and like that first time, I didn't want to spoil the moment, so I simply said yes.

As Larry and I entered the dance floor, Lorraine and Nick were returning to their seats. Halfway there, Lorraine stopped, placed her hand on Nick's shoulder, and removed her shoes. From the relieved expression on her face, I guessed that she would probably be sitting out the next few dances.

Larry took one of my hands in his and placed his other hand squarely on the small of my back. I noticed that he didn't let it slip lower as Ralph Corbin had. I was prepared to be assertive if needed, but Larry was a self-assured partner so I just relaxed and just followed his lead. Soon, I stopped concentrating on technique altogether and lulled myself into floating with the tempo of the music. I imagined myself once again in Frank's arms and relished that feeling of forgetting anything or anyone else but the two of us and the music. Then I realized that I hadn't spoken to Larry the whole time.

"I'm so sorry. I haven't said a word to you since we started dancing. I didn't mean to ignore you. I just felt so … comfortable."

He smiled, "No offense taken. I consider it a compliment. Some of the women I've danced with here seemed more intent on grilling me with questions and sometimes the dancing itself felt more like a test of wills. With you, it was almost like being with Helen again. I used to tell her that dancing with her was like wearing an old pair of shoes."

Larry stopped talking for a moment as the wetness in his eyes caused them to glisten, then he suddenly looked uncomfortable. "Oh, I'm sorry, Maureen. That was an awkward thing to say. I didn't mean to compare you to...."

"Don't worry Larry. I know what you said and I understood exactly what you meant. It sounded sweet. He looked relieved and the smile returned to his face.

I continued, "This is only the second time I've danced since Frank died."

"Are you comparing me to the first?"

"Oh, not at all." I looked around to make certain no one else was in earshot. "The other was Ralph Corbin last year. We didn't even get through the first dance. I never should have gone. I think maybe Ralph was just lonely and I was too sensitive over just losing Frank."

"Sounds like you're trying hard to give Ralph the benefit of the doubt."

I looked into Larry's eyes, "That seems like an odd thing to say."

"Sorry. Ralph was a friend of mine but I had seen him try that lonely widow move more than once. To me, that's predatory. If I had to guess, I'd say he tried to take advantage of you."

"Well, uh, yes, he did. Back then, it seemed like every man did."

"Including me?"

My initial reaction was to say, "No," but I hesitated a moment to consider my answer. I recalled that snowy morning in my kitchen, the way Larry kissed me, and my concern for Ceil.

"To be truthful, Larry, yes, you too."

The pained expression on his face made me wonder if I was too blunt.

"I'm sorry, I didn't mean for it to come out that way." I wasn't being honest. Though I didn't want to hurt Larry, I think my answer came out exactly the way I intended.

My mind started racing. I was a jumbled mix of emotions and couldn't sort out my thoughts.

"To be honest, Larry, I am not completely sure of what I was trying to say."

He gave me a sad but understanding smile. "You had just lost Frank. That day I stopped by, you looked confused and vulnerable and I took unfair advantage. At the same time, you were being loyal to your friend. What I did was wrong and you had every right to be angry. Your sending me away was actually the best thing that could have happened. It made me realize that I wasn't being honest with myself or with Ceil. She's a kind, caring woman who had genuine feelings for me, but I realized that I didn't feel the same way about her. I missed Helen and I was confusing Ceil's companionship with love, so I broke it off. I know it hurt her and I regret that, but it would have been worse to continue. I'm sorry for how I made you feel, Maureen."

As I thought back to that snowy morning, I realized that, to be fully honest with myself, for a moment I had welcomed and returned that kiss. I also realized that, despite my friendship with Ceil, I was actually pleased that Larry had broken up with her.

"Thank you, Larry. I appreciate your honesty. Apology accepted." Then I recalled Larry's reference to Ralph. "You said Ralph *was*, not *is* a friend. Did you have a falling out?"

"No. I understood Ralph. His batting average wasn't that great and he would just say that you can't kill a guy for trying. He had many good qualities too. We were friends right up until he died a few months back."

I halted, "Oh, poor Ralph."

"So are you sorry you didn't sleep with him?"

"Larry!" We both broke out laughing. Somehow, our mutual losses created a common bond that overlaid our conversation and made communicating easier. We stayed on the dance floor and continued talking for

221

the remainder of the set. My concentration was broken only briefly when Doris glided past us on the dance floor with Clem.

"Hey Mauri," she shouted, "check this out!"

Her hand rested firmly on the back of Clem's head and he wore a broad smile as his face snuggled firmly against her breasts.

CHAPTER 47

I HARDLY SLEPT at all that night and I was up by 5:30 the next morning. I hoped that Doris and I would have a long talk after the dance but she dropped me off and left immediately. She and Clem had other plans. I made myself a cup of coffee and held it as I paced nervously around the kitchen.

I kept reaching for the phone to call Bridget or Megan but then realized that it was still dark out so I flipped on the television but that didn't help either. I couldn't sit still long enough to watch anything. I also had these uncontrollable bouts of giddiness. *This is silly*, I told myself. *You're a senior citizen, not some schoolgirl after a summer camp romance.* Romance? It was only a few dances. What was I thinking? I paced some more.

I wished that I had not given up on the driving lessons with Steve. Then at least I could have gone to Denny's and killed some time eating breakfast. I scanned the living room searching for reading materials. In the magazine rack next to the recliner, I found several back issues of *National Geographic*. I was certain there were articles in each that I had missed but I also knew that I couldn't focus long enough to read them. Several issues of the *Bristol Press* were on the lamp table but I had already finished those. Under the newspapers were some store flyers and catalogs. I picked them up and started to scan through them but I was too antsy to concentrate. Then I noticed a stack of small brochures. As I picked up the "CareNotes" pamphlets, I vaguely remembered one of the girls giving them to me shortly after Frank died but I had never gotten around to reading them. I quickly scanned the covers. Each pamphlet dealt with a different aspect of the grieving process. I went through the stack and created two piles: one to read and one to ignore. Selections like *12 Reflections for the First 12 Weeks of Grief; Widowhood—12 Things You Can Do On Your Own;* and *Five Ways to Get Through the First Year of Loss,* went into the discard pile. Thinking about it now, I wished I had made time to read them all earlier. For the read pile, I picked titles like *Cherishing Your Memories of a Loved One; On the First Anniversary of Your Loss;* and *Grieving as a Woman.* Armed with enough distractions, I poured my coffee down the kitchen sink, made myself some chamomile tea, and settled into my recliner.

The ringing phone woke me with a start. As I brought the recliner forward, the pamphlets spilled onto the floor. The clock on the VCR showed 8:15 as I grabbed for the receiver.

"I hope I didn't wake you." It was Larry and I jerked involuntarily.

"No, I was just sitting here catching up on some reading." Why was I lying?

"Does that mean that you've had breakfast already?"

"No. Not at all. I made myself some tea earlier but I wasn't hungry then." My head was spinning. I was talking too loud and too fast so I worked to compose myself and not sound too excited.

"So are you hungry now?"

"Absolutely! I'm famished!" So much for composure.

"Great. Can I pick you up in a half hour?" I thought Larry sounded excited too.

"If you don't mind, forty-five minutes would be better. I'd like to jump in the shower first."

"OK. I'll see you then."

I hung up the phone and then reached down to recover my reading materials. I had highlighted three items in the pamphlets. The first advised not to hide your hardships but to share them. It went on to say how important it was to be "real" with someone. I realized that I found it easy to be honest with Larry and looked forward to continuing our conversations.

A second entry advised that on the one-year anniversary of a loss, the best gift you could give your departed was that of healing yourself and reentering the world. Doris had said that same thing when she suggested the holiday ball, although not quite as eloquently.

I scanned the final highlight and nodded my head in agreement. It was accurate and important but it was also something that I was not ready to do just yet. That step would have to wait for the right time. I circled that suggestion with my pen and placed the stack back on the lamp table. Then I hurried off to get ready for my breakfast with Larry Kowalski.

CHAPTER 48

SUDDENLY FOR ME, time sped up. My breakfast with Larry turned out to be the first of many. During them, there was so much to catch up on that we talked incessantly. Our conversations moved beyond sharing our losses to details about extended family and friends, likes and dislikes, successes and disappointments, and the countless other details that added up to a life. With each exchange, the topics deepened and so did my feelings for Larry. As the winter passed, we saw each other even more until *often* became *constant* and included doing almost everything together. Our focus also shifted from the past to the future as we began creating new memories of our own. The Bristol Senior Center quickly became a hub for many of those activities.

Larry was an enthusiastic bridge player and tried to recruit me for the Thursday morning games. He was the only man in the group and they were always one player short for the two tables of regulars, so he bounced between the two tables playing a hand at each. It was funny to watch. I tried to join in for a while but found that I had other interests, so Larry continued to bounce between the two tables, although I don't think he minded all that much.

In the meantime, I started taking ceramics classes. At first, I was frustrated with how amateur my pieces looked and I considered dropping out of the group. When the instructor taught me dry brushing, however, I began producing pieces of which I was truly proud. I decided that, with enough time and practice, I could create items for the center's annual craft fair and maybe, by Christmas, make handmade gifts for everyone on my holiday list. I also became a regular at the center's Mahjong group while Larry played billiards in the poolroom. The women in our group enjoyed swapping off-color jokes and took particular delight when Larry or other center men happened to walk in during one of the stories.

Larry and I also shared many common interests. Primary among them were the center dances every Tuesday afternoon. Each week we taught each other a few new steps until our reputation for dancing rivaled the one Frank and I had.

Both of us also loved movies. We made it a weekly routine to attend the matinees at the Southington Cinemas where the $2.00 senior admission included a free popcorn and soda. While there, we saw classics like *Gone with the Wind* and *Casa Blanca*. On Wednesday afternoons, we went to the senior center movies to see newer films. Unlike Frank and me, however, we left the work of screening, showing, and reviewing the movies to the younger center members.

With Larry, the emptiness that once defined me left. My life became engaging and full. When my answering machine took a message early one April morning, however, I realized that in at least one way, it had become too full.

CHAPTER 49

I WAS IN the shower when the phone rang at 6:45 a.m. on Saturday, so Doris left me a message.

"Hey, kid, it's me. I was riding around town yesterday and the tag sale signs are up everywhere. It's supposed to rain later so people are going to be desperate to unload their stuff in a hurry. There are some great listings and with the forecast the way it is, we should be able to pick them up for a song. I'll swing by and pick you up. We haven't seen much of each other lately so put on some coffee. I'll bring the bagels and wait until I tell you what I've been up to! See you in about fifteen."

When I finished listening to the message, I breathed out deeply and lowered my head, "Oh, Doris."

She arrived shortly after seven. I was still upstairs getting ready so I left the kitchen door open.

"That coffee smells great," she shouted as she entered the kitchen. The cups were on the counter so she poured one for herself. "I went all the way into Southington for the bagels. Fancy Bagels makes the absolute best and I remembered you liked salt so I brought you two of those. They must have just come out of the oven 'cause they're still warm. I also got some cream cheese with chives."

Doris was removing the butter from the refrigerator as I entered the kitchen. She lowered her volume when she saw me.

"I brought the cream cheese for you. I prefer butter myself," she said as she closed the refrigerator door and turned around. Seeing how I was dressed, she said, "That's a pretty fancy outfit for tag saleing," then lowered her gaze, "and what's with the suitcase?"

I lowered the suitcase to the floor, "I'm sorry but I can't go tag saleing with you today. Larry is picking me up in a half hour."

"Where are you off to? I thought that center trip to Atlantic City was a little pricey for what they were offering. You know if you play it right with those casinos, you can get them to pay you for going there."

"No," I answered. "We're not going on that trip. Larry and I are going to Martha's Vineyard. His friends have a place right on the water and they're going to Virginia for their son's wedding, so Larry rented it for the week."

Doris's expression turned rigid. "For the week, huh? And you didn't think to let me know?"

"Well, like you said in your message, we haven't seen much of each other lately. We've both been busy. In fact, you said you wanted to tell me what you've been up to."

"Oh that. It'll probably seem silly to you. I'm taking a painting class at Wesleyan."

"Not at all. It sounds great, but talk about pricey."

"No, I'm getting it for free."

"How did you manage that?"

"I saw an ad from Wesleyan looking for a model for a course on painting the male nude. I told them I would get them the model if they let me take the course for free."

"You were able to convince someone to pose for them?"

"You remember Clem Avery?"

The image of Doris and Clem dancing together popped into my mind. "When I picture a male model, I imagine the *David*. Isn't Clem a little short for that?"

"The model is seated so height doesn't matter. Actually, Clem's got a pretty solid physique and the students all love him."

229

I burst out laughing, "You're right. It does sound a little silly but it's definitely you all the way."

Doris turned stoic again, "So, you and Larry together on Martha's Vineyard for a week, huh? It sounds serious. Do you love him?"

"Honestly, after Frank died I didn't think I could ever love another man that way again, but yes, I do."

"And does he love you?"

"I believe he does."

Doris paused, "Well, OK, then," and started for the kitchen door.

"Wait, Doris, we haven't had our coffee and bagels yet."

"I guess I wasn't that hungry after all. Give mine to Larry." With that, she slammed the door behind her.

CHAPTER 50

I WOKE TO the sound of ocean waves, the feeling of the sun shining on my face, and the memory of lovemaking with Larry. There was a deep calm inside me and a peacefulness that I hadn't known since Frank died.

Frank....

I checked myself for feelings of guilt but couldn't find any. As relieved as I was by that, I was also puzzled. Everything was happening so fast and on such an emotional level that I couldn't sort out one feeling from another. Was I just fooling myself?

Larry was still asleep, breathing quietly by my side. I gingerly freed myself from the covers, eased myself off the bed, and tiptoed to the dresser. After retrieving my robe, journal and pen, I quietly opened the French doors and stepped out onto the patio.

The sun had already burned off the early morning mist. I stood there for a moment taking in the smell of the ocean and salt marsh and quietly prayed a thank you. At one time, I was certain that my life had ended. Now it felt like it was just beginning again. Then I sat down, opened my journal, and started to write.

Dearest Frank,

I need to sort out my feelings. Can I love another man and still remain faithful to you? Throughout our more than fifty years together, I never thought about another man. Now, someone else has come into my life and I have developed deep feelings for him. I needed to be sure that I wasn't doing this out of anger or revenge because that would feel like cheating on you. When I told Larry how irate I was at losing you without a warning, he shared his experience of losing Helen.

After returning from their trip out west with us, they both knew that it was only a matter of time. The doctors had done all they could for her and then it was only a question of how quickly the disease would spread. Larry said that they discussed how they would spend what little time they had left together and I told him how much I envied that opportunity. Then he described what those last weeks together were like.

He said that at first, while she was alert, they spent most of their time talking about their memories. Then, at Helen's pleading, they discussed her funeral arrangements. That devastated Larry. He agreed to go through the selection of the readings and hymns but it tore him up inside. She must have recognized it and suggested leaving the rest of the arrangements up to the priest and family.

Then Helen could no longer eat and she began wasting away. When the pain became unbearable, she had to be heavily sedated. While she just lay motionless in bed, all Larry could do was to sit helplessly by her side. Even under the medication, Helen moaned from the pain. Finally, Larry thought she might be bearing all that suffering in order not to abandon him and that he might be holding her back by not giving her permission to go.

Larry said that when he wrapped Helen's hands in his, her skin was paper-thin and he could feel her bones moving, even under the lightest touch. Then he leaned in and whispered that she didn't have to fight any more. She could let go. He told her he loved her and always would but he didn't want to see her suffer any more. He asked her to go home to God and said that he would be fine. He was certain that she must have heard him because her body calmed, her breathing softened, and she died shortly after.

After listening to Larry's experience, I realized how selfish I've been for being angry with you. You know that I would rather have died before you or at least, with you. That didn't happen but would I have preferred to watch you suffer? Never! I guess there just isn't any perfect way to die. What I realize now is that instead of concentrating on what I lost, I want to appreciate all that we had and to remember all of the wonderful things we did together. I wouldn't trade those memories for having to go through losing you a thousand times.

So what do you think, Frank? Are you all right with my being with someone else? Is it what you would have wanted for me? I've searched my soul and can't find feelings of guilt or shame. I'd like to believe that you want me to move on with this next part of my life and that I don't have to abandon you in order to love Larry. You are part of me, Frank, and you always will be.

I closed the journal, set it down, and walked to the end of the patio. Even with my robe on, the chill of the April breeze caused goose bumps to form on my arms and I crossed them in front of me to warm myself. Then Larry's arms crossed on top of my own and I felt the delightful warmth of his body against mine. I pulled his arms closer together to snuggle myself deeply inside them.

"Did you sleep well?" he asked.

"Better than I have in a long, long time."

"Good." He kissed me on the top of my head.

As we stood there together in silence, I thought about my anxiety from the night before. I worried about the toll the years had taken. When Frank and I married, I was a young woman with a body that was firm and smooth and I presented it to him as my gift on our wedding night, throughout our honeymoon, and for the many years that followed. Now, it felt to me like whatever was not bulging was either sagging or wrinkled and I dreaded the look of disappointment in Larry's eyes, but there was none. I tried to explain how I was feeling but he just smiled and touched his finger to my lips.

"Shhh," he whispered, "there is nothing to explain. If you could see yourself through my eyes, you would see more elegance, gracefulness, and beauty than I could ever hope for. And I'm certainly no Adonis! We are exactly as we should be right now." Then he drew me into his arms and kissed me gently on the lips. My fears gave way to desire. I returned Larry's kiss with all the passion I was feeling and he responded in kind. What had become familiar with Frank became new and intensely sensual with Larry. My need for intimacy surprised me and I surrendered to the moment.

Now, the morning after, I felt warm and safe wrapped in Larry's arms. Now, I was finally ready to open up to the next chapter in my life.

CHAPTER 51

ON THE MORNING following our return from Martha's Vineyard, I placed three telephone calls. The first was to Doris, offering to get together for tag saleing the following weekend. She sounded less than eager on the phone but agreed. The second and third calls were to Bridget and Megan asking them to meet me for breakfast during the week. Both of them hesitated at first. I guessed it was because they dreaded hearing more of my complaints, but I pressed how important it was to me that we meet quickly and they finally agreed.

Doris's reaction to Larry was unexpected. I was concerned that the girls might also respond negatively. If so, I wanted to get their input right away, although I wasn't at all sure of what I might do if it wasn't positive. I suggested we meet at Luiza's Diner, across the street from ESPN's corporate headquarters in Bristol. Because the restaurant was on the access road to Lake Compounce, we had stopped there often before or after our family outings to the park. I secretly hoped that the girls' memories of past visits would help smooth our conversation.

The diner was normally crowded for lunch and dinner but since the park didn't open until 11:00, it was quieter during breakfast hours and I wanted a place where we could talk easily. On the phone, both girls asked if everything was all right and I assured them it was. We met at nine on Wednesday morning. The girls drove to the restaurant together and when they arrived, I was sipping my second cup of coffee.

"Mom," Bridget asked, "you said there was no problem but you sounded a little desperate on the phone. Are you sure everything is OK?"

"Desperate might be an exaggeration, but yes, everything is fine. There's just something I need your input on."

The waitress greeted us with a warm smile. "What'll you ladies have to drink?"

The girls ordered and Megan asked, "So what's the crisis, Mom?"

I answered more emphatically this time, "There is no crisis. As I said on the phone, I'm fine. I just need your opinion on something."

"OK then, on what?" said Bridget impatiently.

Megan asked, "This isn't about going into a nursing home again, is it?"

"Goodness no. I'm well past that. Actually, I'm feeling better now than I have in a long time."

"Come to think of it," said Bridget, "you look really good, Mom, and where did you get that tan?"

The waitress returned with the drinks and took the breakfast orders. As she turned to go, I continued, "I've been getting a lot of sun lately. Actually, that's part of what I wanted to talk to you about. I've been seeing someone."

"Way to go, Mom!" Megan cheered.

Bridget shushed Megan and then asked me, "Really?"

"Yes, really. I'm old, not dead."

"I didn't mean it that way. I'm just surprised. We assumed you were with your senior center group. You haven't mentioned someone else before."

"It didn't seem that important before, but things have changed lately."

"Are you guys having sex?" Megan asked too loud for my comfort level.

"Now Megan," I started turning red, "that's not an appropriate kind of question to ask."

"So you are!"

"Megan, please … lower your voice," I glanced around nervously.

A man seated a couple tables over was reading the morning papers and I could swear he was chuckling to himself.

After returning with waters and drink refills, the waitress smiled at me and then turned and left. I couldn't tell if her smile was for reassurance or because she overheard Megan's comment.

"Larry and I just got back from a week on Martha's Vineyard."

"Dad's friend, Larry; the one whose wife died?"

"Well, both Dad's and my friend, but yes, that Larry."

"That explains a lot," Megan chimed in. "He's handsome."

"Put a lid on it, Megan," Bridget chided and then asked, "How long have you two been seeing each other?"

"Since Christmas. That's why I wanted to talk to the two of you. Larry and I have become close and we've been talking ... we've been discussing...," I struggled to find the right words but nothing was working so I just dove in, "he's asked me to marry him."

"Did you hear that, Bridget? Mom is getting hitched!"

"Why not, Megan? That's her choice."

Bridget's comment hit home with me, "You're not upset?"

"Why would we be upset? You're a grown woman."

"Yea, Mom," Megan added, "all kidding aside, we're both thrilled for you."

"It doesn't bother you that there's someone else besides your father?"

Both girls sat silently for a moment. My question obviously brought home the reality and it took a while for it to settle in.

Bridget broke the silence. "I miss Dad and I miss your being with him," her eyes began to water, "but most of all I ... we miss you, Mom, the person that you used to be. We were a family and it will seem a little strange to have you with another man." She turned and looked at Megan, "But we've both seen how miserable you've been and neither of us wants that, so if marrying Larry makes you happy, then it will make us happy too."

"Bridget's right, Mom. You love him, don't you?"

"Not in the same way as I loved your father but yes, I love him very much."

I smiled widely. The conversation was going better than even my most optimistic hopes. Then a disturbing thought struck me and I fell silent.

Bridget caught the change, "What's wrong, Mom?"

"It's not what we're talking about but I just realized something. Do you remember that letter I got from my girlfriend, June: the one who was the maid-of-honor at my wedding?"

Bridget nodded.

"When it came, I was still in shock after losing your father. It's hard to explain unless you've gone through it, but I think I understand better now how she felt. It must have been terribly painful for her to see me after she lost Harvey and that pain would have been even worse once Frank returned. In her letter, she tried to explain how embarrassed she was and how that kept her from contacting me until she heard about Frank. When she finally reached out to me, I was so angry that I tossed her letter away. Now I wish that I could answer her but I guess that I've lost that opportunity forever."

I changed the subject and we finished by talking about my wedding plans. Bridget offered to take me home after breakfast, but I noticed that we were heading in the wrong direction. "Bridget, did you forget you were taking me home?" "I just need to make a quick stop at my house on the way." Bridget rushed into her house, quickly returned, and handed me a wrinkled envelope. It was the letter from June with her return address. Bridget explained, "I saw you throw it away that day. After I told you to go upstairs and get dressed, I pulled it out of the trash. I figured that you might want it again someday."

"Oh, Bridget, thank you, honey," I pulled her toward me and hugged her tight. "Right now, this means the world to me."

Thinking about my two grown daughters and their husbands, I reflected on the wonderful people they were. Then, recalling June's letter from Bridget and Steve's stopping me from tossing Frank's pictures away, I silently gave thanks that my children sometimes chose to ignore my wishes.

As if to underscore my thoughts, Bridget interrupted, "So Mom, what do you say? When do we get to meet with Larry?"

CHAPTER 52

AS ARRANGED, DORIS picked me up promptly at seven on Saturday morning. For my part, I had done considerably more research than normal. I looked up each of the tag sale locations and circled any items I thought might be of special interest to Doris. I also listed the start times of each stop and mapped out the most efficient route taking all of the factors into account. I proudly shared my work with Doris when she arrived but the extent of her reaction was a tepid, "Looks OK."

Even though it was out-of-the-way, I asked that our first stop be an estate sale in Burlington. The ad included a reference to several original pieces of jewelry by a local artist that Frank and I had met before we were married. Doris and I arrived at the house fifteen minutes before the advertised start. Typical of estate sales by professional coordinators, no early birds were allowed. A line of people had already formed at the front door. As Doris parked the car, I ran ahead to secure our place in line.

"You realize that by standing here, we're going to miss the start of some of the other sales," she said.

"Please don't feel that you have to stay here with me. You can go to some of the other sales and come back to pick me up later. I don't mind waiting."

"This means that much to you?"

"You'll see why when I show it to you."

As soon as the doors opened, I went to the coordinator and asked

239

about the jewelry. She pointed to a locked glass display case across the room. A couple was already standing at the case looking inside. The female partner asked to have the case opened so she could examine some of the items. I kept nervously looking over her shoulder to see what she was looking at. The first item was a broach, the second a collectible Hummel figurine and the third, a necklace.

"That's it," I whispered to Doris.

"So what's so special about it?" Doris questioned at a normal volume. I motioned for her to whisper. She answered, "Whatever."

The other woman kept examining the necklace and the Hummel. All the while, I couldn't breathe. When she finally settled on the statue, I calmed down again.

After the couple left, I asked the coordinator to let me inspect the necklace. As Doris and I examined it, I explained, "Each piece is fashioned from an actual leaf. The artist treated the leaf first and then dipped it into a 14-carat gold bath several times. Once it cured, she mounted the setting or clasp. It's a very time-consuming process because the leaves are so delicate. Any misstep before it was finished and the whole piece was ruined. Frank bought me the earrings before he left for the military. I've worn them every year on our anniversary. He wanted to get me the matching necklace but he couldn't afford it so we decided to wait until we could. By the time we were ready, the artist had passed away and I never saw another one until now. Isn't it beautiful?"

"If you go in for that sort of thing, I guess. How much is it?"

I swallowed hard, "It's marked $225.00."

"Are you kidding? This is an estate sale, not Tiffany's! There are no diamonds in it and it can't weigh more than a few grams. Offer them seventy-five."

"But what if they say no?"

"Then we'll come back later after they realize how overpriced it is."

"What if they sell it in the meantime?"

"At that price? They won't get half that much."

"OK, then I'll offer them $150."

"Hey, it's your money to waste. Just try not to look too desperate. I gotta pee."

I made the offer but the coordinator said the estate sale was only just beginning and they wouldn't budge. I reluctantly gave up and wandered through the rest of the house until Doris returned. We compared notes on other items we saw and agreed that most were overpriced and so we left.

We made several more stops before I couldn't stand the wait any longer and I asked Doris to return to the Burlington hours. When we got there, she waited in the car. I immediately rushed to the display case but the necklace was gone. When I asked the coordinator about it, she said it had sold. I felt a sinking feeling in my stomach but I had to know; I asked the selling price. The coordinator said it went for twenty-five dollars over the sticker. I had to fight back the tears. When I told Doris what happened, all she said was, "Sorry; tough break, kid." I was seething inside.

We made several more stops and returned to my house shortly after noon. Against my better judgment, I invited Doris in for lunch. As we entered the kitchen, I said, "I hope chicken salad sandwiches are OK."

She returned with a lukewarm, "Whatever."

I had reached my limit, "OK, Doris, what's going on?"

"What are you talking about?"

"I'm talking about your attitude. I'm talking about your cryptic answers to anything I say. I'm talking about your treating me like I've done something terrible to you."

"Just because I didn't jump for joy about chicken salad?"

"You know full well it's more than that."

"Are you still fussing over the jewelry thing? We were only gone a couple hours before you dragged me back there again. How was I supposed to know somebody would be stupid enough to pay that much for it? I told you, I didn't see that coming and I already apologized."

"What you said was, "Tough break, kid": the same thing you said when I told you that Frank died. All morning you've been treating me as if I've done something horrible."

"You mean like your taking off for a week without saying a thing to me or blowing me off since Christmas because you were too busy spending all your time with lover boy? Or did you mean pretending that we're still friends because you don't have the guts to come out and say we're not."

"That's not true, Doris. Where is this coming from?"

"You've changed, Maureen. You used to worry about staying faithful to your husband's memory. Now I'll bet you have trouble remembering his name."

"That's so unfair, especially coming from you. All along it's been you telling me that I needed to accept Frank's death and move on with my life."

"And you think that means jumping into bed with the first man you see? Just because you landed one saint doesn't mean you'll get another. Sooner or later, you'll find that Larry is like all the rest of them. They all have feet of clay."

"Don't hide behind clichés, Doris. The truth is that I've moved on and you refuse to."

"You don't know what you're talking about."

"I'm talking about you, Doris, about your need to put everyone and everything down. I'm talking about the way you push people away, even those who try to like you and about your daughter and the grandchild you've never even seen. Your father was a sick man. What he did to you and your mother was criminal but not all men are like that. You let your experience with your father destroy the relationship between you and your husband. Then you tried to drive a wedge between him and your daughter and in the process, you lost them both, but it doesn't have to stay that way. You have the power to change it, or at least to try. And if you refuse to change, then don't lash out at me because I have."

There was nothing left to say. Everything had been laid bare like an open wound. There was no returning, no taking back what was said. I was too exhausted to sort the truth out from this war of words. Part of me regretted pushing things this far and part of me wondered why it took me so long, but it was done now and it couldn't be undone. I walked over to the kitchen door and opened it.

"Doris, you need to leave."

"Yah, that's the first thing you've said all morning that we agree on."

She got up and walked out. Neither of us said goodbye; neither of us knew how to.

I walked into the living room, collapsed into the recliner, sobbed bitterly, and then fell into a deep sleep. When I awoke, it was already dark out. I glanced at the lamp table and saw the stack of CareNotes pamphlets I had read a few days earlier. I scanned through them until I came upon the final suggestion I had circled in pen. Then I checked the time: 9:08. *Good*, I thought to myself, *it's not too late*. I picked up the phone, called Larry, and asked if he would drive me to the military cemetery in Middletown. There was something I needed to do.

CHAPTER 53

LARRY GRIPPED THE umbrella to shelter us from the steady afternoon rain and draped his free arm around my shoulder to protect me from the chilling breeze and absorb my sobs. We stood motionless in front of the plain white headstone in the center of the row: one of the endless rows of markers, identical except for the inscription. Under the generic cross, it read: Frank Russo, Sgt. U.S. Army, World War II, September 19, 1920 – September 17, 2000, Loving Husband, Father and Grandfather.

The military cemetery in Middletown was the second gravesite we visited that day. Earlier, we went to St. Joseph's cemetery in Bristol. There was an awkward moment when we noticed Larry's name and date of birth on the headstone next to Helen's and the extra space for his date of death. That would have to be a discussion for some future time.

As we stood looking down at the marker, I said, "I'm sorry, Larry. You know that I love you but I still miss him terribly."

Larry wrapped me more tightly in his arms. "No need to apologize. I miss Helen too.

"Thank you for understanding. When I first read that suggestion about visiting the grave to say goodbye, I couldn't even bring myself to think about it. It seemed so final. But the closer we've gotten, the more I felt I needed to make Frank part of it."

"And it doesn't have to be final. We can come and visit as often as you want. They're both part of us and they always will be."

Some people never get to experience the love of a true soul mate, yet here I stood with a second one for me. I looked into Larry's eyes and kissed him on the cheek. "If you don't mind, would you please give me a moment alone and wait for me in the car?" He gave me the umbrella and did as I asked. After he left, I took the single red rose I held, placed it on top of Frank's headstone, and talked to my husband.

"Hello, Frank. I know that it's been too long and I'm sorry. After your funeral, I promised myself that I would never come back here again. I felt like the war had robbed us of our first years together and now this place would keep us apart after we died but I understand better now. I think about how different you were when you returned: how cheerless and distant. I also remember the nightmares that went on for months and the times I held you in my arms and rocked you back to sleep. I know that at first, I resented being shut out of that part of your life. Later, I was grateful that you tried to protect me from the hell you went through. I only hope that here you can finally rest in peace with so many others who went through the same thing you did.

There's another reason that I came, Frank. Larry and I will be married soon. For so long, I resisted getting close to anyone but I felt so depressed and lonely. Then someone told me that if you really loved me as much as I said you did, you wouldn't want to see me suffer, you would want me to go on with my life. It took me the longest time to believe that, but now I do. Larry's a good man, Frank. I know now that you would approve. After all, what I see in him is what I most loved in you, so please, Frank … please be happy for me."

I leaned over and kissed Frank's headstone. As I did, I tasted the saltiness of my own tears on the granite. "Rest in peace, my love."

As Larry drove us away from the cemetery, I looked back toward Frank's marker and whispered, "Goodbye, my love, and thank you. I have always loved you and I always will."

CHAPTER 54

MEGAN SUGGESTED THAT I wear a traditional white gown for the wedding but I nixed the idea quickly and chose a pink floral pattern instead.

"I wore a wedding gown when I married your father," I said. "Once was fine. Besides, at my age I'd look silly."

"You look beautiful, Mom," she said teary-eyed as she zipped up my dress. I turned around and rubbed the back of my hand gently against her cheek, "Now don't you start crying or your mascara will run and you won't look your gorgeous self for the pictures."

"Is this the one?" Bridget asked as she entered, holding a small, black box.

"Yes, that's it. Thank you, honey." I opened the box and looked at the delicate gold-leaf earrings. As I did, I recalled that last terrible day with Doris.

"I don't suppose we've received any last-minute replies to the wedding invitations, have we?"

The girls exchanged worried glances and then Bridget answered, "If you mean from Doris, no. We've called and left messages right until this morning but I'm sorry, Mom, we haven't."

My eyes started to tear and my hands trembled slightly as I held tried to put on the earrings. "Bridget, I'm all thumbs today. Would you mind helping me with these?" I handed her the box.

"There," she said as she finished the last one, "now let me look at you."

Our eyes met as a tear trickled down her cheek. "I've never seen you looking more beautiful, Mom. I'm so happy for you." Then I looked toward Megan who was dabbing her own tears away.

"Now would the two of you stop it," I said with mock sternness while wiping beneath my own eyes, "or none of us will look fit for this wedding.

The doorbell rang and I jumped. "Oh, thank God." I dashed for the door telling myself that it didn't matter who started that stupid argument or who was right or wrong. All that mattered now was the day was complete. I started talking as soon as I reached for the knob, "Doris, I'm so glad you decided to...," but when the door opened, I was looking at a tall, slender man in a brown uniform.

"Maureen Russo?" he asked.

"Yes, that's me," I sighed.

"The instructions were that this had to arrive by 9:00 a.m. and be delivered to you personally. Please sign here." He extended an electronic signature pad and I scribbled my name on it.

"Thank you, ma'am. Have a nice day," and he was gone.

I unwrapped the package and opened the box. Inside was an envelope addressed to me sitting atop a bed of cotton. I removed the letter from the envelope, sat down, and began to read.

Hey Maureen,

If you're all dolled up while you are reading this, then you're probably about to go through with your wedding. Actually, I never had any doubt that you would. I'm going to be really bad at this writing thing, so give me a break while I try to figure out where I'm going with it. What I mean to say is that I really screwed up the last couple of times we met. When you told me that you and Larry were leaving together, something just snapped. I don't know if I was jealous or angry or what. All I know is that I didn't like what I heard and so I lashed out at you. I have a tendency to do that in case you hadn't noticed. Now I'm trying so hard to say something intelligent that I'm even boring myself. Let me start over.

Ever since that day I've been thinking about this bird I had when I was a kid. I found it in the snow a few months after I moved in with my aunt. It wasn't able to fly so I brought it home and nursed it back to health. I would sit with it in my lap by my bedroom window and feed it. Then one day in early spring, it just flew out the window and I never saw it again. Sometimes I wondered why I didn't just leave the little ingrate to die in the snow. Now just in case you think this story is about you, you're wrong. Actually, it's about me.

When I said I had something to tell you that morning you left for the Vineyard, it wasn't about that stupid art course. I did take the course and it turned out to be a heck of a lot of fun (I can't believe I just wrote "heck." You have me censoring my own language) but that only popped into my head after you told me about you and Larry.

What I meant to say was that I called my daughter like you suggested. I figured she was probably going to hang up on me even before I finished saying hello but she didn't. She did say some pretty nasty things at first but I had that coming so I braced myself for it and managed to keep my mouth shut. That must have surprised her because pretty soon she simmered down enough to listen to what I had to say. That's when I got really nervous but I took your advice and told her about my father, Henry and me, my mom and her. I slipped a couple of times when I started ragging on Henry but she cut me short. Anyway, she listened long enough for me to get it all out. Then she was just quiet for a really long time. When she did talk again, it was to say that she had to go and then she just hung up on me.

I figured right there and then I had lost any opportunity to ever connect with my kid and grandkid again. I paced around for most of the day until I started balling like a baby and couldn't stop. I finally looked up and screamed, "Don't you do this! Don't let me lose her." Then, out of the blue, she calls me back! She had talked to Henry. Even though I hadn't told him about what happened with my old man after the funeral, he said it kind of made sense. He told her that he believed me and only wished he had known earlier. She sounded as though she had been crying a lot too. We must have talked for another couple hours. Since then, we've talked almost every night. It hasn't always been easy, but we've connected again in ways I would never have thought possible.

Now here's the rub. A few days before you and I met that last time, Colleen asked me to come out west and move in with her so I could spend time with her and my granddaughter. I told her flat out no way was I living with her. Her marriage would never survive it and besides, I can't even stand myself sometimes. But we did agree to look into some nearby apartments while I'm there. I seriously doubt it can work out, but I at least have to give it a try.

I just couldn't figure out how to tell you. I've never been comfortable with goodbyes but this time was worse than most. Then, when you told me about you and Larry, I think I kind of unloaded my own guilt feelings on you, if that makes any sense. Anyway, my plane takes off from Bradley this morning so I'm sorry but I'm not going to make it for the wedding. Also, all that stuff I said about Larry: that was just a pile of crap. He seems like a really great guy and based on the way he treated Helen, he'll probably spoil you rotten. I don't know how you do it but somehow you always manage to end up with the keepers.

I owe you, friend: a lot. I don't know how or why you managed to stick with me but you did. You're a great listener, Maureen, though you're not nearly as great at talking. You said some things that really bugged me, but you got me to think. I realized how much I've allowed my past to screw up my present and maybe even stop me from believing in the future (Now doesn't that sound profound!). Seriously, I'm gonna work to live like every day is my last. I don't know if I'll ever be able to believe the way you do, let alone trust as much as you do. But, if there is a God, then I'm guessing that maybe I've shortchanged him. Anyway, thanks a bunch. If you wouldn't mind, I'd maybe like to call you sometime.

I'd better stop here before I start bawling and I don't want to mess up my makeup. Who knows? I might get a seat on the plane next to some young stud and maybe both of us will get lucky. Maureen, you and Larry go out and make a wonderful life together. You deserve it.

Doris
P.S. Look beneath the cotton

I carefully folded the letter, returned it to its envelope, and placed it on the lamp table. Then I picked up the box and lifted the bed of cotton out. My whole body trembled and I started crying uncontrollably. Tears streamed down my cheeks carrying my mascara with them. "What is it, Mom," Bridget asked, "what's the matter?"

"Nothing, honey," I answered while lifting the gold-leaf necklace that matched my earrings. "Nothing at all."

CHAPTER 55

LARRY AND I held our wedding ceremony in the Bristol Senior Center courtyard. While it was an unusual event for the municipal building, the location came as no surprise to anyone who knew us. The center connected most of the people in our circle of friends. We had wanted Chet Hartman to lead the music for the reception, especially since he played when we first danced together, but Chet passed away shortly after the holiday ball. Rather than dissuade us, it only underscored the importance of starting our married life together and making the most of each day we had. We quickly booked the center's new bandleader for our reception.

The center staff went all out decorating for the wedding. When they finished, it looked as beautiful to us as any full-time banquet hall. As the staff prepared the courtyard for the ceremony, Betsy, the center director, asked me if I would like them to remove the angel statue because of the broken wing. I insisted that it stay. I felt a special bond with that statue and I told Betsy that, if anything, the broken wing made it even more endearing to me. I took special care to include it in many of our wedding photographs.

It was a picture-perfect day. Bright sunshine poured into the courtyard and the high walls blocked the autumn breezes. Immediately following the ceremony, Megan invited the guests into the gym for the reception while our small wedding party stayed behind for pictures.

Before we began, I felt a tap on my shoulder and heard a timid,

"Hello, Maureen." With only those few words, I recognized the voice and immediately turned around.

"Oh, June," I said as we reached out and hugged each other, "thank you so much for coming."

"Are you kidding? Nothing in the world would have prevented me from making it. Maureen, I'm so happy for you. You look so beautiful and your dress is gorgeous. When you get back from your honeymoon, I hope that maybe we can get together."

"There's no need to wait that long. Let's talk inside and make a time to get together right away. Larry and I aren't leaving for a few weeks and you and I have a lifetime of catching up to do."

"I'd like that, very much," June said, tearing up.

"Now don't you start too or you'll get me going all over again."

"OK. I'll see you inside. And by the way, your earrings and necklace look perfect with that dress." I instinctively reached up and touched the necklace leaf. Then I recalled Doris's excusing herself at the estate sale to use the bathroom and I smiled.

When the photographer finished the group photos, Larry and I dismissed everyone else. Bridget and Megan wanted to stay but I asked that they care for the guests until Larry and I made our entrance.

As we sat for the last photo in front of John's angel statue, a jet flew overhead, traversing the courtyard in the clear blue sky. Its metal fuselage glistened in the late morning sun and a dazzling white contrail billowed out behind it. Larry looked at his watch, "Right on time as usual: the 11:00 a.m. from Bradley to Arizona."

That was Doris's plane. I asked Larry, "Have you ever noticed how much an airplane in flight looks so much like an angel?" He smiled, wrapped his arm around me, and kissed the top of my head. We followed the plane until it disappeared over the courtyard wall. Then I squeezed his hand and looked into his eyes. Mine glistened with wetness but I didn't mind.

"For the longest time after Frank died, I thought God was deaf to my prayers. Now it seems He was answering them all along."

"I think that maybe He had an even bigger plan in mind." I gave him a puzzled look.

He smiled and continued. "Like she said in her letter, you're the reason she's on that plane. If anything, you were angels to each other and very strange ones at that."

The sound of Frank Sinatra's *Second Time Around* poured out of the open door and filled the courtyard space.

Larry extended his hand to me. "That's our cue. What do you say, Mrs. Kowalski? May I have this dance?"

— End —

ACKNOWLEDGEMENTS FOR
WOUNDED ANGELS

I PENNED THE first line of *Wounded Angels* almost fifteen years ago and while the writing is mine, the input of many people over many years helped shape it into the story you read here. First and foremost, I am indebted to the people who inspired this book, especially Fred and Charlotte Frasario, Michael Fanelli, Rosaria MacDonald, Cataldo Miceli, Nicholas Miceli, and Anthony Scapelatti. Special thanks to my wife, Judy, my final reviewer and to my sons Michael, Jason, and daughter-in-laws, Jennifer and Jolene: my primary critics and supporters.

My sincere gratitude goes to the family, friends and associates who provided support, encouragement and detailed and substantive feedback. They include: Jonathan Blais, Dan Blanchard, Ruth Boss, Mimi Bouyea, Stephen Bustamante, Mary Casey, Nancy Castonguay, Carmella Chawner, Becky Chawner, Cindy Eastman, Ed Ebert, Janet Ebert, Diane Ellis, Gordon Ellis, Dr. Helen E. Ellis, Antoinette Escott, Ralph Famiglietti, Grace Grab, Penny Goetjen, Jennifer Haigh, Martin Herman, Darrin Horbal, Brian Jud, Jan Kardys, Carol Keeney, Joseph Keeney, Jack Lander, Deborah Levison, Jared Look, Patricia Dwyer Mellitt, Barbara Miceli, Dawn Miceli, Charles I. Motes, Kathryn Orzech, Diane Smith, Peter G. Smith, Dorothy Sterpka, Joan Tardif, Delma Way, Sharon Welton, Nancy Whitney, Jeff Wilson, Anne Yuhas and Robert Zaslow.

Much of *Wounded Angels* takes place in and around the Bristol CT Senior Center, where I did much of the writing. My profound thanks go to Executive Director Patricia Tomascak, Assistant Director Jason Krueger and all of the center members for their hospitality and support.

The Osher Lifelong Learning Institute at UCONN has been a consistent source of education and inspiration for my writing journey. I thank the administrators, presenters and my fellow members. A special thank you goes to the members of Ilvi Dulack's "Writers' Table" group.

Seven Angels Theater in Waterbury, CT hosted the first reading of *Wounded Angels*: the play based upon the manuscript. That reading influenced the further development of the story. My sincere appreciation goes to Artistic Director, Semina DeLaurantis, and the staff. Thanks also to the very talented cast, including Ilvi Dulack, Luke Lynch, Jean McGavin, RM McCarty, Michael Medeiros, Bonnie Plourde, and Kelly Smith.

Feedback from several Writing Conferences made significant improvements to this story. I am indebted to the organizers, presenters and members of the Wesleyan and Unicorn Writer's Conferences and the Connecticut Authors and Publishers Association's CAPA University.

Moving from a printed draft to a professionally finished, marketed and distributed book is a monumental task. My profound thanks go to the Elm Hill and HarperCollins Christian staff who worked with me every step of the publishing journey.

And to you dear readers, I offer my deepest appreciation. You are the reason I write.